JULIE HEARN

IVY

OXFORD
UNIVERSITY PRESS

OXFORD
UNIVERSITY PRESS

Great Clarendon Street, Oxford OX2 6DP

Oxford University Press is a department of the University of Oxford.
It furthers the University's objective of excellence in research, scholarship,
and education by publishing worldwide in

Oxford New York

Auckland Cape Town Dar es Salaam Hong Kong Karachi
Kuala Lumpur Madrid Melbourne Mexico City Nairobi
New Delhi Shanghai Taipei Toronto

With offices in

Argentina Austria Brazil Chile Czech Republic France Greece
Guatemala Hungary Italy Japan Poland Portugal Singapore
South Korea Switzerland Thailand Turkey Ukraine Vietnam

Oxford is a registered trademark of Oxford University Press
in the UK and in certain other countries

The poem on page 213 is *Sudden Light* by Dante Gabriel Rossetti

Database right Oxford University Press (maker)

First published 2006

British Library Cataloguing in Publication Data
Data available

Printed in Great Britain

ISBN: 978-0-19-275431-8

5 7 9 10 8 6 4

For my mum and dad, with love

One face looks out from all his canvases,
One selfsame figure sits or walks or leans;
We found her hidden just behind those screens,
That mirror gave back all her loveliness,
A queen in opal or in ruby dress,
A nameless girl in freshest summer greens,
A saint, an angel;—every canvas means
The same one meaning, neither more nor less.
He feeds upon her face by day and night
And she with true kind eyes looks back on him
Fair as the moon and joyful as the light.

From 'In An Artist's Studio', Christina G. Rossetti

Part One

When she was born her father took one look at her and spat into a corner.

'Red 'air,' he wheezed. 'Like Judas, an' the whores down Ratcliff Highway. She'll 'ave a temper to match the Devil's, strike me if she won't. An' no decent man'll keep company with 'er, you mark my words.'

Then he went stomping and wheezing into the night to spend the coal money on beer.

'Take no notice, missis,' sniffed an elderly neighbour, parking her rump on a rickety chair in order to light her pipe. 'Some men just ain't good at senty-ment. 'E don't mean nothin' by it.'

The woman on the heap of flock and sacks that passed for a bed tried to smile but was too weak.

And the flame-haired infant in her arms lay very still and quiet as if she knew she had just been written off as a hot-headed trollop and it pained her.

After a while the woman and the baby snuggled closer and the baby's fist escaped from its shawl of rags to wave and bang against the woman's breast.

'Little thing,' crooned the woman, stroking the tiny hand with one finger. 'Little tiny thing.' It was no bigger than a leaf, that baby hand, but its grip as it curled around the woman's finger was surprisingly strong.

Ivy.

They called her Ivy. And no one expected her to blossom. Not in the slums of south London. And certainly not with red 'air.

CHAPTER 1

In which Ivy is treated rather badly by
philanthropists in ridiculous dresses

Mrs Hortense Merryfield and Mrs Christiana Larrington of the Ragged Children's Welfare Association (South London branch) chose a bitterly cold spring morning upon which to patronize the deserving poor of Lambeth.

Picking their way along filthy streets, the hems of their crinolines blotting up slush and the beads on their bonnets tinkling like ice, they were so obviously out of their element that by the time they reached the corner of New Cut a sizeable crowd of ragged children was on their tail, hopping and flapping and begging for coppers.

'Jus' a ha'penny, missis. Jus' enough for a hot 'tater.'

'It's for me bruvver, missis. Me little bruvver wot's sick.'

'Shoo!' cried Mrs Merryfield. 'Scram!' And she waved her umbrella and stood her ground until all but one of the little imps had given up the clamour and scattered.

Mrs Larrington, who was younger than her companion, drew a mohair shawl tighter round her shoulders and tried not to seem afraid. This was her first time out among the deserving poor and she was beginning to wish she had stayed in Norwood, among snowdrops and servants and the undeserving rich. Where had they come from, all those ragamuffins? So pale, so dirty, and so clearly half-frozen that they might have sprung fully formed from the slush. Yet they'd had the strength, all of them, to run like bunnikins from the point of Mrs Merryfield's umbrella. Even the *girls* had scarpered.

It was the sight of those scarpering girls, Mrs Larrington realized, that had disturbed her the most. For she herself had never run anywhere. Not even as a child. It wasn't ladylike; it wasn't *natural* for the female of the species to move so fast.

She was about to say as much to dear Mrs Merryfield when she felt a tugging at her sleeve. And '*Ugh!*' she shuddered, shrinking away. 'Don't *touch* me, you . . . you insolent creature.'

'I live 'ere, if you please,' piped a voice at her elbow. 'Only your dress is blockin' the way.'

Looking down, over the slope of her crinoline, Mrs Larrington found her gaze being met by a little scrap of indeterminate age. A small girl with huge hazel eyes and a veritable halo of tangled hair. It was a cross between a nest and a cloud, that hair, and such an extraordinary colour that Mrs Larrington's gloved hand moved instinctively to stroke it.

'Stop! My dear Mrs Larrington. What can you be thinking of? There will be more lice on this child than you'll find crumbs in a biscuit barrel. First rule of home visits—keep your distance.'

And with a prod and a twist, the redoubtable Mrs Merryfield hooked the crook of her umbrella under the ragged girl's collar and yanked her up and away.

'Oh my,' declared Mrs Larrington, as the child rose into the air, flailing like a raggedy fish. 'Oh, my goodness me.'

But the child said not a word; only struggled and gulped while her face turned very pink beneath several layers of dirt and her extraordinary hair whipped around her head in a flurry of tangles and tendrils.

Now had Mrs Merryfield's umbrella been a dainty contraption of ruched silk and spindled ivory it would have snapped for sure. But this umbrella was like its owner—sturdy. Its point had seen off pickpockets, bull terriers, and many a drunken sailor. And its hard wooden handle, carved to resemble a bird with its beak open, was more than equal to bearing—temporarily, anyway—the weight of a skinny underfed little girl.

'Oh my,' Mrs Larrington repeated, as her companion swung the child expertly across the cobbles and landed her, with a barely audible 'thwunk', in a puddle of muck and melting snow. 'Oh, my goodness me.'

'There!' Mrs Merryfield unhooked the umbrella. 'That's more like it.' And from somewhere about her person she whipped a rag; one of the many squares of calico she carried for the specific purpose of wiping whichever bit of her umbrella had been used to prod, poke, or occasionally lift the undeserving poor to a distance where neither their lice nor their thieving fingers could threaten her own person.

The little girl seemed too stunned to move. Her bottom would have been turning as wet and cold as a polar bear's, yet she remained in the muddy puddle, staring up in hurt astonishment at the one who had dumped her there.

Mrs Larrington dithered.

Mrs Merryfield carried on wiping. All around the handle she went, pressing the rag into every dip and dent of the carved bird, and taking particular care with the open beak in case it contained a microscopic helping of lice.

'Oi! What's goin' on? Git up offer them wet cobbles. And 'oo said you could wear me jacket? Me snazziest jacket wot I bartered me ticker an' chain for down Petticoat Lane and ain't worn meself no more than once, an' that only to check the fit of it.'

Mrs Larrington gave such a start that she almost snapped something in her corset. Mrs Merryfield (who never bothered with corsets, preferring ease of movement, particularly in Lambeth) turned and raised her umbrella.

'Young man,' she scolded, 'I must ask you to mind your manners. Such bellowing and agitation is exceeding rude, and quite . . .'

'Git up, I said. And if me jacket's spoiled you'll get an 'iding you won't forget in a month of Sundays, strike me if you won't.'

And before Mrs Larrington could unflutter her nerves, or Mrs Merryfield do any more bashing, prodding, or hooking, a ragged boy darted across the cobbles, grabbed the child in the puddle and whisked her back onto her feet.

'Give it 'ere.'

The jacket in question was a soiled but still gaudy blue with brass buttons the size of jam lids down the front. On the child it looked more like a coat. Miserably she shrugged it off and handed it over. Underneath she wore a cotton dress with a pattern of roses faded to smudges. It was tissue-thin that dress and she shivered silently in it and swayed a little, her feet still planted in the puddle.

The boy was holding the jacket aloft, inspecting it carefully. He himself wore dark cord trousers, good-ish boots, and a plush velvet cap. His waistcoat had two

8

mother-of-pearl buttons left on it, and he had arranged a scarlet neckerchief to cover the place where the topmost buttons were missing. Skinny and grubby though he was, he was clearly a bit of a dandy.

'*A rip!*' he hollered. '*A big rip under me collar! Right—now you're for it.*'

Lifting one hand he made a lunge for the child. Quick as a cat she ran all the way round Mrs Larrington's crinoline and disappeared down an alleyway.

The boy tried to follow.

Thwack!

'Not so fast, young man.'

Mrs Merryfield's right arm and the length of her furled umbrella blocked the entrance to the alleyway as effectively as any three-barred gate.

'What's your name?' she demanded.

The boy gaped at the umbrella and then up at Mrs Merryfield as if he couldn't quite believe they were in his way. Mrs Merryfield regarded him, ferociously, until he backed down and averted his own scowl. A charity monger. That's what she was. Uglier than a butcher's dog and with a snarl to match, but a do-gooder nonetheless.

He had no time for do-gooders. No time at all. But they could be soft touches, if you played your cards right, he knew that much.

'Your name?' Mrs Merryfield demanded again.

The boy appeared to hesitate.

Then: 'Jared,' he replied, doffing his cap and flashing her a sudden grin. 'Jared Roderick Montague Jackson at your service, ma'am.'

Mrs Merryfield's expression remained flinty.

'Ma'am,' he repeated, swivelling to bow to the other lady who, he noticed at once, looked like being a much softer touch.

Mrs Larrington risked a nervous smile. *What a long name*, she thought, *for a pauper*.

'Well then, Jared Roderick Montague Jackson,' said Mrs Merryfield, lowering her umbrella. 'And you are what—nine, ten years of age?'

The boy puffed out his chest in its partially-buttoned waistcoat.

'I turned twelve on Christmas Day, ma'am,' he said. 'Not that there was much rejoicin' of it. No, nor of our dear Saviour's birth, neither. Not with my dear mama an invalid and my papa so sorely reduced in circumstances that there ain't a moment goes by when we ain't all workin' and contrivin' as best we can to pay the rent an' put bread on the table.'

Mrs Larrington's mouth twitched. The boy had pronounced 'invalid' as in 'completely without merit' when he had surely meant 'invalid' as in 'person suffering from chronic ill health'. How on earth, she wondered, had he arrived at such an error?

Jared didn't notice, or chose to ignore, her little sneer. 'Not that we 'as a table no more, ma'am,' he continued. 'For it went for firewood a fortnight since when it were freezin' so bad the little 'uns turned blue an' we 'ad no money for coal.'

Then he gave a huge sigh and held his jacket to his cheek.

'An' now me jacket's torn,' he moaned. 'Me best jacket wot I'd intended sellin' on to pay for a bit o' fuel. Me brand new jacket wot I'd sooner barter to keep the little 'uns warm than wear on me back for so much as a minute. All torn under the collar it is now, an' good for nothin' but the rag man.'

With a sorrowful shake of the head he folded the jacket beneath his armpit and patted it once, twice, three times as if it had hurt feelings, or a pain in its sleeves . . . Then he scowled towards the alleyway and shook his fist. 'An' there's one 'oo's still to cop a good thrashin' for rippin' it. So excuse me, ladies . . .'

'Oh dear,' said Mrs Larrington, 'I rather think . . . there might have been . . .'

'HALT!' Mrs Merryfield slapped her umbrella back across the entrance to the alleyway. Her other hand she held up at Mrs Larrington, for silence.

'. . . some mistake.'

Jared paused, obediently.

'Young man,' said Mrs Merryfield. 'It sounds to me as if your family might—and I stress the word *might*—benefit from an assessment of its current situation.'

'It would benny-fit from the price of a sheep's 'ead or a bit o' bacon for the pot,' the boy declared, solemnly. 'And from summat a bit warmer than 'tater sacks to wrap the babby in.'

'Well then,' said Mrs Merryfield, her smile only a little sweeter than vinegar. 'Perhaps Mrs Larrington and I should acquaint ourselves with your entire clan. I suggest you lead the way.'

11

CHAPTER 2

*In which Mrs Larrington suffers a terrible
ordeal in an extremely confined space*

The name Paradise Row did not exactly suit the
collection of houses that lined the alley the way rot-
ten molars fill a smelly mouth. Hell's Hovel would
have been better. Or Purgatory Place at the very least.

'Not far, ladies,' Jared promised. 'Mind yer skirts now.'

Mrs Larrington had trouble immediately. 'I'm stuck,'
she whimpered. 'My dear Mrs Merryfield, I fear I am
stuck quite fast.'

And so she was, for alleyways and crinolines are about
as compatible as tea parties and elephants and anyone
daft enough to wear a hoop the size of a giantess's wedding ring to go visiting the poor fully deserved to get
wedged between two damp and sooty walls.

'Lift it up, woman!' snapped Mrs Merryfield. 'Like me.
And in future wear a smaller one. Tenth rule of home
visits—dress sensibly.'

At this, Mrs Larrington felt quite faint. Had she heard
correctly? Had dear Mrs Merryfield *seriously* implied that
she should re-arrange her clothing in a manner that
would surely reveal her *ankles*? And not just her ankles
either but . . . but . . .

Evidently, Mrs Merryfield had implied precisely that, for
she herself was trotting along quite briskly with the hoop

12

of her rather more sensible crinoline flipped all the way up at one side. And what, in doing so, had she revealed to the world? Nothing more startling, actually, than a long flannel petticoat as thick, dark, and modest as any winter skirt.

Oh dear . . . Oh, mercy me . . .

Mrs Larrington was also wearing a petticoat, and a very pretty one too with hand-embroidered violets on it and white lace round the hem. Only, her petticoat wasn't *underneath* her crinoline. No, indeed. It was, as fashion dictated, being worn over the top, to soften the line of her skirt. Which meant that should her own hoop rise up, accidentally or otherwise . . .

Oh, deary me. Oh, dreadful prospect . . .

At a complete scarlet-faced loss as to how to proceed, Mrs Larrington glanced anxiously all around. She could hear babies wailing and a man shouting. But they were indoors, thank goodness, not out. Above her head broken windows were shuttered, or blocked with planks, to keep out the biting cold. Ahead of her, only Mrs Merryfield and the ragged boy with the unsuitably long name appeared aware of her predicament.

'Come along, Mrs Larrington, do!' Mrs Merryfield ordered. 'We're here now.' So saying, she prodded Jared Roderick Montague Jackson in through an open doorway, so that his cheeky grin would not deter her companion from doing what was clearly necessary if she wasn't to remain wedged in Paradise Row until her ringlets turned to twirly icicles and her blood froze in her veins.

Somewhere close by a dog began to bark. A nasty, guttural sound it was; the kind of noise a very *large* dog might make should it find itself hungry enough to bite the knuckles off its owner—or the toes off a silly woman sandwiched obligingly between two walls.

Mrs Larrington turned deathly pale.

Mrs Merryfield, losing patience, raised her voice to a most unladylike pitch.

'NOW!' she bellowed. 'Mobilize yourself immediately, my dear Mrs Larrington, or there may well be consequences.'

There was nothing else for it. Terrified of being set upon by a rabid lurcher, Mrs Larrington grasped the left side of her crinoline and tugged.

Nothing happened.

With trembling fingers she tugged again, this time pushing down equally hard on the other side. Still nothing. Again and again she tugged and pushed, wrestling and heaving her two handfuls of material until, finally—*whump*—up shot the left side of her skirt, petticoat, hoop and all.

'Goodness me!' exclaimed Mrs Merryfield. '*Most* unusual . . .'

And, 'Cor, what an eyeful!'. . .'Gawblimey, there's a sight!'. . .'Giddy-up, love!' cried the tenants of Paradise Row who, alerted by Mrs Merryfield's strident tones, had materialized at doorways and windows, to see what all the fuss was about.

As consequences go, this gale of merriment was nowhere near as painful for Mrs Larrington as being savaged by a starving dog would have been. It was, however, the most agonizing humiliation.

'Move faster, my dear,' Mrs Merryfield encouraged her, above whoops and snorts of laughter. 'If you possibly can.'

14

But Mrs Larrington, accustomed only to walking, gliding, and tiptoeing, couldn't possibly move any faster. She could only hobble stiffly along, holding her head even higher than her crinoline and doing her utmost to pretend that the guffaws and pointing fingers were all part of a ghastly dream.

At last, at long last, she reached Mrs Merryfield who, grabbing her by the elbow, muttered a most unsympathetic 'Quickly now', and bundled her into a dark hallway that was only slightly wider than the accursed alley.

Smelling salts, thought Mrs Larrington, breathing rapidly through her nose. *I fear I may require smelling salts.* Her crinoline was still tipped to one side, like a pretty, falling saucer. In the dark, and half-swooning from her ordeal thus far, she found herself past caring.

'Can you manage the stairs, ladies?' asked Jared, his voice solemn but his mouth twitching. 'Wivout attractin' another crowd, I mean?'

'It's like your impertinence to say so!' declared Mrs Merryfield, crossly. 'And yes, young man, we can most certainly manage the stairs. Mrs Larrington—walk behind me, if you please, to save yourself further shame.'

Mrs Larrington fell shakily into step. Dimly, she noticed that the banister beneath her right hand was sticky with dust and filth. Her glove was going to get badly soiled and a soiled glove, as everyone knew, was quite inadmissible when you were paying a call.

Letting go of the banister, though, was not an option. Not with the stairs so rickety and her left hand still controlling the tilt of her hoop. Her glove, she reassured herself, would be thoroughly cleaned by a maid that very

15

evening. Washed in tepid rainwater, with plenty of Castile soap, it would doubtless be rendered as good as new.

Her husband's crotchless woollen drawers however—saggy, moth-eaten, and the grim colour of an old rice pudding—would go straight out for the rag man. For, warm as they were when the north wind blew, she had no intention of borrowing them, or of even setting eyes on them, ever ever again.

CHAPTER 3

In which the third rule of home visits gets well and truly broken

The elder members of the Jackson family, oblivious to the approach of charity mongers, were arguing at the very tops of their voices:

'Throw 'im in the pot, I say. 'E'll add a bit o' flavour to the stew.'

'Ha-ha! Good idea, father—let's cook 'im!'

'No! Mother, don't listen to 'em. Poor Jimminy. It's *too cruel*.'

'Oh, my thumping heart and pounding temples! My dears—please . . .'

'But there ain't more'n two mouthfuls of meat on 'is bones, all of you, so why bother?'

'Two mouthfuls is two mouthfuls, is wot I say . . .'

'But . . . but I LOVED 'IM.'

It was so cold in the room that each shout came out of each mouth in visible puffs of breath. In the grate, a small fire was barely licking the sides of a cooking pot or warming the hands of the boy and girl huddled side by side, their backs turned to the argument.

'Ivy,' said the boy, tugging the girl's sleeve. 'If Jimminy gets put in the stew will you eat any?'

The little girl shook her head, vehemently. She had barely said a word since running in ten minutes earlier,

17

minus the blue jacket, and her wet bottom and evident distress had gone entirely unremarked.

'What, not even if you fished bits of 'im out, so it was just the turnips left?'

No, said a second shake of the head. Never in a month of Sundays. Never, never, never.

Behind their backs a man, a woman, and three big girls leaned closer over the object of their disagreement. The man kept his face straight and licked his lips as if he could wait no longer for his dinner. He was pulling the legs of this lot, but they were all too dim to see the joke. *Women!* he thought. *As thick as fog, the lot of 'em . . .*

'Poor Jimminy,' wailed the middle girl. ''Ow could *any*one think of eatin' 'im. It would be . . . it would be . . .'

'Savage,' declared the woman, raising one hand weakly to her brow. '*Savage* is the word you are rummaging for, Mad, my dear. And I do declare, Mr Jackson, I never thought . . .'

But no one got to hear what it was she never thought, for into the room burst Jared, followed, at a more sedate pace, by Mrs Merryfield and Mrs Larrington.

'Now then, me nearest an' dearest!' Jared called, clapping his hands for silence. 'We've got important visitors, so look sharp an' let's be showin' 'em wot little 'ospitality we can, given our sadly reduced circumstances.'

'Orlando!' he added. 'Ivy! Git away from the fire so these ladies can warm theirselves. An' if there's any of our table left, even so much as a splinter, throw it in the grate so's they get the benny-fit. An', Horatia, see if there ain't a few tea leaves still stuck to the sides of the old caddy, an' two cups wot ain't cracked to pour tea in.'

'Wait!' Mrs Merryfield held up her umbrella, for silence. 'There is no need for anyone to move, or to provide refreshments. Mrs Larrington and I are perfectly comfortable as, and where, we are.' Quickly, she checked to see if Mrs Larrington had managed to lower her crinoline. Mercifully, she had. 'Now,' she continued. 'May I address myself to the head of this household?'

Obediently, the three big girls shuffled away, leaving their father, their mother, and a very dead canary all by themselves in the middle of the room.

The father cleared his throat. 'Elmer Nicholas Montague Jackson at your service, ladies,' he said. 'An' you'll forgive us, I 'ope, for bein' all out of sorts, but little Jimminy 'ere was a fine singin' bird an' much doted on by me daughter, Madeleine. An' now 'e's froze to death—jus' like we all will be, if me circumstances don't improve before the weather does.'

Mrs Merryfield grunted in what sounded like sympathy but could just as easily have been boredom. Or disbelief. Mrs Larrington, however, had barely acknowledged either the man's speech or the presence of a small feathery corpse on the floor. She was distracted—mesmerized, almost—by the third member of the group.

Mrs Pamela Letitia Montague Jackson was making no effort whatsoever to be civil. Indeed, she had not even risen to her feet but was reclining, like a raggedy duchess, on what looked like . . . what *was* . . . a dilapidated, but still serviceable, chaise longue.

And what a peculiar spectacle she made in her 'good' brocade gown that had been patched so many times in not-quite-the-same materials that the original pattern could have been of anything from dots to daisies.

Her frilly cap, too, was ludicrously outdated and, like the disintegrating gown, really *not* the kind of thing one would expect to see on a pauper. Round her shoulders she wore a fur—a big tatty swathe of the stuff, in several shades of grey. It certainly wasn't ermine, that fur. Or chinchilla. Or mink. Perhaps, thought Mrs Larrington, it was cobbled-together rabbit. Or, *oh dear*, cat.

Haughtily, Mrs Jackson returned Mrs Larrington's gaze.

'Is this a visit of condolence, m'dear?' she enquired. 'For our sweet-departed canary-bird? Or is it a social call? For whichever it is I ain't in no mood to receive yer. I'm an invalid woman, as you can surely see, an' I don't take kindly to folk jus' droppin' in without an invy-tation or so much as a by your leave.'

There it was again. That word 'invalid' incorrectly pronounced. This time Mrs Larrington just about managed to turn her sneer into a cough.

'Now then, mama!' Jared was at his mother's side in a trice. 'These ladies 'ave come to assess our wants an' needs. So let's just give 'em an' honest account of ourselves, shall we? So they'll know that every penny they sees fit to give us is sorely needed and truly deserved.'

Mrs Larrington looked at Mrs Merryfield and Mrs Merryfield frowned back. *Third rule of home visits*, said the look and the frown. *Do not be tricked into parting with money*.

'Young man,' rapped Mrs Merryfield. 'I think you misunderstand the nature of our Association's . . .'

20

'AHA!' Quick as a wink, Jared whirled away from the chaise longue and pointed across the room. 'Don't think you can creep away unnoticed, Ivy, me girl. An' don't think I've forgotten what yer did neither. It's a wallopin' you're about to get, for rippin' the collar of me brand new jacket. So COME 'ERE!'

Ivy jumped. She hadn't been creeping anywhere. She hadn't moved so much as a snail's slither from the hearth.

'COME 'ERE, I said! I'll learn yer t'be so careless with the only warm piece o' clothin' we possess between the lot of us!'

Agonized, Ivy gazed beseechingly at the charity monger who had hooked her. She didn't deserve a walloping. It was their fault the jacket had got torn, not hers.

Mrs Larrington and Mrs Merryfield exchanged another glance. *Oh dear*, said that glance. *It could be we have a moral obligation, just this once, to break the third rule.*

'Did you bring a purse, my dear?' murmured Mrs Merryfield. 'For I tend to travel light.'

Mrs Larrington opened her mouth to protest, but closed it as, with a furious roar, Jared bore down upon the hearth.

'Oh, for a second's blessed *peace*,' was all the mother said, while the father seemed to want no part in the issue and the three big girls merely huddled and shrieked in mock alarm. Only the little boy—the one they called Orlando—appeared to mind as Jared reached the fireplace and swung his right arm in a great walloping arc.

'WAIT!' cried Mrs Merryfield, in the nick of time. 'How much? How much will it cost to replace the jacket?'

Jared paused, his hand still up in the air. 'Ten bob,' he said.

Mrs Merryfield's face turned dark. 'Ten *shillings*,' she spluttered. 'For that threadbare piece of tat?'

'It's good quality cloth,' declared Mrs Jackson, sitting up remarkably fast for an invalid. 'I can vouch for that, my dear madam. *And* it's lined.'

'That's right,' added Mr Jackson, blinking rapidly. 'A *gentleman's* garment it was, an' barely worn. 'Ow didjer ruin it, Ivy? What the Devil was yer playin' at?'

'Eight shillings,' snapped Mrs Merryfield, before Ivy could answer. 'The Association will allow you eight shillings—but only if you will forgive the little girl her . . . her carelessness, and dwell no further on the matter.'

'Nine,' Jared shot back. 'To be sure of gettin' one wiv all its buttons.'

'Eight shillings and sixpence,' said Mrs Merryfield. 'And that is my final offer. Mrs Larrington—the purse, if you please.'

CHAPTER 4
Concerning marvellous opportunities

*E*ight shillings and sixpence . . .
The chink of those coins falling into Jared's palm was like music to the family's ears.

Rent an' coal, Mr Jackson told himself. *An' enough left over for a few beers!*

Coal an' rent, Mrs Jackson decided. *An' meat in the pot for a week!*

The big girls smiled and sighed and made silent wishes: *A pink ribbon for me bonnet . . . Another canary . . . A rattle for the babby . . .*

Even Orlando Bartholomew Montague Jackson, for all he was only eight, dared to hope for a very small twist of liquorice.

Only Ivy expected nothing whatsoever.

'Thank you, ladies,' said Jared, patting his pocket once the transaction was complete. 'We won't detain you no longer. Orlando'll show you out. Good day.'

'Not so fast, young man.' Mrs Merryfield leaned forward, both hands resting on the handle of her umbrella. 'What's that noise?'

Mrs Larrington, too, had been thinking she could hear something. A faint mewling coming from a far corner of the room, where rolls of dingy bedding had been stowed out of the way.

Mrs Jackson sighed. 'Hor,' she whined, ''e's awake.'

Horatia Dolores Montague Jackson, the eldest and lumpiest of the big girls, gave an exaggerated tut of annoyance. Then she flounced across the room to where her baby son had been left to sleep, swaddled in sacks and wedged in a gooseberry sieve.

'Oh!' said Mrs Larrington as the girl strode back to her sisters with the baby hiccuping sadly on her shoulder. 'Oh, my. So you've recently had a happy event, Mrs Jackson? He must be . . . let me see . . . your seventh?'

'Ha-ha!' laughed the family while Mrs Jackson pursed her lips and winced at the very notion. 'No, indeed!' she declared. 'That's our Hor's little-'un—Salvador Francis she calls 'im. An' 'e weren't no 'appy event neither—much as we all loves 'im—for 'e weren't planned for, if y'get me meaning, an' the father ain't got the prospects of a toothless comb, for all 'is flash talk.'

Mrs Larrington felt her face turn hot with embarrassment. Had this little baby been born out of wedlock, then? If so, it was surely shameless to admit as much to visitors or to even acknowledge his *presence*.

'And Ivy ain't mine neither,' Mrs Jackson continued, adjusting her furs imperiously. 'She's me dead brother-in-law's child wot we took in, out the kindness of our 'earts, three years back.'

Aha.

Mrs Larrington did no more than incline her head. *Cat*, she thought, having caught a glimpse of tail, swinging from the back of Mrs Jackson's attire. *Definitely cat.*

Mrs Merryfield was considering the small girl beside

the hearth with something verging upon interest.

'Where's your mother, child?' she asked.

Ivy looked up, warily.

'Gone,' Mrs Jackson answered, promptly. 'Leavin' little Ivy all alone in the world, God love 'er.'

'I see.' Mrs Merryfield snapped her fingers towards her companion. 'The list,' she demanded. 'If you please.'

Mrs Larrington looked back at her, baffled. Then the penny dropped. Of course . . . the list.

Quickly she reached for a second time into her beaded reticule and produced a rolled-up piece of paper which she passed to Mrs Merryfield.

Without a word of explanation, Mrs Merryfield unfurled the paper and scanned its contents.

What is it? the Jacksons wondered. *What is this list? And what does it have to do with Ivy's mother?*

'Hmmm,' went Mrs Merryfield, as she considered the words on the page—words set down by the founders of the Ragged Children's Welfare Association to help its volunteers reach a very important decision:

Who is Most Deserving of a Place at Our Schools?

1. Children of convicts who have been transported
2. Children of convicts in our prisons at home
3. Children of thieves not in custody
4. Children of the lowest mendicants and tramps
5. Children of worthless drunken parents
6. Children of those suitable for the workhouse but living, instead, a semi-criminal life
7. Orphans, deserted children and runaways

25

8. The children of poor Roman Catholics who do not object to their children reading the Bible

Mrs Larrington peeped excitedly over Mrs Merryfield's shoulder.

'Number seven,' she declared. 'I do believe number seven is *quite* appropriate in this instance.'

Mrs Merryfield rolled up the list and passed it back. 'Indeed,' she replied.

'And the little boy?' Mrs Larrington felt encouraged to ask, nodding towards Orlando. 'Might he also be deserving?'

'Hmmm,' Mrs Merryfield hummed again. 'I suspect numbers three, six, and possibly five might all prove fitting in *his* case.'

Mrs Larrington turned towards the big girls. She was beginning to enjoy herself. She was starting to feel like a ministering angel, bringing light to dark places and succour to the needy.

Mrs Merryfield tugged sharply on her shawl.

'Enough,' she muttered, through the side of her mouth. 'There's a limit.'

And so the Jackson family was told that little Ivy and her cousin, Orlando, were to be granted a marvellous opportunity—namely, an education. And that this education would enhance their expectations no end, to the extent, perhaps, that they might one day find employment as servants.

Mr Jackson wasn't keen.

'Never mind no educashun,' he grumbled. 'It's out sellin' fruit an' flowers they oughter be, like our Jared an' the girls. An' that's what they'll be doin', come the spring,

26

if I 'as any say in the matter.'

Mrs Jackson fluttered her hand at him, dismissively.

'They will need boots for school,' she said to Mrs Merryfield. 'Both of 'em. An' what about their dinners?'

'The Association donates footwear to pupils in particular need,' Mrs Merryfield replied. 'And a midday meal is provided at the school—a very *good* meal, with meat more often than not.'

'Hah!' whooped Mrs Jackson. 'Y'hear that, Ive? A meat dinner more often than not. That's summat for yer t' look forward to, ain't it?'

Ivy lowered her eyes as the rough laughter of her aunt and her big girl-cousins rang around the room. Her hair fell in red snarls down over her face, hiding her expression.

'That's settled then,' said Mrs Merryfield. 'The school, as I'm sure you know, is directly behind the vinegar factory. These children should report there at eight o'clock sharp on Monday morning. Mrs Larrington? I believe our business here is concluded. You must brace yourself to re-enter the alleyway.'

Mrs Larrington gulped.

'Eh? No need for that.' Mr Jackson turned towards the hearth. 'Orlando—show these good ladies down the stairs an' out through the courtyard. It's just as quick, the courtyard is, for gettin' back onto New Cut. Unless, if you'll pardon me boldness, ladies, you *prefer* squeezin' down the alley wiv' yer skirts up by yer ears?'

'No indeed,' squeaked Mrs Larrington. 'We will go by the courtyard. Most definitely.' Her relief was immediately tempered by the realization that young Jared

Roderick Montague Jackson had neglected to mention, earlier, the existence of a far wider and less humiliating route into and out of Paradise Row.

But Jared smiled so winningly as she and dear Mrs Merryfield took their leave, that she was inclined to give him the benefit of the doubt.

'The jacket!' squealed Cynthia Evangeline Montague Jackson (the youngest and least lumpy of the big girls) as soon as the door creaked shut. 'I'll 'ave it for meself. I don't care about no torn collar. I ain't fussy.'

'Shhhh.' Jared held a warning finger to his lips. 'Wait.'

And so the family waited until the sound of the charity mongers' boots had faded away down the stairs. For Ivy the waiting was as fearful as it was silent, for she half-expected a thrashing, still, for the thing she hadn't done but could never explain because no one would listen, or believe her if they did.

But then—'Oh my stars, what a caper!' burst out Jared, doubling over with mirth, and chortling until tears sprang from his eyes. 'What a ruse!' And he held up the blue jacket by the collar and shook it once . . . twice . . . three times.

Ivy stared, her eyes growing rounder and rounder as the jacket flapped and twitched.

There were no rips in it at all. Not even a tiny one.

Jared grinned and winked at her.

''Ow smart was that then?' he bragged. ''Ow clever am I? I saw the way that big old charity monger hooked yer, wiv that brolly of 'ers. An' so I thought to meself, "Jared, me lad, there's a bob or two to be made out o' this. We could bennyfit from this if I plays me cards right."'

'That's my boy!' declared his father, rubbing his hands

together. 'That's my smart lad.'

And Mrs Jackson beamed fondly at her eldest son while the big girls giggled and clapped and baby Salvador tried and failed to go back to sleep on his mother's jiggling shoulder.

Then Madeleine Aurora Montague Jackson said that since they now had more than enough money to buy mutton for the pot could they please, please, *please* give darlin' Jimminy a Christian burial before the ground outside froze too solid to dig?

And Mr Jackson, with a twinkle in his eye, said he would give the matter some serious thought but he still had a hankering for a mouthful of canary meat.

And then the big girls began to shriek and argue all over again. And Mrs Jackson sank back on her tatty chaise longue crying, 'My dear Mr Jackson . . . Mad . . . Hor . . . Cyn . . . remember, if you will, my poor aching head . . .'

And Ivy turned away from the chaos to stare sadly into the ashes under the pot of cooling stew.

School.

Perhaps it would be a good place. Perhaps she would like going there, in spite of the dinners. And Orlando would be with her. She was glad about that, at least.

Prodding the ashes, to see if they would flare, Ivy tried not to think any more about the blue jacket. Only . . . would Cousin Jared really have thrashed her, she wondered, if the charity mongers hadn't stopped him?

Yes, he would.

Even knowing, full well, that she had done nothing wrong?

Yes.

And would he have kept on belting her, in front of everyone, until the charity mongers had either gone away or been shamed into paying up?

Yes. Undoubtedly.

Ivy was five years old and already resigned to life being unfair most of the time. She couldn't quite see how school might change that for her. But she dared to hope . . . couldn't *help* but hope . . . that perhaps . . . if she was lucky . . . it might.

CHAPTER 5
In which Ivy becomes a scholar

The first thing Ivy learned at school was that the back of her neck was so filthy it was amazing that nothing had grown in it. The second thing she learned was that her head might have to be shaved, like a convict's, and marked with the letter 'V'.

'V' for verminous.

This second piece of information was particularly frightening and completely untrue. The big strong-fingered woman, whose job it was to check heads, simply enjoyed saying it to scare new pupils. And she got a special thrill out of saying it to little pauper-girls who had hair far thicker, curlier, and brighter than their station in life seemed to merit.

'Disgraceful,' this mean-minded old fossil muttered, bending Ivy forwards over a sink and tugging and pulling at the knots in her hair until Ivy thought she would swoon from the pain of it. 'Absolutely disgraceful. When were you last combed through, child?'

Ivy couldn't remember. There was no comb at home, but there was a brush which the big girls and Aunt Pamela sometimes used in an attempt to bring a shine to their dust-coloured locks. It wouldn't go through Ivy's hair, though. And anyway, Cyn and Mad said it turned their stomachs to see horrible red strands clogging up the bristles of 'their' brush so the less often she borrowed it the better.

'Tsssk,' hissed the lice woman, tugging even harder as she searched for infestations.

Nothing.

No creepers. No eggs. Nothing except tangles and dirt.

'Humph!'

Ivy found herself back on her feet, being told to go through to the schoolroom. Other children, waiting in line to have their own scalps examined, looked at her and giggled.

'Mop-'ead,' someone sniggered.

Anxiously, Ivy raised a hand to her hair. Her curls, unruly at the best of times, had been teased by the lice woman's fingers into an even bushier shock.

An oddity, she thought to herself. *I am an oddity after all, just like Hor and Mad and Cyn are forever tellin' me I am.*

Miserably she looked along the line for Orlando, but he had already gone ahead of her into the schoolroom. The waiting children stared back with varying degrees of mischief or malice in their eyes. Some of the girls had heads so verminous that their plaits were twitching. But none of them had hair that was red, or mop-like. None of them were *that* different.

The door through to the schoolroom was solid and heavy and hard for Ivy to push open. The noise of it closing behind her made everyone turn. Big children. Little children. Ivy recognized some of them from the streets and felt less alone.

The room was vast and the windows too high to see out of. Warm, though. It was nice and warm in there. And the lady who told her to come and sit down spoke kindly enough.

Ivy would have liked to sit next to Orlando, but he was halfway down the room, among the bigger boys, while she was being pointed to a bench not far from the door, where the youngest pupils perched, their faces wan, their feet weighed down by second-hand boots.

Meekly, Ivy went where she had been told. Her scalp was stinging and she thought she might need the privy. No one had told her where the privy was. No one had told her anything at all except that she was disgraceful and a mop-head and should sit down.

And so she sat. And she waited.

'Hands in laps, children,' the kind lady said. 'And no fidgeting.'

It was hard not to fidget, when you needed the privy.

Eventually all the children on Ivy's bench were given tin trays with a thick layer of damp sand in them. Ivy held hers between both hands and wondered why. There was no desk or table to put it on, so she rested it on her knees.

The kind lady moved away and began pointing with a cane at some shapes on the wall. 'Watch and listen, children,' she said. 'A, B, C . . .'

Letters, Ivy realized. The lady was teaching them their letters. And if she paid enough attention, like the charity mongers had said, she would learn how to read and write and might one day be somebody's servant.

'D, E, F, G . . .'

The tray felt awkward on her lap. She pressed into it with one finger. The sand was gritty but an interesting colour—not grey like the ash or black like the mud that she usually traced her pictures in but a salt and peppery mix of lightish and darkish browns.

'H, I, J . . .'

The hole she had made looked like an eye, or the middle bit of a daisy. An eye, she decided. It was definitely an eye. But whose or what's? Gently, carefully, she began to make other marks.

'K, L, M, N . . .'

A curve here, a line there . . . It was interesting how, if you patted some of the sand together in just the right way it made a big fat tummy look exactly *like* a big fat tummy.

'Little girl. *Little girl!*'

The kind lady had stopped chanting letters and was pointing her cane across everybody's heads at . . .

Oh.

Ivy took her finger out of the sand so fast that the tray almost slid from her lap.

The children nearest to her twisted round to gawp. Even some of the older pupils, further down the room, turned to see who was in trouble. 'Eyes front!' their own teacher commanded and they swivelled back again.

The kind lady was striding towards Ivy, her face grim.

'Stand up,' she said.

Ivy stood.

'Now follow me. And bring your tray.'

The boots Ivy had been given had belonged to a rat catcher. They were serviceable enough, but way too large, and they clumped, slopped, and grated Ivy's heels as she followed her teacher to a corner of the room, holding her tray out in front of her as steadily as she could.

'Stand there and don't move.'

There was a pile of rags in the corner which the teacher began to sort through. Each rag had a red flannel shape stitched onto it—a letter of the alphabet, Ivy realized, just like the ones she was going to learn.

'I,' said the teacher, pulling a rag from the pile. Her voice was stern, and loud enough for everyone to hear. 'The letter "I". What might that stand for, school, in relation to this child?'

Several hands shot up at once.

Ivy considered the shape on the rag. It looked like a stick, this letter 'I'.

'Yes, you . . . you there.'

'Idiot, miss.'

'It could. It could mean "idiot", but not in this instance . . . Yes? Boy in the yellow waistcoat?'

'An eyesore, miss.'

'No. That would be the letter "e". . . and it is *no* cause for merriment, school.'

Ivy hung her head.

'Idle.'

'No. Not idle. Not in this case.'

These were all older children speaking out. They sounded very wise and Ivy couldn't help but wonder if she would ever be that clever. She wasn't to know that these children were no great shakes as scholars. That they had merely spent enough time in the corner themselves, or watching others being punished, to have memorized the school's entire A to Z of transgressions.

Then Orlando raised his hand—the youngest child to do so.

Orly, thought Ivy, in hurt surprise. *Wotcher doin'?* Orlando didn't understand letters any more than she did. And besides, why would he, of all people, want to add to her misery by suggesting a bad thing about her beginning with 'I'?

'Yes,' her teacher said. 'You . . . new boy.'

Orlando's voice rang clear across the room. 'I know,' he said. 'I know what the word is. It's "Ivy", ain't it? "I" for "Ivy", I, V, E.' He sounded excited, as if he had just discovered the key to something vital—something that would eventually mean far more to him than anything else in the world.

'Nonsense,' the teacher rebuked him. 'Ivy—and that's I, V, Y, by the way, young man—is neither an adjective or a misdemeanour, so how could it possibly apply?'

Orlando shrank back, the excitement draining from his face.

The teacher turned to Ivy, and took the tray from her hands.

'Inattentive,' she pronounced, slowly and loudly. 'This child was not paying attention to her lesson. Her very *first* lesson. She is "I" for "inattentive" and will remain here, in this corner, until she is "R" for . . . ?'

'Repentant,' chorused half the school; 'remorseful,' chanted the others, the sound of the words clashing and jumbling above their heads.

And so Ivy was left standing in the corner, clutching the letter 'I' and wondering what it meant to be remortant. Or had they said repenful? And the tray of sand was

36

placed on the floor beside her, its surface swiped smooth by the flat of the teacher's hand so that no trace remained of the happy hillocky person that Ivy had so enjoyed creating.

CHAPTER 6

Concerning additional shame and humiliation

Had Ivy's mortification ended there, all might yet have gone well for her—academically, that is. She might have knuckled down, toed the line, and taken to reading, writing, and doing sums faster than any other ragged child in London.

And who knows? By the time her Uncle Elmer decided to put a stop to it (and he would have done, eventually, on the grounds that education makes the female brain boil) she might have learned enough about the art of wheedling and coaxing to talk him round.

Still, that is not the way her life unravelled.

For approximately ten minutes, on her first day at school, she suffered her punishment in the corner meekly and well. But the longer she stood there, holding the letter 'I', the more urgently she felt the urge to visit the privy. And the more urgently she needed to go, the harder it became to feel repentance, remorse, or anything at all apart from the growing pressure on her bladder.

Eventually, when the discomfort had become painful, she glanced desperately around the room. If someone—the teacher, Orlando, the lice woman, *anyone*—would only catch her eye she would get them to come over and tell her where the privy was.

But the little children were bent over their trays, tracing the letters 'D', 'E', and 'F' in the sand. And the older ones were staring into space, chanting multiplication tables like a dull prayer. No one was watching Ivy. No one was paying her any attention whatsoever. And it was rapidly becoming too late to ask about the privy. Too late to leave the room, even.

She had to go.

She really, really, had to go.

And so, with a quick sideways step, a twitching up of her dress, and a wide standing squat—she went.

Really, it was 'I' for ingenious the way she avoided making a big puddle on the floor—or even a small splash. And it was nothing short of 'M' for miraculous that nobody noticed what she had done. No one, that is, until the lesson ended and the teacher came over to tell her she could join the other children in the yard, and then go for her midday dinner. For the teacher noticed straightaway that the tray of sand on the floor had become more than a little waterlogged.

To Ivy's astonishment not a word was said. The teacher merely took her into the yard and pointed out the privy. Then she left her with the other little ones, who taunted her for a while about being a mop-'ead, but eventually included her in a noisy game of tag.

No word was said later, either. Nor would it have been. Ever. For the teacher was not so unkind as to openly shame a five-year-old child for having had a little accident, particularly when the said five year old had shown enough 'I' for 'initiative' to do it in a tray instead of all over the floorboards.

Ivy, however, did not think for a minute that peeing on one's tray of sand might be considered less of a misdemeanour than drawing a person in it. To her it seemed by far the worst thing to have done and she felt certain that her punishment, when it came, would be brutal.

It was like waiting for an axe to fall. By the time her midday dinner was plonked in front of her she was too twisted up with anxiety inside to even sniff it.

'Go on,' whispered Orlando who had squeezed next to her on the dinner bench. 'It's mostly cabbage, I *think*.' He and the other children were eating their own broth so fast that the clatter of spoons sounded like a race of tin horses.

The lice woman was waiting to remove the empty bowls.

'What's wrong with you?' she said to Ivy. 'Finish that soup. There's good bacon in there.'

Orlando looked anxiously at Ivy and then up at the woman.

'She . . . she don't eat no meat,' he said. 'Not if she can 'elp it she don't.'

The woman peered at Ivy in amazement. She had never heard the like.

'Why not?' she said.

The sound of spoons diminished as other children stopped to listen.

'I . . . I can't rightly say,' Orlando muttered, heat rising in his face. He had already spoken up once, in front of the whole school, and been made to feel ridiculous. And that had been about Ivy as well. He was tired, now, fed up with his odd little cousin and too confused by the wonder and horror of education to want to debate this, or

40

anything else, for longer than absolutely necessary. 'Maybe she just don't fancy it right now,' he mumbled, hoping it would be enough.

The lice woman placed both hands firmly on her hips. Her face was red, sweaty, and as big as a basin as she towered over the bench. 'Well la-di-da,' she exclaimed. 'And 'ere's me thinkin' beggars can't be choosers. Perhaps 'er ladyship would prefer a nice baked sole, with a jug o' parsley sauce, and then raspberry cream for afters? Or shall I ask cook to coddle 'er an egg, with a bit o' nutmeg in the yolk, and some bread an' butter on the side, cut thin?'

Ivy kept her head down, her mouth shut and her gaze just slightly to the right of her unwanted dinner. Orlando nudged her.

'She *does* eat eggs,' he volunteered, hopefully. 'Don'tyer, Ive? You'd eat an egg, wouldn't yer? If the kind cook were t'do one for yer?'

The lice woman bent closer and lower, until Orlando could see all the hairs up her nose. 'Give me strength!' she roared, thumping the table so hard that bowls jumped and spoons trembled. 'I ain't serious, you daft blighter. No. This picky miss stays right where she is until every morsel of that broth gets eaten. The rest of you—back to your lessons. "Don't fancy it", indeed . . . The plain ingratitude! The bloomin' cheek!'

And so, for the second time in less than two hours, Ivy found herself in disgrace. *School ain't no fairer than 'ome,* she thought to herself. *Probably nowhere is.*

The lice woman waited until the last child had clomped away before thrusting a spoon into the bowl of congealing broth.

41

'You give me one good reason,' she said, 'why you ain't touched this lovely dinner.'

Ivy stared at the spoon, standing straight up in the mess of food. She had good reasons all right, but no one ever listened to them without laughing or getting cross so what was the point in explaining?

She could hear the lice woman breathing right in her ear. But she wouldn't look round at her, nor would she speak.

'Then eat!' the lice woman ordered. 'Go on. I ain't got all afternoon.'

Slowly, Ivy took hold of the spoon and lifted a morsel of cold cabbage to her mouth. It was slimy and cold but at least it wasn't meat, so she chewed it up and swallowed it quickly down.

'And the rest.'

Mercifully, the broth contained more cabbage than bacon. But with every reluctant mouthful the bacon-taste grew stronger until Ivy had to fight to keep from retching. She couldn't be sick. She couldn't. She had already wet in her sand tray and that was bad enough. If she vomited as well they would surely send her into the corner for at least a week, with enough letters in her hands to make an alphabet quilt.

'Eat. That. Bacon,' said the lice woman.

And then Ivy's luck changed—not much, but enough—as the lice woman was called away to deal with two little girls throwing sand from their trays into each other's eyes.

'I'll be straight back,' she warned. 'And if that meat's still there when I do, there'll be trouble. Understand?'

Yes, Ivy nodded. *I understand*.

But when the lice woman returned, the bacon *was* still there—uneaten, pink, and stringy at the bottom of Ivy's bowl. Of Ivy herself there was no sign.

She had vanished.

CHAPTER 7

In which a stranger gets ready to pounce

There had been frost on the cobbles again, that morning, but it had soon melted and for the first time in a long time the air didn't feel as if it was going to freeze your face off.

No fog, either, to clog the lungs and dampen the spirits. In fact the sky, above the chimney tops, was very nearly hyacinth blue and the afternoon sun, although weaker than a beggar's tea, was almost warm.

Perhaps it was this brightening of the weather that stopped Ivy from going straight back to Paradise Row after she had abandoned her bacon and marched out of school. Perhaps it was the tiny hint of spring in the air that made her turn left instead of right at Beaufoy's vinegar and wine works and go clomping down unfamiliar alleyways, as bold as a troll in her rat catcher's boots.

Whatever the reason, she was soon hopelessly lost.

I'll ask, she told herself. *I'll ask a bluebottle the way back to Paradise Row*. 'Bluebottle' meant a policeman. 'Watch out for them bluebottles,' Uncle Elmer always told Jared before the boy went out on the town. When she was smaller, and had known no better, Ivy had imagined real bottles raining down from the sky and thought her cousin very brave indeed to venture out among all those shards of breaking glass.

She felt knowledgeable now, in comparison to her three-year-old self, as she scanned the immediate vicinity for a figure in a top hat and distinctive blue coat.

It was a wide and busy thoroughfare she had found herself in. The sun had brought the street sellers out and their voices mingled with the clatter of wheels and the clop of hooves to form a sing-song sales pitch for plum cake and violets and packets of pins.

The big girls sold violets. Perhaps, Ivy thought, she would see Mad or Cyn or Hor and whichever one it was would swoop over to her, all of a scold, and keep her close until enough flowers had been sold to make supper more likely.

But the violet-seller turned out to be an unknown blowsy person who passed by without so much as a glance in Ivy's direction. No bluebottles around, either, so far as Ivy could tell. Only strangers in a hurry, their legs, skirts, and carriage wheels racing by in a blur.

From somewhere—a pie shop, perhaps, or the cake-seller's barrow—a heavenly smell of pastry made Ivy's stomach growl. She would eat a plum cake all right. Or muffins or crumpets or a gingerbread-nut. For none of them had ever been creatures, and she had long since walked off any energy she might have gleaned from seven nasty mouthfuls of school cabbage.

Orlando had told her, once, about a street boy who would have starved only he knew of a big house where a lady put food on a windowsill for the birds. A ground floor sill it was, because the lady was an invalid, like Aunt

Pamela, and never left her parlour. And it wasn't just crumbs she put out either, or crusts gone hard and green, but hunks of bread so big and soft and warm you'd think that the lady was waiting for some magical beast to fly down and tap on the glass.

Ivy would have given anything, at that moment, for a piece of warm bread. But she didn't know where to find the house with a feast on the sill. It could have been anywhere in London. It could have been anywhere in the *world*.

For a moment, the passing legs and skirts and carriage wheels became an even bigger blur. But crying was for babies who wanted to be fed, or for silly girls like Mad who did it for attention. Crying had never got Ivy very far, so there was no point doing it now.

Three blinks, a snotty sniff, and the urge to weep went away. And, with the tears gone, Ivy saw that she was being watched.

It was a woman gazing at her, from across the street. A very tall woman with—*oh*—red hair.

With so many people to-ing and fro-ing, it was odd to see someone else—particularly someone else with red hair—standing stock still as if they too were lost and hoping to see a bluebottle. Perhaps, Ivy thought, this was someone she knew. Someone from Paradise Row.

But no. She was just another stranger. So why had she stopped and why was she staring?

Eventually it dawned on Ivy that this woman hadn't actually paused for her benefit. Nor was she really staring—at least not in a *seeing* kind of way. She had stopped to peel an orange. She was just a woman resting her feet for a moment or two, while she ate her fruit. And she,

46

Ivy, happened to be in her line of vision the way a statue or a gas lamp might have been.

Ivy didn't like being looked at in that way. It made her feel like a ghost; transparent and forgotten.

So she hunkered down on the paving stones, with her back against the chill of a wall, and let her head fall forward so that all *she* could see was her own lap.

Then the red-haired woman really did notice her.

Small child alone. Aha!

Briskly, in a matter of seconds, she assessed Ivy from top to toe.

Hat: none. Scarf: none. Coat: cream-coloured but grubby and thin—wouldn't fetch more than thruppence. Gloves or muff: none. Dress: faded and unfashionable—fit only for the rag man. Petticoat: none visible. Stockings: probably none. Boots: adult sized and . . . hmmm . . . not at all bad, despite the missing laces. Good leather. Just need to check for holes.

Right then.

Ivy looked up. The woman was smiling at her now—really smiling—and holding out a slice of orange.

Ivy liked oranges, although the taste, she knew, could be variable. The ones Cousin Jared got from the market were usually small and wizened until he pricked the skins and boiled them up. Then they swelled to double their size and he quickly sold them on.

If this woman had bought her orange from Cousin Jared it would be like eating a sliver of water. Still, it was food, and of the kind Ivy ate, so she got up and crossed over the road.

The woman watched her drawing closer. *That's right, my pretty*, she thought. *Come to Carroty Kate. Come an' say*

47

hello. Keeping her smile fixed, and her hand outstretched, she plotted her next few moves. The street was busy (*bad*) and there was no fog (*bad*) but the girly was alone (*excellent*) and it couldn't be very far to the nearest Suitable Place.

In fact, now she came to think of it, there was a highly Suitable Place just off to the left—the kind of alley law-abiding adults never entered for fear of losing their lives, their wallets, or both. It was the simplest act in the world to lure a small child into a place of that sort, so long as it didn't struggle or scream.

This one didn't look like a struggler or a screamer. It looked meek and trusting; dealing with this one would be as easy as peeling the orange. No mess, no bruised flesh, and nothing badly torn.

Carroty Kate leaned towards the approaching child the way an angel might lean from the heavens. And the piece of orange between her fingers could have been fashioned from the second stripe of a rainbow, or cut from purest gold, so graciously did she offer it.

There, she thought as Ivy's small hand reached up. *Gotcher.*

CHAPTER 8

In which snap decisions are made

It was a very tasty orange after all.

'Thank you,' said Ivy, licking the juice from her lips and wishing there had been more.

The tall red-haired woman was pointing down at the rat catcher's boots. 'I think, little girl, you might 'ave stepped in somethin' unspeakable,' she was saying, holding her nose as if mortally offended by a terrible smell. 'Shall we check? You wouldn't want to be treadin' whatever it is into your nice 'ome now, would you?'

Baffled, but obedient, Ivy lifted first one foot then the other. She couldn't smell anything. And why would it matter to this person what she'd stepped in or where she trod it?

'Actually, they're both fine,' she heard the woman say. 'Perfect, in fact.'

'Thank you,' Ivy repeated, at a loss to know what else to say.

'I can buy us another orange,' the woman added. 'If you like.'

Ivy hesitated. She wasn't used to people offering her good things. The woman yawned and glanced away down the street, as if it didn't *really* matter two hoots to her what Ivy wanted to do. Then she said: 'I know *I* could eat some more. But not a whole one. A whole orange'd mess me innards up summat chronic, but another half would just about see me through till suppertime. How about you?'

Ivy thought about suppertime in Paradise Row. There would be mutton in the pot, without a doubt, now that they had all those shillings from the charity mongers. More mutton than turnips, probably, which would be truly horrible. And what if Uncle Elmer and Aunt Pamela were cross with her for running away from school? They weren't hitters and wallopers like Cousin Jared, but they were great yellers and shriekers and that would be bad enough.

She didn't want to face the smell of boiling creatures and the clamour of angry voices. Not both at the same time. Not yet.

So she looked up at the red-haired woman and nodded.

'Very well,' said Carroty Kate. 'Take my 'and, and we'll go and find the fruit seller.' She offered her fingers, still sticky with orange juice.

Ivy took them.

What a strong grip, thought Carroty Kate. *Trusting, though. They were always so trusting . . .*

Quickly she turned and began to hurry, half-leading and half-pulling Ivy towards the Suitable Place.

'Please . . .' Ivy's voice was timid. 'I can't go very fast. Me boots won't let me.'

Carroty Kate ignored her and tightened her hold.

'They ain't my boots, that's why,' persisted Ivy, trotting and stumbling along as best she could. 'If you'd only wait a minute, missis, I could take 'em off. Then I'd go quicker.'

'What?'

Ivy almost fell over as Carroty Kate stopped dead in her tracks. But at least her hand had been released, so she plonked herself down on her bottom and tugged off first her right boot—*umph*—then the left.

'There,' she declared, waggling her bare toes. 'That's better. I'll leave 'em here, shall I, for some poor man to find? For I ain't wearin' 'em again. They hurt.'

Carroty Kate stared down at the rat catcher's boots, dumped on the cobbles like the droppings of some big leathery animal. Then she stared at Ivy's sore and stocking-less feet . . . at her peaky little face above the collar of the almost-worthless coat . . . at the halo of hair that, beneath all the dirt, was an even richer, brighter red than her own. And she felt something—an affinity, almost—that made her throw back her head and laugh so loud that passers-by stared in surprise and were moved, although they didn't know why, to smile briefly themselves as they hurried by.

'You're a rum little object, ain't yer?' Kate chortled. 'A funny little so-an-so.'

Ivy shrugged and stood up. 'I can go as fast as you now,' she said. 'To find that fruit seller.'

Carroty Kate rolled her eyes. *Gawblimey*, she thought. *I've picked a right one 'ere.* The air was colder now and the sun would soon be setting. It was time for her to be getting back to the lodging house where her bloke would be waiting to pick over the spoils of her day.

'Run along 'ome,' she said to Ivy. 'Go on. Scram.'

Ivy looked up at her, hurt.

'I can't,' she said, her lower lip starting to tremble. 'I don't know where to go.' *And what about the orange?* she wondered. *I thought we was gettin' another orange to eat?*

'Too bad,' snapped Carroty Kate. 'But none of my concern. Scarper—go on. Get lost.'

She began tapping her feet on the cobbles as she willed the child to go. The lodging house was a good few miles away, in another part of London, and her bloke would be fractious if she wasn't back soon. A long and weary walk it would be from here, but in Kate's line of business it didn't do to look for victims too close to home. Hit and run, that was her policy. Or hit and trudge anyway.

'Right, well, I'm off then,' she said. 'An' I'm takin' these with me.' Quick as a whip she bent down and swiped up the rat catcher's boots.

'What about our orange?' Ivy dared to ask.

'Never mind no orange.' Carroty Kate was refusing to look any more at this girly's sweet, stubborn face. Instead, her glance was caught by a lady going by. A well-dressed lady holding an equally well-dressed child by the hand. The lady smiled before carrying on. The child looked over her shoulder, and kept on looking until she disappeared round a corner.

Carroty Kate was quite taken aback. The lady's smile had been companionable—sisterly almost—and the girly's brimful of trust. The lady's look had said, 'Children— what trials they can be!' and the girly's had said, plain as anything, that she could have been made to linger.

And if a child lingered it could be lured. Snatched. Taken and gone. It was all in the timing.

Carroty Kate returned her attention to Ivy and began thinking fast. She had always worked the streets alone. It suited her temperament and situation. But folk were getting wiser to her kind of ruse. Children were being warned to beware of women, as well as men. So maybe . . . just maybe . . .

'Where's yer mam and dad then?' she asked, gruffly.

'Dead,' Ivy replied, mournfully, 'and gone.'

'So there ain't no grown-ups to care for yer? No one waitin' anywhere? To feed yer and suchlike?'

Ivy paused. What to say? Did Uncle Elmer and Aunt Pamela care? She doubted it. And would they be waiting for her or even wondering where she'd got to? Probably not. And would they feed her later, if she went back to them? Not if she could help it they wouldn't. Not if it was mutton.

So: 'No,' she said. 'There ain't no one.'

It wasn't a lie. Not really. In Ivy's mind it was kind of the truth, for even her precious Orlando had finally let her down. And she was only five, don't forget—too young to know that words, once said, can change the pattern of a life for ever.

'You'd better stick with me then,' said Carroty Kate. 'But I'm warnin' yer, it's a long walk and I ain't carryin' yer for all of it.'

Carrying?

Ivy couldn't remember what it felt like to be carried. Would it be like being cuddled or squashed? Either way it would stop her from being lost for a while. She was tired of being lost.

'Here,' said Carroty Kate. 'Only don't get too excited cos I'll be takin' 'em back in a bit.' And from somewhere up her sleeve she produced a pair of slippers. Small leather slippers as red as cherries and softer than a second skin.

Ivy put them on and was surprised to find that they fitted.

'Scuff 'em up and you're in trouble,' said Carroty Kate. 'Now let's go.'

And as they took the road out of Lambeth, heading hand in hand towards Westminster Bridge, Ivy had only one concern.

'Can we get that orange now?' she said.

CHAPTER 9

*Concerning potatoes and prayers in
dubious company*

C arroty Kate's bloke had a face like a bulldog
chewing a wasp. His name was Finn Nolan but he
was known among his peers as Fing, short for
Fingers.

The night Ivy first met him he was roasting chestnuts
on a shovel. This was unusual, for Fing's fingers, after
dark, were usually wrapped around a chisel, a jack, or a
brace and bit as he jemmied a window or forced a lock.

A recently bungled job, however, coupled with a narrow escape from the bluebottles, had obliged him to lie
low for a bit. And so he was cooking supper—chestnuts,
potatoes baked in hot ashes, and a sauce made of pulped
tomatoes, onions, and bits of the parsley he had grown
himself, in a dented colander suspended like a birdcage
from an overhead beam.

So exhausted was Ivy, as she half staggered and half
toppled into Fing's presence, that she failed to pick up on
telltale signs that she had fallen into a den of thieves. And
not just petty pilferers either, but criminals so hardened
that they made the Jackson family look like a tribe of
saints. All she understood, at that precise moment, was
that the lodging house kitchen was blissfully warm and
that supper smelt divine.

''Oo in the Devil's name is this?' Fing turned so abruptly that two of his chestnuts rolled off the shovel and burst into flames.

Carroty Kate continued unwinding her shawl.

'Keep yer 'air on,' she said. 'I'll explain in a bit. Ivy girl—sit down before you fall down. Go on. Over there with the lads. Ain't no one gonner bite yer.'

Peering dazedly around, Ivy focused on a table with half a dozen or so shadowy beings gathered round it. She hadn't noticed it, or them, straightaway, for they were partially screened by strings of laundry stretched across the room.

Damp sleeves, dangling ribbons, and frayed trouser legs brushed against her cheeks as she tottered to the end of the table. The bench was too high for her to climb onto, but one of the lads helped her up, grinning to show that there weren't enough teeth left in his head to bite.

'Right,' continued Carroty Kate. 'Here's me day's pickin's—for what they're worth, which ain't much.'

And from about her person she drew the scarlet slippers, the rat catcher's boots, and a baby's woollen bonnet, all of which she flung in a very small pile beneath the darkening gaze of her bloke.

'*Pah!*'

Fing spat contemptuously into the fire.

'Is that all? Wot was yer doin' all day then? Takin' the air—or tippin' the wink at young sailor boys?'

'Sailor boys, my eye! I walked the skin off me feet to get this little lot, Fing Nolan. Times is 'ard, that's all. Brats ain't as trustin' as they used to be. Or maybe me face don't look so sweet to them no more. Could be I'm losin' me knack.'

Muttering, Fing reached for a poker. 'These 'taters are done,' he said, prodding each one. 'An' I ain't sharin' mine with no brat. Wot's it doin' 'ere? This ain't no place for a little 'un.'

'She fits the Plan,' said Carroty Kate. 'The Mighty Grand Plan. So shut yer gob an' serve the grub. She can share my 'tater.'

Still muttering, Fing flung his 'taters onto a platter and carried them to the table. Then he shuffled back to the fire for the chestnuts and the sauce.

'Hats off, lads,' he said.

The shadowy beings removed their oilskin caps to reveal heads that were bald as eggs or as roughly stubbled as autumn fields. *Jail crops*. These lads were fresh out of prison.

Maybe they've all had the lice, Ivy thought. *Maybe some woman's gone and shaved their heads for 'em. Maybe Kate did it.*

Carroty Kate had plonked herself opposite Ivy and was dolloping tomato sauce onto a halved potato. Now that she was sitting down, with her bonnet and shawl off, Ivy could see that she was a biggish woman and not really very pretty. Her hair was more ginger than copper-coloured and the long ringlets had gone frizzy in the cold night air. It was this hair, Ivy realized, that had made Kate seem young. Closer to, she looked knobbly, like the potatoes, and easily as old as Aunt Pamela.

Ivy reached for a spoon.

'*Not yet*,' whispered the toothless lad on her left.

At the head of the table, Fing had removed his own cap and was standing with his big hands steepled together and his eyes scrunched shut.

'For wot we are about to eat,' he intoned, 'may we be truly grateful. And forgive the lads their trespasses, particularly today's ones, wot, as ye surely know, they only did for the sake of the Grand Plan and so's we wouldn't starve.'

Ivy peeked through her own steepled fingers, expecting that to be all.

'Forgive the Crow in partic'lar,' continued Fing, solemnly, 'for wot 'e did to that toff down Drury Lane. An' may the gentleman in question survive an' continue to prosper wivout too much of a scar. Amen.'

'*AMEN*,' chorused the lads, their heads nodding and gleaming in the firelight.

'*Amen*,' whispered Ivy, wondering which one was the Crow.

For a few seconds there was silence, as if the prayer needed time to settle. Then everyone began eating and talking at once.

Nobody was speaking to Ivy, however, so she ate her potato quietly. It was one of the best things she had ever been given. Carroty Kate passed her a handful of chestnuts, already peeled, and she ate those too—nibbling each one slowly, to savour the sweet nutty taste.

When she had finished she didn't know what else to do. It was too late to go back to Paradise Row. And she had walked a long way—right across London, it seemed—to get to this place.

Her eyes were closing . . . it was so warm. And since it had been a strange and exhausting day, and since she actually felt safe here, as well as snug, she rested first her arms, then her head, on the table top and went fast asleep.

One by one, the lads fell silent. The Crow. The Muck Snipe. Flash Michael. Dan-of-the-Ditch. Bludger McNab. One by one they looked at Ivy, slumped small and pale among them with tomato sauce on her chin and contented baby-snores whistling through her nostrils.

'Carroty,' said Fing, in his gruffest voice. 'You've got some explainin' to do . . .'

CHAPTER 10

Concerning some peculiar modifications to the thieves' lodging house

When Ivy eventually opened her eyes, she hadn't the faintest idea where she was. *Heaven*, she thought at first. And then, as she grew more awake: *or somebody's lovely cupboard.*

Her second impression was nearer the mark; for the space she had been tucked into was definitely cramped. If she pointed her toes they touched a wall. And if she wriggled backwards, just a little way, she hit her head. Reaching out with her right hand she touched a third wall. With her left she encountered a fourth only this one wasn't made of brick, it was all splintery.

There was daylight filtering in from a tiny barred window way above her head. It wasn't much, nor was it bright, but it was enough for Ivy to see that this confined space had been draped with gauzy material in different shades of blue, stitched all over with silver sequins the exact shape of stars.

Cocooned as she was, in a squishy eiderdown, it was a lot like being up in the sky. Had the whole place started to float away she would not have been at all surprised.

She felt around some more with her left hand. The splintery thing was a plank, and it was just high enough to stop her rolling out of her cloud-like bed. Above it hung a heavy curtain which, when she poked it, seemed to have nothing solid the other side.

Well.

'Ivy? You awake, girly?'

Carroty Kate's voice seemed to be coming from somewhere low down, on the other side of the plank.

'Come on. Rise an' shine. We got work to do, an' I ain't holdin' on to this blessed ladder for ever.'

Intrigued, Ivy shrugged off her bedding, lifted one side of the big heavy curtain and peeped out.

'Careful,' said Carroty Kate. 'Knock that thing off the wall an' Fing'll have the Devil's own job nailin' it back.'

Peering down, Ivy realized that her peculiar sleeping area was attached to a room with a lot of rolled-up mattresses in it. Away to the left, a cracked window, as big as a barn door, looked out over frosty rooftops. Someone had strung tin stars in front of the broken panes and they were twirling in the draught, like dancers.

It seemed an awfully long way to the floor.

''Urry up,' insisted Carroty Kate, jiggling the ladder. 'Or you won't get no breakfast.'

Breakfast? Now there was a treat.

The top rung of the ladder was just about reachable. The plank had a gap cut into it, close to where it joined the wall at Ivy's feet, and it had clearly been fashioned that way on purpose, so that the ladder would fit.

Quickly, Ivy crawled to the bottom of her makeshift bed, and opened the curtain at that end, enough to inch round it. Then . . . very carefully, so as not to wobble the ladder or do anything else wrong . . . she eased herself down and out. The heavy curtain fell back into place as she descended, rung by rung. Only, it wasn't really a curtain, Ivy realized, as her feet touched the floor. Not from this side, anyway. It was a picture daubed on a massive piece of sailcloth. And it was scary.

Round-eyed, Ivy stared and stared at the image of a vast, spreading tree. It looked like an oak, only with huge thorns instead of leaves. And, in place of acorns, there were *horrible things* weighing down the branches and heaped around the trunk. It was a black, menacing composition and it made Ivy shudder to think she had slept, unawares, right next to it.

'The Muck Snipe did that,' sniffed Carroty Kate. 'Silly sod. We could've made six pairs o' trousers out o' that piece o'cloth an' sold 'em at five shillin's a pair. But we needed summat to keep pokers an' priers from findin' our Secret Place an' it does *that* job all right . . . Gruesome, ain't it?'

Ivy hid her face against Carroty Kate's skirt and reached for her hand.

'Now then,' growled Kate. 'No goin' soft on me over nothin'.You've a few tricks to learn today, girly, and learn them you will otherwise Fing'll 'ave you dumped in the Thames before you can say a prayer.'

'I ought to go 'ome, really,' said Ivy.

'Home?' Carroty Kate's bumpy face was on an exact level, suddenly, with her own. 'You told me that you ain't got no 'ome,' she hissed. 'That there ain't no one in the world who'd ever miss yer and come lookin'.You weren't lyin' to your old pal Carroty, was you, girly? Cos if you was, best you say so right here and now.'

Ivy's heart began to race, but she kept her face empty. 'No,' she lied. 'I weren't lyin'.' She tried not to think about Paradise Row but found she couldn't help it. *Orly . . . I want my Orly*. Then she remembered the glee in Orlando's voice as he'd tried to guess the bad thing about her beginning with 'I'. He had school, now, to fill his days and his mind. He wouldn't want her any more.

Behind her, the tin stars tinkled and snickered. And the terrible things the Muck Snipe had painted on the tree had noticed her, and were interested. She could feel it.

Carroty Kate's eyes were boring into her too. Had she believed the lie? Ivy couldn't tell. The truth was tingling on the tip of her tongue but it felt too late, now, to say it.

Eventually, Carroty Kate gave a big heavy sigh. Her knees creaked as she stood up and for a moment she seemed at a loss.

Then she looked down at the top of Ivy's head, the way a weary bird might look upon a cuckoo in its nest. *I ought to throw you out*, said the look. *But we've let you in now, so you might as well stay*.

'All right,' she said. 'All right then, Ivy girl. Let's get you fed and properly dressed. Then you'd better start earnin' your keep.'

CHAPTER 11

*In which Ivy foolishly assumes that a Suitable Place
is where children are given free sweeties*

For as long as Ivy could remember, getting fed and
dressed had never been anything to get excited
about. At Paradise Row she had been lucky to start
the day on a cup of gruel. As for her clothes, every last
rag had already been worn, torn, and grown out of by
Mad, Cyn, and Hor. She had never owned a bonnet and
undergarments were an alien concept.

As usual, she had slept all night in her faded cotton
frock. So far as she was concerned, she only needed to
put her old coat back on, and maybe those wretched
boots, to be 'properly dressed'.

But first: breakfast; which, in the thieves' kitchen, consisted of an omelette fried in butter and sprinkled with a
fistful of cheese.

'Kidneys?' asked Carroty Kate, producing a platter of
the things from the heart of the oven.

Ivy shook her head. *No!*

'Please yerself,' said Kate, shoving them back.

Apart from the two of them the kitchen was deserted.
The dangling clothes had gone as well, all except a green
velvet dress and a pair of frilly drawers. Ivy looked at
these and wondered whose they were. They were pretty,
but way too small for Carroty Kate.

64

Was there another little girl staying here, then?

The omelette was very tasty, and there was a mug of milk to wash it down. 'What are these tricks I'm to learn, if you please?' Ivy asked, through a final mouthful of egg.

'All in good time,' said Carroty Kate. 'Are you finished? Right. Get that raggedy garment off yer back and put these on.' She had unpegged the pretty dress and the frilly drawers and was holding them out in a manner more purposeful than generous. 'Go on,' she said. ''Urry up. And there's a good green cape in that pile by the door, with a bonnet to match. Oh, and a muff—the black one. And a pair of stockings. You can wear the red slippers again for now. They ain't right, but they'll do.'

There were so many hooks and eyes on the dress that Ivy needed help getting into it. The stockings made her legs feel like someone was breathing on them and the drawers just felt *strange*.

'I don't want no cape on,' she puffed. 'I'll be too 'ot.'

'You'll do as I say,' snapped Carroty Kate. 'You've gotter seem respectable or you won't fit the Grand Plan.'

What's a grand plan when it's at 'ome? Ivy wriggled unhappily in her fancy layers. *What's she on about?*

The pile of clothes over by the door looked big enough to live in. The cape, bonnet, and muff were on the top. Carroty Kate whisked them up, one by one, and got Ivy into them so fast she barely had time to blink.

'Me head feels all squashed,' Ivy said. 'An' this dress is pricklin' me.'

Carroty Kate stepped back to observe.

'Hmmm,' she said.

Then she spat on the corner of her shawl, and used it to wipe Ivy's face.

'We should've put you under the pump first thing,' she grumbled, as the child squirmed beneath her grip. 'It's like wrappin' slops in silver tissue. Better hope nobody notices what a grubby urchin you really are, under these fine clothes, or cares much if they do. There now—let's go.'

It was a bright sunny day outside. (*Good*, thought Carroty Kate, *a bit o' sunshine brings boys and girlies out like worms after rain*.) But there was still the bite of winter in the air. (*Excellent. They'll be well wrapped up those boys and girlies—rich pickings for sure*.)

'Where are we goin'?' asked Ivy, hoping it wouldn't be far. She had never felt so uncomfortable in the whole of her life.

'First thing? To the smartest grocer's in London, I reckon. And then to a Suitable Place. Yes . . . I know, for a fact, there's a Suitable Place round the back of that smart grocer's.'

'What's a suitable place?' Ivy wanted to know. 'And what are we goin' there for?' She was trotting along with her arms outstretched, to avoid touching the fur muff with her fingers. To use that muff properly would have seemed, to her, like putting both hands into either end of a poor dead kitty-cat.

'I'm a canary bird,' she said, flapping the green cape. 'Flyin' along—wheeee! What *IS* a suitable place, I wonder?'

Carroty Kate yanked both of her arms down, smartly. 'Ask me no questions and I'll tell yer no lies,' she scolded. 'Just do what I say when I says it and no arguin'. And walk properly, will yer? And mind where you're treadin'. Those shoes ain't yours for keeps.'

It took a long time to get to the grocer's with the Suitable Place behind it. When they finally did, Carroty Kate said they were to stand outside for a while, watching the doors to see who went in. Ivy gazed in awe at the imposing facade of Fortnum & Mason. It was hard to believe that such a vast building was somewhere people only went to buy food.

'Don't no one live in there?' she wondered. 'Not even at night?'

Carroty Kate ignored her. She had spotted a potential victim trailing its feet behind a harassed-looking woman whose mind was clearly fixed on luxury foodstuffs.

Aha. Let's see . . . hat: sealskin with ribbon ties. Cape: blue (a good fashionable colour). Dress: dark blue corded silk, with orange braiding and yes . . . orange silk petticoats underneath. Stockings: white; probably silk. Boots: bright blue morocco with tasselled trim. And . . . oh yes, excellent . . . Carroty's lucky day . . . it's carrying its own little bag. A blue one with orange beads.

Quickly she rummaged in one of her voluminous pockets and took out a peppermint candy cane. 'Take this,' she told Ivy. 'Only don't you dare eat it. Not even a lick. Now follow me. Come on—move. And listen hard to what I tell yer on the way.'

Confused, Ivy clung on to Carroty Kate's skirts with her free hand as they dodged and wove their way across the street. 'When I tip you the nod,' Kate was telling her, 'you smile at the girly in blue and orange, all right? You smile at her like she's yer own flesh an' blood wot you ain't seen in a month of Sundays. An' you offer her that sweetie when her mama, or whoever it is she's with, ain't lookin'. All right?'

'Yes,' Ivy agreed. 'But why? And can I lick me hand after?'

'No. Listen. You ain't to give 'er that candy cane. You're to tell 'er—and you do it quiet, no shoutin'—that the shop is givin' 'em away, and barley twists and bull's-eyes too. And that if she follows you double quick she can take as many as she can eat and be back in a trice. All right?'

'Yes,' said Ivy, hoping it was true.

'An' then you bring 'er here. Straight to me. You got that?'

'Yes,' Ivy said again. They were pushing open the door to the shop. She could smell spices and lemons and the rich aroma of coffee. There were gentlemen and ladies moving as leisurely as butterflies from one display of groceries to another as if they had all the time and all the choices in the world.

Carroty Kate lowered her voice to an urgent whisper:

'After that, you stick to me like spit. Even if this goes 'orribly wrong we're in it together, all right?'

'All right,' said Ivy, although she was too busy drinking in the rich sights and smells to be listening any more.

'Good. Now go and stand by the pickles and wait for the nod.'

Ivy did as she was told. The little girl in blue and orange was slouching mutinously against a counter while the lady she was with checked the price of beef tea. She noticed Ivy immediately and stuck out her tongue.

Confused, Ivy looked towards the door, for guidance.

Now. Carroty Kate nodded. *Quick sharp—before the lady turns round.*

The little girl had pale hair and a pale haughty face. She was taller than Ivy and perhaps a year or two older. When Ivy smiled she did not smile back. But when she saw she was being offered a candy cane she licked her lips. Then she flounced across the shop and held out her hand.

'This one's mine,' said Ivy, quickly. 'But there's lots more. And . . . and bull's-eyes and barley sugar too. This kind shop's givin' 'em away. But we gotter hurry or they'll all be gone. Come on.'

And so impatient was Ivy to get to the Suitable Place herself—for that was surely where all the sweeties would be—that she took hold of the older girl's hand and began tugging her towards the door. She didn't have to tug very hard. For the girl in blue and orange had more petticoats than sense, and was herself greedy for as many free sweeties as she could cram into her dainty little bag.

Well, look at that, marvelled Carroty Kate, flexing her big hands as both children hurried towards her, their eyes shining and their mouths watering for the taste of peppermint and the crunch, crunch of sugar. *She did it. First time an' all.*

And if the pale haughty girl was at all unnerved by the sight of the odd-looking woman beckoning them out of the shop and into the busy street, she doubtless assumed—as Carroty Kate fully intended her to—that she was the red-haired child's red-haired mama and, as such, to be trusted completely.

CHAPTER 12
Concerning the stuff of nightmares

I vy screamed.
   She screamed so loud that she hurt her own ears and throat. And, as she screamed, she struck out with her hands and feet as if warding off a swarm.

It had taken her a long time to fall asleep, tucked once again into the thieves' Secret Place. For a start, she had been scarily aware of the horrible things daubed on the canvas-curtain, just a spider's leap from her head.

Worse, she had been unable to stop dwelling on the thing that had happened in the alley behind Fortnum & Mason.

Jolted awake, by her own yells, Ivy couldn't tell, at first, what was real among the jumble of images in her head and what wasn't. For a memory of the pale haughty girl being stripped of all her blue and orange finery seemed exactly like the echo of a terrible dream.

Only, it hadn't been a dream. It had really happened . . . so unexpectedly that both Ivy and the girl had been too stunned to cry out . . . so fast that the girl had been down to her frilly drawers before Ivy's brain could tell her mouth to stop watering for the sweets that had never existed.

There had been a lot of rubbish in the alley behind Fortnum & Mason, and a strong smell of rot.

'Well?' the girl had demanded, stamping one leather-clad foot. 'Where are these barley . . . *Eeek!*'

As swift as a wink or a spit or a curse, Carroty Kate's big strong hands had filched the bag from the little girl's arm, the hat from her head, and the cape from around her shoulders. The dress should have been trickier but Kate's well-practised fingers had rippled, faster than a concert pianist's, *twiddley-diddley-diddley*, down the girl's spine, undoing the hooks and eyes seconds before stripping both the dress and the petticoats right down to the ground. Then up into the air the unfortunate child had gone, held firmly round the waist and almost upside-down while Carroty Kate tugged off her boots and her stockings.

The speed at which each item disappeared into the specially-designed pockets and linings of Kate's own clothing had been slick enough to mesmerize as well as appal young Ivy, as she stood bearing witness to every pull, twist, and tug.

A skinner.

Carroty Kate was a skinner. A mean and horrible person.

'Right!' Kate had snapped, shoving the dangling toe of a stocking back up her sleeve. 'We gotter run like the wind now, before it hollers. Come on—move.'

And Ivy had moved; responding to the order like a soldier, a servant, or a person in a trance—automatically and without question.

'Hurrah!' Carroty Kate had whooped, once they were six streets away and could be said to have got away with it. 'You're a natural, you are, Ivy girl. Fing and the lads'll be chuffed to bits.'

And Ivy hadn't known how to explain herself to this seemingly new and incredibly scary Carroty Kate . . . hadn't dared admit that she had truly believed in the barley sugars and the bull's-eyes and never *imagined* being part of a heinous plan to skin that girl of her lovely clothes.

So she had said nothing. Not then and not later. She had even taken the candy cane Fing had offered her, as a reward, once he'd discovered that the girl's blue and orange bag contained five shillings and sixpence, a jewelled pin shaped like a four-leafed clover, a scent bottle with a silver stopper, and a pair of kid gloves. She hadn't eaten it though. For it would have tasted rank in her mouth, like bait.

Carroty Kate, assuming Ivy was full of supper, and dog tired, had put the candy cane back in a jar and sent her early to bed.

Now, lying fully and fretfully awake, Ivy found herself worrying worse than ever about what might have happened to the skinned girl after she and Kate had scarpered. What if she had been too scared, or too ashamed of being seen in her drawers, to make her way back into the shop? What if she was still huddled in the Suitable Place, getting colder, hungrier, and even more frightened as the night closed in?

The guilt was awful; heavy, like a second eiderdown, and too troublesome for sleep. Ivy began to whimper, then to cry, and it wasn't long before the thud of feet entered the room and the top of the ladder came crashing up against the wall.

'*Oi! What's with the din?*' The canvas-curtain twitched and Carroty Kate's knobbly head loomed into view. In the light of the moon, filtering in long strips through the tiny barred window, her nose looked like Mr Punch's and her hair seemed oddly askew.

'That . . . girl . . .' Ivy hiccuped. 'What if . . . what if she . . .'

'So that's it, is it? *Pah!* It'll be dreamin' sweetly in a big 'ouse somewhere, wiv a fresh set of clothes laid out for the mornin'. So don't you go losin' shuteye over *that* . . . And don't look at me like I'm damned to Hell, girly, for there are worse than me in the skinnin' trade. I left its drawers on, didn't I? We could've got two shillin's at least for them drawers—more if we'd cut the lace off and sold it separate . . . But I never skins the drawers. And if they ain't wearin' any . . . why, I chucks 'em a big handkerchief, for modesty's sake.'

Ivy continued to sob. Crying, as we know, had never got her very far but in this case she simply couldn't stop.

'Now you listen to me,' growled Kate, losing patience very fast. 'We can't 'ave no caterwaulin' in our Secret Place or it won't be a secret much longer, will it? So shut yer trap and thank yer lucky stars that there was only me an' the Muck Snipe downstairs this time to hear yer.'

But Ivy was too far gone to shut her trap.

'*I want . . . to go . . . home,*' she wailed '*I want my Orly. I want Uncle Elmer and Aunt . . . Pam . . . and . . . Mad and Cyn . . . and . . . Hor . . .*'

Carroty Kate sighed. That was a lot of names, she thought, for a girly who had sworn blind she had no one to miss her.

'*I want Cousin Jared an' . . . an' . . . baby Salvador. But I want Orly the most . . . I do . . . I do . . . I want . . .*'

73

'Right, you lyin' little brat . . .' Carroty Kate grabbed both Ivy's ankles through the bedding—grabbed them so hard and fast, in just the one hand, that Ivy was shocked into silence. 'We gotter get things straight between us once an' for all. So best you come down to the kitchen for a bit of a chat with me and the Muck Snipe. Right? But before you do that, I'll tell you one thing for certain-sure. You're part of old Carroty's Grand Plan now. So there ain't no way you're goin' anywhere—unless it's down the river in a sack for makin' so much as a squeak up 'ere from now on. Got that?'

Ivy gulped.

Orly . . . she wailed, in the secret silence of her head. And then she pushed back her bedding, and did as she'd been told.

Down in the kitchen the Muck Snipe was heating cocoa. He had a little whisk made out of twigs which he was using to froth the milk. When he saw Ivy tottering into the room he dabbed a bit of the froth on his upper lip and pulled a crazy face. It was meant as a joke but had the opposite effect.

'*Shut yer noise, girly*—it's yer last warnin'!' Carroty Kate plonked Ivy on a bench and towered over her, hands on hips. 'Otherwise it won't be Fing throwin' yer in the Thames, it'll be old Carroty. Mucks—give 'er some milk. An' put a few drops o' laudanum in it, for Gawd's sake . . .'

Laudanum. Aunt Pamela took laudanum for her nerves. And Hor gave it to baby Salvador sometimes, to make him go to sleep. The ironmonger sold it and so did the barber and you could get it at the markets. It was a

74

cure for whatever ailed you, although nobody had bothered dosing Ivy with any up until now.

''Ow many drops?' asked the Muck Snipe.

'Dunno,' said Kate. 'Just splash it in, man. This girly's overwrought.'

The Muck Snipe splashed it in and Ivy drank it down.

'That's the way,' Kate nodded, approvingly. 'Syrup of opium—it'll calm yer down a treat.' Her face loomed lower. 'Now listen to me, Ivy girl,' she said, her voice becoming deeper and more urgent. 'This is 'ow it is. You know that smart grocer's we went to—that Forternum an' Mason? Well, William Forternum—the *late* William Forternum—'e weren't no rich man, girly. Not to start with. Not by a long chalk . . .'

The opium in Ivy's milk began to do its work. Her eyes grew heavy and she started to feel as if she was floating.

''E were a servin' man, was Will,' Kate continued, 'in the court of Queen Anne. And every day 'e took the used candles out o' their sticks an' put in new 'uns. That was 'is job, see?'

Ivy didn't see. Not really. But it was pleasant, being told a story—even a dull one about a grocer—so she nodded and did her best to seem interested.

'Only, instead of chuckin' them old candles away he kept 'em and sold 'em on. And that's 'ow come 'e started to better 'imself. You followin' this?'

Ivy nodded. She was staring up at the blue and orange dress which was hanging above the fire and steaming in the heat. The orange petticoats were pegged alongside it . . . one, two, three of them . . . all flounced out like curtsies.

'Now . . .' Carroty Kate sat herself down on the other side of the table and stared Ivy full in the face. 'Look at me. There are some would say those candles weren't Will's to sell. That 'e didn't deserve to prosper from stolen goods. But think on . . . Queen Anne, God rest 'er, 'ad enough candles at 'er disposal to light up the world. So d'yer reckon she missed the ones she'd already 'ad some use of? Or cared tuppence whether they got chucked out for ratties to gnaw, or sold on?'

Ivy shook her head.

'No,' crowed Kate. 'She didn't. No more than some stinkin' rich little boy or girly is gonner care about losin' a few garments wot they probably ain't gonner wear no more than twice before their wealthy papas buy 'em new 'uns.'

Ivy blinked and frowned.

It wasn't the same, she thought. *Pinching candles was nothing like stripping the clothes right off a person's back. Nothing like. For candlesticks didn't care, did they, about being skinned? They didn't feel shocked or cold or ashamed after their candles had gone.*

She glanced back up at the washing line. The Muck Snipe had stoked the fire so the blue and orange dress was steaming even more, like something about to chug away. In her mind's eye Ivy imagined it shunting off the line and straight out of the door, heading back to its rightful owner—wherever she was.

Carroty Kate was talking about the Grand Plan now. Or, rather, she was telling Ivy what the Grand Plan was all about. The *Mighty* Grand Plan. A shop. That's what she and the lads were working towards, with their skinning and

76

their house-calls and all their other dodges. A nice little shop, selling quality garments to the gentry. Nothing as big as Forternum and Mason, mind, but something a lot better than their stall down Petticoat Lane. All legal too and strictly above board, with no need for a Secret Place nor for any more ducking and diving from the bluebottles.

'My Fing,' Kate sighed, ''e was a tailor before fallin' on 'ard times. 'E could stitch you a ball gown out o' cobwebs an' sugar sacks an' you'd think yerself finer than royalty, swishin' around. 'E's as clever and as canny a man as that old candle-snaffler Will Forternum ever was, you mark my words. 'E deserves to better isself by and by. We all do.'

She sighed again, and began clearing away empty cups.

'So we'll 'ave no more talk from you about goin' 'ome,' she said to Ivy. 'Specially not in front of Fing. This is your 'ome now, girly. We're a good team, you and I. We'll make us a profit from skinnin', an' a few other dodges, in no time at all. And one day, when old Carroty and the lads 'ave got their nice little shop, why—you can serve in it an' be proud.'

The door from the street banged open and in stamped Fing. 'Where's the Crow?' he growled. ''E should've bin back by now, from 'is 'ouse call. And what's she doin' up? I wants me supper and I wants it in peace.'

'She's just goin' to bed,' Carroty Kate replied, quickly. 'Ain't yer, Ive?'

Ivy looked from one person to another. It was hard to focus. She could barely keep her eyes open. But she knew that if she went back to the Secret Place, the things on the tree would be waiting.

'Please,' she half-said, half-whispered. 'Can't I sleep down 'ere?'

'Not likely,' snapped Fing.'Now scram.'

Ivy's face crumpled. *'I want my Orl . . .'*

Carroty Kate whisked her up under one arm. For one dizzying moment Ivy thought she was going to be skinned. But in a trice she found herself back upstairs and being chivvied up the ladder.

'Now SHUT IT!' Kate yelled, reaching up to prod her off the ladder and into the Secret Place. 'And no kickin' around in there. The Crow'll 'ave some loot to stash by yer feet when 'e gets in.'

Ivy's head was spinning. She heard the ladder being taken away and a sob caught in her throat. She didn't dare lie down, next to the things on the painted tree. So she scrunched herself up in a corner, determined to stay awake so the things wouldn't get her. She thought Carroty Kate had gone away so was startled to hear her say:

'It's for yer own protection, Ivy-girl, bein' up there in the Secret Place. Cos it ain't always just me an' the lads sleepin' in this 'ouse, if you gets me drift. Others stay, if they needs to. Strangers, some of 'em, and real nasty types. It wouldn't be proper nor safe for a little girly to be down 'ere on those nights, fast asleep and unawares.'

Ivy gulped and wiped her nose on the back of her hand.

'So that's why you gotter be quiet as a mouse,' Kate continued. 'Not just to keep the Secret Place secret, so's no one steals our loot, but so's no nasty types gets to learnin' that *you're* up there an' all. You got that?'

78

Ivy whimpered that she had. And then she fell asleep.

Luckily, there were no nasty types bedding down in the lodging house that night. Although that's not to say that, had there been, they would have automatically recognized the terrible cries that rang around the place shortly before dawn as the yells of a frightened child.

Indeed, they might just as easily have assumed, upon being jolted awake, that those screams were issuing from the Muck Snipe's ghoulish picture. For at least a dozen of the horrible things on the tree had mouths, after all.

As it was, only Carroty Kate and the lads were disturbed. But disturbed they most definitely were as Ivy babbled and wept about the things on the tree and swore she would sooner be thrown in the Thames before daybreak than sleep another hour where she was.

'We gotter do something, lads,' muttered Carroty Kate. 'She can't do this again. We got loot up there now.'

'I'll sort it,' growled Fing. 'First thing in the mornin'. I'll fix it so she won't scream no more.'

And he did fix it.

He fixed it beautifully.

Part Two

CHAPTER 13

In which we find ourselves some years on, in a more affluent part of London

Oscar Aretino Frosdick took three steps back from an easel the size of a giraffe and wiped his paintbrush on the seat of his trousers.

He had been working at this canvas for almost five hours and had only stopped because the light had grown so poor that he could no longer see where his flesh tones ended and his petal-colours began.

Cold, too. It was ridiculously cold, out here in his Chelsea garden. So cold that the blossom on his plum tree might have been clumps of snow. So cold that he could no longer feel his fingers and the dabs of paint on his palette were starting to freeze.

'Are we done for t-today, d-d-dear boy? D-do say we are. For if I st-stay here much longer I will sh-sh-surely perish.'

'We're done, mother. You can get down now.'

'Well, I will need help with that, d-d dear boy, won't I? With untying the b-b-b-blindfold anyway . . .'

Oscar continued to assess his painting. Was it good? Was it good *enough*? It was hard to tell. The blossom was all right. Nice and luminous. And he was moderately happy, now, with the texture of the bark. But the figure of the woman . . . her expression . . . her proportions . . . her whole *being* was not . . . quite . . .

'Osc-c-c-ar?'

Tearing his gaze from his work, Oscar considered his mother as she leaned from the plum tree, shivering like a nervous wreck. It was no use, he decided. *She* was no use. She meant well, and it was true what she said about proper models costing more money than they were worth. But, really, she was too old for this kind of caper—and far too closely related. He needed someone fresh and lovely up that tree. Someone to inspire him. A stunner.

And it wasn't as if he was short of the readies. Indeed, since turning twenty-one he had more money coming in from his trust fund than he knew what to do with. He could afford to pay a model, and handsomely too should she prove capable of holding a pose for as long as necessary, without complaining or looking fed up. A lovely girl; a sweet, compliant girl—if only he knew where to find one.

'Oscar!!'

'Don't fret, mother. I'll just clean my brushes and see to my palette. Then I'll be right with you.'

In the house next door, a young servant looking down from an upstairs window chuckled to see poor Mrs Frosdick being rescued, at last, from the tree. The unfortunate woman's skin was almost as blue as her robe. And how she had managed to balance among those branches for so long, particularly while clutching a lute, was beyond imagining.

This servant—whose name was Alfred—couldn't see much of Mr Frosdick's canvas. He could only ask himself what could possibly be the point of painting a woman

84

stuck up a plum tree with a stringed instrument in one hand and a silk scarf around her eyes. That there *was* a point to it was not to be doubted. For Alfred had learned enough about Pre-Raphaelite painting techniques to know that every prop in Mr Frosdick's painting would have some clever meaning attached to it.

Symbolism. That's what Alfred's master would have called it. And he should know. For Alfred's master was a genius, everyone said so. A wildly talented artist who never painted so much as a ladybird, or a falling sycamore key, without it being hugely significant. Take, for instance, the poppy in his latest work—a white poppy being dropped by a bird into the hands of a swooning woman. That poppy meant sleep of the deepest kind. It meant death.

Young Alfred shivered and turned away from the window.

His master would not be home tonight. He was rarely home nowadays and the house, without him in it, seemed morose and full of shadows. The cook and the maid-servant were no longer in residence. It wasn't worth it. But someone had to be here, to keep dust and unwanted callers away. And to feed the armadillos, of course.

Ho-hum. Alfred wasn't used to silence. But then, he hadn't been used to armadillos either, once upon a time, and now they seemed as common to have around as cats. There was a peacock in the garden, too, and a jack-daw in an elaborate wire outhouse. They were no trouble; only quiet and miserable like the house (which in the peacock's case was just as well, since its cry, when it could be bothered, put Alfred in mind of a desperate call for help).

Carefully, Alfred drew a heavy crimson curtain back across the window so that neither the fading afternoon light or the following morning's brightness would filter into the room. His master had been most explicit about that. Go in twice a day, he had said. Just to check. But don't let in any light. And if you are struck by anything at all unusual send word to me at once.

'Unusual in precisely what respect, sir?' Alfred had felt compelled to ask.

His master had raised his shaggy head and looked at Alfred without really seeing him.

'I cannot say . . . pre*cise*ly,' he had said. 'It may be a gap in the curtains, that wasn't there before. Or a sound . . . yes, quite possibly a sound, even a tiny one . . . a sound as faint as the tearing of wings. It may simply be the quality of the air . . . a vibration, if you will, as if someone who was in the room but seconds before has only just departed.'

Alfred had not thought any of this much to go on. Still, he had done his duty for three . . . four . . . five days in a row now, checking the room at daybreak and once again before dusk. He had yet to notice anything remotely amiss. All the same, he never liked to linger. And he never checked after dark.

Today he almost hoped he *would* see or hear something strange. For then his master would come home and the tempo of each day would revert to something closer to normal. At the very least the animals would cheer up.

Straining his eyes and his ears Alfred watched, listened, and waited. He thought he saw the curtain twitch but decided it was probably wishful thinking. Bored though he was, and lonely too, he would never summon his master home under false pretences. That would be cruel. The poor man had suffered enough.

He looked for perhaps the two hundredth time at the picture above the mantelshelf. It hadn't been framed yet. It hadn't even been seen—not publicly anyway.

Despite the dimness of the room the vast canvas glowed with the rich jewel-like quality Alfred's master was famous for. The woman's face glimmered and the light around her mass of red hair resembled a halo. She had her eyes closed and her face raised and she was leaning forward as if yearning for something. A revelation. A kiss. Or maybe just the poppy being delivered into her lap by a red and dangerous-looking bird.

The woman's expression was that of someone who was either falling fast asleep or completely away with the fairies. Alfred didn't think she looked very well. Beautiful, though. She was certainly incredibly beautiful—or had been.

Alfred's stomach gurgled. There were cold meats and pickles down in the pantry and the remains of a rye loaf. It would be a solitary meal but he would make the best of it. Perhaps tomorrow a message would come from his master, telling him to air the studio, order a pheasant, and summon the cook because he was coming home.

In the meantime those wretched armadillos needed feeding before they began ploughing through hedges and causing havoc. Mrs Frosdick had threatened court action should one pop up again next door. She was a fine one to talk though, considering her own son's penchant for strange and exotic creatures.

There were rumours that Oscar Frosdick had commissioned Jamrach, the animal importer, to find him a unicorn. That he truly believed these mythical beasts existed, somewhere to the north, among forests and lakes and ancient caves. No doubt, once he got tired of waiting, he would bring a white horse into his garden, stick a cardboard horn above its eyes, and paint that in place of the 'real thing'.

Oh, these artists . . . Alfred could never understand why the Pre-Raphaelite painters didn't just copy from a book; why everything from a bird to a blossom had to be reproduced from life.

He glanced one more time upon the woman in his master's most recent work. It was strange, he thought, as he turned to leave the room; strange and sad how she of all people could continue to look so lifelike. But that's what art did. It preserved a person, like a fossil in a rock, or a dragonfly in a jar. It made them last for ever.

Shutting the door behind him, he turned the key in the lock.

Then he went downstairs, thinking sadly about supper.

CHAPTER 14

In which Oscar finds himself a stunner

O scar needed some air. Or rather, he needed to get away from his mother before she drove him round the bend. Strolling towards Battersea Bridge, the scent of the river bunging up his sinuses and the rough calls of bargees and shrimp vendors offending his ears, he found himself yearning for more beauty in his life.

A statue for the garden. A dish of perfect blue. A new poem by Lord Tennyson. His heart wasn't set on anything in particular. He just knew he was all out of sorts, and that a spending spree in town might cheer him up and make him feel more like doing a bit of work.

This morning, although the light had been good and his mother more than willing to shin back up the plum tree, he had found all kinds of excuses to avoid setting up his easel and preparing his palette.

How will I ever paint a masterpiece, he asked himself now, turning up his collar against a nippy breeze, *when the only person I can get to model for me keeps complaining about chilblains and demanding cups of tea? I am a sensitive soul. A talented artist. If I am reduced to painting my own mother then so be it. But I need beautiful objects around me to compensate for that and, by Jove, I intend to find some.*

After crossing the river, Oscar took an omnibus to his favourite part of London, where antique and curiosity shops brimmed with objects guaranteed to delight his eye and lighten his wallet. He bought a willow-patterned jug, a bone china plate shaped like a seashell, and a brass statuette of a young shepherd carrying a lamb. Then, because he still didn't feel like going home, and even less like doing any work, he decided to head for Lambeth market.

It was late afternoon. The street sellers, he knew, would be setting up their stalls along New Cut, ready for an evening's trading and, as an early bird, he might find a bargain or two. And thinking of birds . . . ah, *yes* . . . the con man might be there; the one who had sold him a canary so ancient it had expired within a week.

The damned cheek of the fellow. And the little bird had looked and sounded so chipper too. Oscar had seriously considered hanging its cage in the plum tree, next to his blindfolded lute-playing mother, and including it in his masterpiece to symbolize . . . well, something to do with being caged.

'You've been swindled there, sir,' young Alfred from next door had told him, upon learning of the canary's demise. 'These bird duffers, they go to the colour-shops and stock up on paints and brushes. Then they give an old canary a nice fresh coat of "The Queen's Yellow" and get it so tipsy on hemp seed that it's twittering fit to bust. Then they pass it off as a young 'un. It's a common ruse, sir, I'm afraid. And, if I may make so bold as to say so, you've been had.'

Oscar didn't like being had. It got his dander up. So, yes, he would keep a sharp lookout for that bird-seller fellow and, if he came across him, would let him know, in no uncertain terms, that Oscar Aretino Frosdick was not a man to be made a monkey of.

There was rain threatening by the time he reached New Cut, but it would have taken more than a pile of clouds to keep the vendors of everything from pigs' trotters and Christian tracts to shaving brushes and nutmeg-graters from scrabbling and vying, all along that street, for enough money to stay alive on.

Oscar, because of the way he looked, was assailed almost immediately by men and women pressing this and that upon him and babbling so fast and loud that he couldn't tell who was selling what. Smiling in what he hoped was a kindly but dismissive manner, he walked a little faster, scrutinizing every stall and pedlar that he passed.

'*Git yer finches here. Italian finches only two shillin's each. Canaries an' linnets too. Take yer pick, ladies and gents. Fine singin' canaries . . .*'

It wasn't the person Oscar was searching for. It was a boy of perhaps ten or eleven staggering a little under the weight of a large slatted crate in which several dozen small birds were trilling away as diligently as a male voice choir.

'Young man—a minute, if you please '

'A linnet for you, sir? Right you are . . .'

'No, no. You misunderstand . . .' Oscar positioned himself directly in front of the boy and looked sternly down his nose at the crate. 'Put that bird back. It won't live beyond Thursday and you know it. Where's your father?'

The boy looked startled, but only for a moment. 'Me father, sir?' he said.

'Yes. Or maybe no. The man who was here a fortnight ago, anyway. The fellow who sold me a bird so heavily daubed in yellow paint I could have used the feathers from its pathetic little corpse as fine brushes for the depiction of daffodils.'

The boy looked up at Oscar as if he was a lunatic, or talking double-Dutch.

'Can't help yer sir,' he said, adjusting the straps of the crate where they were chafing his bony shoulders. '*Linnets and finches, ladies and gents. Fine singin'. . .*'

'Wait!'

Oscar grabbed the corner of the crate, jerking it and the boy to a standstill. The crate tilted, causing a minor landslide of the contents which began cheeping and chirruping all the faster in dismay.

'*Oi! What's your game? Unhand my boy, sir. Unhand him this instant!*' A scrawny woman with flinty eyes and a weathered complexion leapt from the sidelines and prodded Oscar, hard, in the chest with one bony finger. She had her own tray suspended round her neck, piled high with posies of violets.

Oscar let go of the bird crate. 'M-m-my *game*?' he spluttered, looking distastefully down at the spot on his waistcoat where the woman had *dared* to lay her less-than-pristine hands on him. 'My *game*, madam, involves settling a score with the fellow who sold me an ailing geriatric canary from this crate. And no . . . don't pretend it wasn't so. You see that broken strut in the crate's right hand lower corner? The part held together with blue twine . . . ?'

The woman shrugged. Other people, who had gathered

to watch, craned their necks and pushed closer to see the strut.

'Well, I am an artist, madam, which means I have a fine eye for detail. My dead bird came from this very crate and I demand my four shillings back.'

'Where's the corpse?'

'I beg your pardon?'

'The corpse. I am a tradeswoman, sir. which means I have a fine eye for a toff wot's tryin' to pull a fast one.'

'But . . . but . . .'

'No corpse, no refund.' The woman stuck her nose in the air and turned abruptly on her heel. 'And if you pesters my Salvador again,' she yelled back over her shoulder, 'you'll 'ave 'is dad and 'is uncles to answer to. They ain't far away. And we don't like your type comin' 'ere, makin' false accusations and shoutin' the odds.'

Oscar gawped after her, his face turning a deep shade of pink. He opened his mouth to protest, but the right words weren't there so he snapped it shut and scratched his chin instead.

His little scrum of witnesses was in no hurry to disperse and one or two people were sniggering. Oscar scratched his chin again.

Should he collar the bird boy and make him turn out his stock of canaries? A quick rub with a handkerchief would surely prove that each hapless creature's attractive buttercup hue was nothing more than a fresh coat of paint.

Yes, he told himself. *Go to it, sir!* He had been conned, after all. And prodded. And *slandered*, by Jove, in front of all these people. And while he hadn't much liked the sound of the dad and the uncles, his honour was now at stake.

The bird boy was still in sight, but only just, for he had clearly decided to scarper while his mother distracted the crowd. Oscar set off after him. 'The birds in that crate are duff!' he cried out, shaking his fist as he ran. 'And I can prove it.'

If he had expected anyone to follow him, or to support his accusation, he was seriously misguided, for a toff's honour meant nothing whatsoever to most people shopping or trading along New Cut that afternoon, and his audience was already drifting away.

By the time Oscar caught up with the boy, he was far enough along the street for no one in the vicinity to be aware of the confrontation that had given rise to the chase in the first place.

'Raspberryade, sir? Nice and cool. Only a penny a glass. Looks like you could do with some refreshment . . .'

'Silk hanky, sir? Just right for moppin' a damp and sweaty brow. Any colour you fancy, sir. Red, green, a nice bright yeller . . .'

Panting, Oscar skidded to a halt. He had a stitch in his side and a blister on one of his heels and his sense of righteous indignation was not what it had been a couple of hundred yards ago.

Motioning the raspberryade and handkerchief vendors away, he closed his eyes and bent forward, resting his hands on the knobbles of his kneecaps while he waited for his breathing to slow down.

'Canaries and finches, ladies and gents. Fine singin' birds . . .'

The bird boy's voice, so sweet and confident, seemed to be taunting him.

94

Aggravating little con artist. Oscar's dander was well and truly up now. He would seize that crate, empty it out and expose the plight of those paint-covered, hemp-sozzled birds come hell, high water, or a veritable army of dads and uncles all built like bison and swinging their fists.

Straightening up, he took a deep breath and got ready to defend his honour.

And that was when he saw her. There . . . less than a coin's toss ahead of him, putting a handful of moss between the bird boy's shoulder and the crate strap, to ease the chafing of the weight. A stunner. An angel. A pearl among swine.

The most beautiful object he had seen all day. And one he became determined, immediately, to acquire.

CHAPTER 15

In which Oscar's enthusiasm is not very catching

'I know little of her background,' Oscar admitted to his mother. 'I only know she is the loveliest creature I have ever set eyes upon and that, with her as my model, I would paint pictures that would make next door's look like the daubings of a chimp.'

Mrs Frosdick sniffed and poured herself another cup of China tea. The sun was almost warm and the blossom on the plum tree at its most heart-stoppingly gorgeous. Soon the blossom would start to fade and then to wither and fall. *Here today and gone tomorrow*, sighed Mrs Frosdick. *Like youth*.

'More toast, dear boy?' she said, pushing forward the appropriate plate. 'And then we must send out for a supply of arsenic. There have been tunnellings again, from next door, and I absolutely will not have it. We will lay poisoned meat tonight, or tomorrow at the very latest. It really *ought* to be tonight, for I hear the Italian is expected home any day and I simply haven't the will to confront him with further evidence of gnawings and tramplings. He takes no account of complaints and his manner, quite frankly, borders on the offensive. A fait accompli, dear boy, is what we will present the man with, upon his return to Cheyne Walk. And I will not feel in the least bit sorry. For what he or *anyone* sees in those armour-plated little beasts is beyond my comprehension. Are there any in his paintings? I believe there are not. And besides . . .'

'Mother, *please*! Never mind the blessed armadillos. Listen to me.' A gust of wind rustled the boughs of the plum tree sending petals into the jam and onto the top of Oscar's head.

'The girl,' he said firmly. 'She lives in Paradise Row, close by the Old Vic. I want you to go there, mother. Today. This very morning. The family is expecting you and will, I am sure, allow the girl to return with you straightaway. Refer often to the fee. That should do the trick. For this family's circumstances, so I'm led to believe, are sadly reduced.'

Mrs Frosdick stood up, leaned forward slightly, and plucked each speck of blossom from her son's head.

'You are frizzing, dear boy,' she said. 'And thinning too, just like your poor dear father, God rest his soul. Bald as a croquet ball he was, by the age of thirty. Such a shame . . .'

Oscar jerked his frizzed and thinning head away. *'Mother!'* he snapped.'The girl! Will you kindly go and get her. I would go myself if it wouldn't be seen as improper. I would go like a shot, for the very thought of her sweet face makes me eager to start painting again.'

Mrs Frosdick cupped her hand around the petals from her son's hair, as if they were precious, or living. Then she threw them onto the lawn.

'This "girl",' she said, irritably. 'Does she have a name?'

Oscar flushed.

'I didn't ask,' he confessed. 'She had so many relatives milling around, all questioning me at once, that I had precious little opportunity to ask anything for myself.'

'I dare say these relatives were suspicious,' said Mrs Frosdick, drily, 'of your intentions.'

Oscar threw her an injured look.

'They wanted details of her fee, mother,' he said. 'And having ascertained the going rate they hustled the girl away, pausing only long enough for one of them—a good-looking fellow, but too cocky by half—to shout out an address. Paradise Row. Number eight. Top floor. The first door you come to. That is where you are to go, both to guarantee payment and to vouch for my integrity as an artist and a gentleman.'

Mrs Frosdick picked up a knife and began spearing petals from the jam pot.

'You will do that, mother, won't you?' Oscar pressed on, anxiously. 'Make it quite clear, I mean—particularly to the girl herself—that my intentions are honourable? For they most definitely are, as well you know, and I would knock down any man and shun any woman who dared to suggest otherwise, by Jove I would!'

Mrs Frosdick wiped the knife, somewhat viciously, on a napkin of finest linen, leaving a sticky smear of stabbed petals and strawberry jam.

'You can depend on me, dear boy,' she said, 'to act entirely in your best interests.'

'Good-oh.' Oscar heaved a sigh of relief. 'And while you are gone, I will take stock of the canvas. I will leave the tree alone. I'm happy with that. But the figure of the blindfolded woman ... *hmmm* ... with this girl as my new model the fluidity of the pose is bound to alter, and the skin tones will be brighter as well. Yes, I believe I will paint over the figure of the woman and start it again, from scratch . . . Mother? Are you going already, without finishing your pot of tea? Well, that's very kind . . . I'm sorry, I didn't quite catch . . . Oh, the arsenic. No, mother, I won't forget. And four pounds of beefsteak? Right you are. And, mother . . . good luck. She really is the most beautiful girl in the world. You'll be entirely won over, I'm certain of it.'

CHAPTER 16

*Concerning negotiations
to everyone's advantage (allegedly)*

P aradise Row had changed very little in the ten years since Mrs Larrington, the charity monger, got wedged in it. Fashion, however, had changed a lot so Mrs Frosdick had no trouble sweeping disdainfully along the alley, although she wrinkled her nose in the process and cursed the day her beloved son set eyes on the piece of trouble who lived there.

A hovel, she muttered, stepping into the dark and dirty entrance hall of number eight and bracing herself for the stairs. *My darling boy has sent me to a hovel! Paradise Row indeed . . . She will be a vulgar little trollop for sure, this wretched stunner of his . . .*

Up the stairs she went without breaking her stride or losing her breath (for any middle-aged woman who can sit for five hours up a plum tree, in sub-zero temperatures, is nothing if not fit). *Bang, bang, bang*, she rapped on the appropriate door. *Five minutes*, she told herself. *That's surely all the time I'll need to put the kibosh on this ridiculous enterprise . . .*

'Enter!'

It was a woman's voice inviting her in. Mrs Frosdick pushed open the door and entered.

The girl. Oscar's stunner Where is she?

The room was surprisingly large and seemed bright

after the dimness of the landing. Blinking, Mrs Frosdick peered all around. There was a skinny young man hunched over a table, lank hair falling over his eyes. He was busy writing something and hadn't even looked up. There was a woman of the most jaded and comical appearance reclining on a . . . how *very* amusing . . . on a chaise longue; and a jaunty fellow standing by the window, cleaning his fingernails with a toothpick.

Mrs Frosdick sniffed. A weakling, a harridan, and a tuppeny ha'penny dandy. This wouldn't take long at all . . .

The only girl in evidence was bent over the fireplace, waiting for a kettle to boil. She regarded Mrs Frosdick with blank disinterest before wiping her nose on the back of her hand and returning her attention to the kettle.

Is that her? Surely not . . .

The woman on the chaise longue had levered herself into a sitting position. She wore the most ludicrous day gown Mrs Frosdick had ever seen, and a bonnet that might conceivably have been fashionable, for about five minutes, back in 1807. 'My dear Mrs Frosdick,' she was saying. 'We have been expecting you. Pamela Letitia Montague Jackson at your service. And may I say how delighted I am that my niece is to be gainfully employed at last. For I don't mind telling you, she ain't much cop as a flower girl.'

Mrs Frosdick looked, again, at the young woman by the fire. Was Oscar mad? Or losing his sight as well as his hair? For this one was no stunner. Not by any stretch of the imagination.

It was just as well, she thought, that it wasn't going to matter.

'So, Mrs Jackson,' she said, briskly, 'is there a senior

male relative—a father or an uncle—I should address myself to?'

'There is not,' declared the woman. 'Not since my dear husband passed away three years back.' She held a grubby handkerchief briefly to her eyes. 'And it's Mrs *Montague* Jackson, if you don't mind. Double barrelled, like them guns. Now. Let us have a wet of tea and get straight down to business. My son, Orlando, will script an agreement. He writes a beautiful hand, Orlando does . . . And we've got my eldest boy, Jared, as witness. Take a seat at the table, madam, do. And forgive me for not rising to join you, but I am an invalid woman and the effort would quite finish me orf.'

Mrs Frosdick's head was beginning to spin, but she held it high while she said: 'There is absolutely no call, Mrs *Montague* Jackson, for further negotiation. For I cannot, in all conscience, allow your niece to model for my son.'

Everyone fixed her with identical frowns.

'Why not?' they chorused.

Mrs Frosdick pressed her gloved fingertips to her temples, as if her thoughts were suddenly painful.

'Because . . .' she began, 'because . . . oh, goodness . . . this is such a *delicate* matter I am at a loss to know quite how to explain it . . .'

'Just spit it out, my dear madam,' snapped Mrs Jackson. 'We ain't none of us easily shocked.'

'Well then . . .' Mrs Frosdick kept her eyes closed and her expression suitably grieved. She wondered whether to swoon a little, but decided not to overdo it. 'The truth is,' she sighed, 'the *lamentable* truth is . . . that he is not to be trusted. My son, that is. With young girls.'

She waited for the inevitable gasps of horror. For indignant exclamations from the menfolk and all kinds of flutterings from the women. She waited to be asked to leave—indeed, her feet were already braced for the going, and her body half-turned towards the door.

'But does 'e paint 'em?'

'And does 'e pay 'em?'

It was the woman and her oldest boy speaking. The younger lad—the scribe—had returned to his writing, bending so low over the table top that his nose seemed almost welded to it. The girl had taken up a cloth and was lifting the kettle from the fire. 'I'm brewin' the tea,' she said, sullenly, 'if anyone's bothered.'

'Well? Is 'e a painter man, like 'e said, or not? And 'as 'e got the readies?'

Mrs Frosdick glowered at the oldest boy, Jared. She didn't like his manner, his face, or the violent colour of his waistcoat. Nor did she appreciate being questioned so abruptly by one so uncouth that he had actually dared address a lady while continuing to pick dirt from his fingernails.

'My Oscar is indeed an artist and a very fine one,' she replied, unable to prevent a note of pride creeping into her voice. 'He is a member of the Pre-Raphaelite elite, no less. And his financial situation, young man, is none of your concern.'

'It is if 'e's entered into a contract with me cousin,' Jared replied, leaning back against the window and splaying the fingers of his left hand to check the appearance of his nails.

'There is no contract, sir, that I am aware of.'

Jared turned the toothpick over and began pressing back his cuticles.

'Oh, but there is,' he said, cheerfully. 'Only a verbal one for now, I grant you, but as bindin' as sticky-paste nonetheless. The word of a *gentleman*. And witnessed, I might add, by at least a dozen honest trades-folk.'

For a second or two Mrs Frosdick could only open and shut her mouth, like a songless bird, while the lout and his mother beamed triumphantly and the girl rattled teacups onto a battered tin tray.

'But . . . but . . . how *can* you,' she spluttered eventually. 'How can *either* of you so much as *contemplate* placing your own flesh and blood in such grave moral danger? For I really *cannot* over-emphasize my son's depravity in relation to the young and the beautiful. It would be like sending a lamb to a lion! A chick to a fox!'

Mrs Jackson frowned, thoughtfully. 'You have a point there, madam,' she conceded. 'A definite point.'

'Thank you,' breathed Mrs Frosdick. 'I'm delighted that you think so.'

'Orly!' called Mrs Jackson. 'Stick an extra two shillin's on the fee, will yer. And note that it's in recompense for any unseemly attentions our girl 'as to fend off in the course of an honest day's work.'

Mrs Frosdick flinched. Like a ball of yarn being pawed by a bunch of alley cats, her neat and cunning plan was unravelling very fast.

As a final resort, she turned to the girl by the fireside. 'Dare I hope,' she said to her, 'that you yourself have some say in this matter? And that you would rather sell posies for the rest of your days than have your virtue besmirched and your reputation ruined by a feckless artist who has yet to take no for an answer?'

If my dear boy could hear me now, she thought, with an almost-guilty shiver, *he would disown me for sure. But needs must when the Devil drives. For just look at the little trollop. Not only is she no beauty, but I do declare she appears more interested in loading that tray than in any threat to her most precious possession . . .*

Ah. Oh dear . . .

The girl was smirking. She had paused in her search for the sugar and was grinning from ear to ear. And the others were grinning too. 'Ha-ha!' burst out Jared, slapping his thigh. 'What a joke! You're barking up the wrong tree there, missis . . .'

Mrs Frosdick felt her stomach lurch. What a fool she had been. What a complete and utter chump. Of course . . . the wretched girl was a trollop through and through. You only had to look at her to see it. Pah! She had clearly lost her virtue long ago, for the price of a small dinner.

What a mess I have made of this. What a complete and utter mess! And my poor darling boy. What have I done? What have I said? This wanton hussy will think him fair game now and play fast and loose with him as sure as my name is Priscilla Joan Frosdick. Oh, I should never have maligned him so falsely. Never! Never! Where will it all end?

Then the smirking girl opened her mouth and said: 'It ain't me.'

'I beg your pardon?'

'It ain't me the painter man's after.'

Mrs Frosdick turned momentarily faint.

'Then who . . .' she said, resting the palm of one hand on her skittering heart, '. . . is it?'

The woman and her boorish son continued to snigger, in no hurry, either of them, to bring such rich entertainment to a close. It was the other son who, raising tired pink-rimmed eyes, looked over to a far corner and called, gently but firmly: 'Ivy! Ivy, wake up.'

Astonished, Mrs Frosdick followed his gaze. There was a tatty screen in the corner, dividing a sleeping area from the rest of the room. She couldn't see round it, nor was it *quite* tattered enough to be transparent. And because she really could not wait a moment longer to see the girl—the right girl this time—she began to move towards it.

Excuse me, she murmured, skirting the chaise longue. *Excuse me* . . .

'Be my guest, do,' said Mrs Jackson, drily. 'Only she'll need a good pinch, and mebbe a kick for good measure, to get her up an' movin'. A lazier gal never did exist, you mark my words. Always in a blessed trance and wouldn't say boo to a goose. Not that the painter man will mind, by the sound of 'im. Most likely 'e prefers 'em half asleep. Ha-ha!'

'Ha-ha!' laughed the lout with the toothpick. 'Hurry up with that tea, Cyn. All this jollity has got me fair parched. And, Orly—stop scribblin' them miserable verses of yours, and get the contract ready.'

Mrs Frosdick ignored them all. She had reached the far side of the room, and was standing by the screen. On the other side: complete silence. Whoever this 'Ivy' was, she was certainly a heavy sleeper. Or could it be she was wide awake and listening to every word? Without more ado, Mrs Frosdick stepped neatly around the screen.

Later—even years later—Mrs Frosdick could not have said what it was, exactly, that made her catch her breath when she first set eyes on the girl her son so yearned to paint.

It wasn't that she was pretty. Not in a conventional sense. Some might even have called her odd-looking, with that mass of flame-red hair, and her chin and her cheekbones so sharply defined they looked set to pierce through the alabaster-whiteness of her skin.

That she was deeply asleep was quite obvious. A light flickering movement beneath closed lids suggested vivid dreaming and the thin counterpane she had cocooned herself in rose and fell gently in time with her breathing.

She was tall. Mrs Frosdick could see that. And slim too; as slim as a willow wand. But being young and tall and thin didn't always add up to great beauty, and red hair and sharp features rarely did.

So what is it then? What is it about this girl? Why do I feel I could look at her forever?

For some reason, Mrs Frosdick was reminded of the plum tree in her garden . . . of the perfect spring blossom that wasn't going to last.

You wait, she thought, with a flash of spite. *You won't always look like this.*

Ivy stirred. She was dreaming, as she often did, of starry skies that weren't quite real . . . of running endlessly and for ever with a bag of clothes on her back . . . of a path she tried to follow but couldn't . . . just couldn't . . . because there were things in the trees and a voice calling, *'Go home, girly. Now! As fast as you can. Run.'*

'Ivy! Wake up. Come on. The painter man's mama is here for you. Wake up!'

Ivy opened her eyes.

'My dear,' cooed Mrs Frosdick, forcing a smile. 'How delightful to meet you.'

CHAPTER 17

In which young Alfred is given cause to fret

A lfred was busy polishing spoons when he heard a rat-a-tat-tat at the front door. It had been so long since anyone had called that he almost jumped out of his skin.

On the step stood Mrs Frosdick, and she wasn't looking happy.

Alfred's heart sank.

'Oh dear,' he said, before he could stop himself. 'The armadillos.'

'Actually, no,' Mrs Frosdick replied. 'I'm here with a proposition. The Italian—is he back yet?'

'No, ma'am,' Alfred said, cringing at her definition of his master. 'He's still in Oxford. But I'm expecting him home by the end of the week.'

Mrs Frosdick frowned. *Wretched man.*

'Oh, well,' she shrugged. 'Never mind.' She paused, just for a moment, while the scheme in her head shifted and re-formed. 'But you . . . you must be rattling around this empty house like a farthing in a bank vault, and with precious little to do once the—*ahem*—once the dear little animals have been fed and watered. Am I right?'

Alfred, unsure where this was leading, moved his head in what could have been either a shake or a nod.

'So—am I to be invited in, then? For I have an additional proposition. One that may well interest *you*.'

Alfred stepped aside, allowing her to sweep through into the sitting room. She was a formidable woman, Mrs Frosdick, and he always felt wary around her. This proposition was bound to be almost entirely in her own interests, with precious little in it for him. It might even be immoral. Or dangerous. For they were all off their rockers, these arty people, and did as they pleased most of the time with scant regard for the opinions or feelings of others.

If she wants to 'borrow' something, he thought to himself, *I mustn't let her. And if she needs help procuring a white horse, for her son to do up as a unicorn, I must say that I am busy.*

Mrs Frosdick was throwing open the shutters. 'Let some light and air in, Freddie, do,' she cried. 'It's like a mausoleum in here.'

She whirled round, her eyes beady. 'How *is* your master?' she asked. 'Is he well?'

'Well enough, thank you, ma'am,' Alfred told her, carefully. 'Under the circumstances, I mean.'

'Ah yes . . .' Mrs Frosdick ran a gloved finger over the top of a Chinese cabinet, checking for dust. 'The circumstances . . .'

Alfred braced himself for a barrage of questions, all of which he would deflect. But Mrs Frosdick's mind was on other things.

'Now, Freddie,' she said, the familiarity of her tone adding to his discomfort. 'Mr Oscar, as you may be aware, has found himself a stunner.'

No, Alfred said. He wasn't aware of that.

'Well, she's very young—around your age. And I

would be most obliged if you would escort her home this evening, and every evening for the foreseeable future. I will make it worth your while, of course. Financially.'

Alfred was surprised. This was indeed an unexpected proposition.

'Where does she live?' he asked.

'Lambeth.'

Lambeth? It was a fair old step to Lambeth and back.

'Would it not be quicker, ma'am,' he said, 'to send her home by carriage?'

Mrs Frosdick tapped her foot impatiently. She could see her face in the dozens of mirrors hanging on the sitting room walls. Oval mirrors, rectangular mirrors, mirrors shaped like crescent moons, and mirrors the size of puddles, all glimmering against walls the sorrowful green of water-weed and reflecting bits of her back at herself in a strange disjointed fashion.

'It might,' she agreed, 'be quicker, but that is not the point. I will pay you three shillings per trip. Not a bad sum, Freddie-boy, for a pleasant evening's stroll with a beautiful young girl; most of it along the riverbank and by moonlight, more than likely. What do you say? Doesn't that sound delightful?'

Alfred remained quiet while he mulled the idea over. Never mind moonlight. The fee *was* generous.

Mrs Frosdick was adjusting her shawl, preparing to take her leave.

'Well?' she said. 'Will you escort our beautiful maiden home or not?'

'All right,' Alfred agreed. 'I will, yes. At least, until my master returns and then we will have to see.'

'Good. And your master, I'm sure, will be as entranced as we are by this lovely girl of ours. We must make sure that he meets her one day. Perhaps he would wish to paint her. Um . . . there is no . . . *special* . . . model in your master's life right now, I take it?'

'No,' Alfred replied. 'Not really.'

At least six mirrors caught the satisfied smirk on Mrs Frosdick's face before she swept from the room. The fringe of her shawl brushed Alfred's fingers as she passed, and he winced as if the silky tassels had been tarantula legs.

Quickly, he opened the front door. It stuck a little, where damp had seeped in. *I must see to that*, Alfred thought. *Before my master comes home.*

'Please call for her at seven,' Mrs Frosdick said, as she descended the stone steps. 'And you may wish to spruce yourself up a bit and perhaps memorize a little poetry to recite. For the girl is, as I've said, very beautiful, and it would please me—oh, more than I can say—if the two of you got along.'

Left alone, Alfred went back to the sitting room intending to close the shutters. A particularly grand mirror, in a frame of gilded leaves and passion flowers, reflected his approaching figure. *What did she mean, 'spruce myself up a bit'?*

Alfred prided himself on always looking neat. Even with his master away, and no one else to notice or care, he would sooner have gone without food and drink than neglect to wash himself, or comb his hair.

Going closer to the mirror, he was relieved to see that his hair was still tidy and his face devoid of smudges. Tentatively, he sniffed his armpits. Pears soap. That's all he smelt of. No traces of spinach between his teeth either. No dandruff on his shoulders. No jackdaw droppings on his boots.

His personal hygiene, he was certain, could not be faulted. *So what else could Mrs Frosdick have meant?* Puzzled, Alfred considered his reflection. He had never wondered, much, about being handsome. He knew he wasn't ugly and that had always seemed enough to be going on with.

Now, though, he found himself scrutinizing every bit of the face he presented to the world. His nose . . . was it too big? And those freckles . . . little spatters of brown as if God had flicked a paintbrush at him . . . were they something a young girl might find unattractive . . . repulsive even? His eyes seemed all right to him. Unless, perhaps, they were a bit too widely spaced. And his hair was . . . well . . . just ordinary hair.

What did 'handsome' mean, anyway? His master was considered handsome, even though he was no spring chicken and had a stomach the size of a bolster. *His* hair was frequently wild and his beard a magnet for midges and crumbs. Yet ladies—even beautiful ones—never seemed to mind. The woman in the painting upstairs had loved him to distraction.

Distraction. Alfred wasn't sure he wanted to be loved like that. Not by anyone, ever. So perhaps it was just as well that he had freckles, and was ordinary. And yet . . . if Mr Frosdick's stunner was beautiful . . . truly beautiful . . .

Turning sideways, Alfred found he had a choice of several dozen mirrors in which to view his profile.

Will she like me? he wondered, turning this way and that. *Will she want to walk across the river with me, this beautiful*

girl? Or will she laugh in my face and insist upon a carriage to
take her back to Lambeth?

Alfred had sisters at his home near Oxford whom he
loved dearly. And, once, he'd had a sweetheart called
Mary whom he had kissed. Twice. Here in London,
though, there had been little opportunity for him to meet
anyone his own age. His master's own models were older
girls—in their twenties at least—who flitted in and out of
the studio without noticing Alfred or even thanking him,
sometimes, for taking their cloaks. And *they* got sent
home in carriages. Or stayed.

Turning back to the big mirror with passion flowers
round it, Alfred gave his features one final appraisal. And
this time he was ruthless. *If I'm to alter my appearance*, he
thought to himself. *Where exactly should I start?*

CHAPTER 18

In which Ivy suffers an unexpected loss

'Are you tired? Or cold? Would you like to finish for the day?'

Oscar had been painting manically all afternoon. So manically that he hadn't noticed the sun slipping lower behind the plum tree, or the shadows of twigs reaching further and further across the lawn, like fingers about to steal his paints.

He had been right. *So* right. This girl was perfect. Not only stunning but compliant and quiet, with an aura of almost saintly calm. And how still she had managed to stay, up there in the tree. So still she seemed quite otherworldly, like a figment of his imagination.

'Come down now,' he coaxed her, gently. 'Come down and get warm.'

It didn't do for fragile young girls to get too chilled. It had happened to the Italian's wife, while she was posing for Millais. Dead of winter it had been, and her floating on her back in a tin bath tub, with just a few little candles underneath to keep the water warm. Ophelia. She had been posing as Hamlet's Ophelia . . . hands outflung, head tipped back, lips parted in silent song . . . And Millais hadn't noticed the candles going out. Poor Lizzie. Poor thing. The chill she had caught from lying so long in all that cold water was so severe it could have killed her. It hadn't though. Not that. Not then.

Ivy moved slowly. She had the beginnings of a headache but it was nothing she couldn't put up with until she had her own clothes back on and could get to the bottle of laudanum in her skirt pocket.

'Let me help you.' Oscar strode through the twiggy-shadows on the lawn and reached to take her hand. He meant only to be courteous, but Ivy waved him away.

'I can manage,' she said, tugging the blindfold from her eyes before sliding dizzily to the ground. 'Here—here's yer lute back.'

Oscar took the lute.

'You are s-so beautiful,' he stammered. 'I could gaze at you forever. Would you consider joining me for supper?'

Ivy looked at him. His face was flushed pink and he seemed painfully shy. Was this how painter men behaved, then, before they pounced? Did they pretend to be bashful and ready for a meal?

Aunt Pamela had said this man would pounce on her for sure, and sooner rather than later. 'Keep 'im at arm's-length for a bit, Ive,' she had hissed. 'Make sure the price is right before you lets 'im 'ave 'is wicked way.'

'High,' Cousin Jared had interrupted. 'Make sure the price is high.'

Orlando had said nothing. He had simply continued to write. And the painter man's mama—sent to wait down-stairs with the carriage—had said nothing either, when Ivy had finally joined her; only turned away, as if travelling alone, and looked out of the carriage window all the way to Chelsea.

Ivy wasn't sure how she would react when the painter man pounced. Except to say 'no', of course. Or 'maybe'. Or 'not yet'. She blinked and flexed her fingers, which were stiff from holding the lute. Oh . . . what did it matter what got said? This man . . . this place . . . this garden . . . none of it mattered and probably never would.

She had a headache. She needed her laudanum. She wanted to sleep. Sleeping was what Ivy liked to do most of the time and, thanks to Fing Nolan, it was something she did well.

'Laudanum . . . syrup of opium . . . just the thing for fixing a noisy brat and making certain sure it sleeps . . .'Ow much didjer give 'er last night, Mucks? Well, it weren't enough to shut 'er up till mornin', were it? Nowhere near enough . . .'

I am an artist's model now, Ivy told herself, gazing beyond Oscar Aretino Frosdick into the shrubbery. *I am being paid to sit in a tree all day and dream.*

It would have been funny if it had only seemed real. If she hadn't felt so groggy and in need of her drug.

There were wallflowers in the shrubbery and a lot of forget-me-nots. Ivy thought she saw something moving there. Something brown and cumbersome. A big old cat, probably. Or a fox.

'Supper?' Oscar repeated, hopefully.

'All right,' Ivy agreed, since it was the easiest thing to do. 'But first I gotter change out of this robe.'

She waited for him to start drooling at the thought of her taking the robe off. She waited the way someone in an audience might wait, to see if an actor is going to do something interesting to liven up a dull play. She waited without really giving a sparrow's tweet what he did

117

because whatever happened was bound to seem unreal and therefore unimportant.

'Of course,' Oscar said, without the slightest hint of drool. 'There is a small parlour next to the conservatory which you may use from now on as a dressing room. The drapes are always closed, so it is completely private. I keep all my clothes in there—my models' clothes, I mean. That blue robe you're wearing goes in the trunk marked "Robes". Come. I'll show you.'

Slightly bemused, Ivy followed Oscar across the lawn and in through the glass-panelled conservatory. She had never been in such a comfortable home before; never seen so many feathery plants or pretty trinkets taking up so much space. And it was so quiet . . . the silence broken only by an ancient clock that ticked and whirred some-where out in the hall, like a solemn geriatric chuntering on and on without anyone taking much notice.

Oscar indicated the door to the small parlour. 'Supper will be served in fifteen minutes,' he said. 'It's the cook's half day, but mother so loves to potter in the kitchen that she has offered to do the honours. Au revoir, then—for now?'

Ivy nodded and he left.

Fifteen minutes . . .

It was, as Oscar had said, completely private in the room where he kept his clothes. Stepping from the diamond-bright conservatory, Ivy had the impression of entering another element altogether, until she realized that the shifting underwater sensation came from the way the light came in through thin green-patterned cur-tains that were moving, slightly, in a breeze. Compared to the room upstairs, where she had changed earlier, this space was refreshingly plain. No frills or flounces. Just a tall chest of drawers, several trunks and a number of boxes, all labelled as if for a voyage.

Ivy wondered which trunk said 'Robes'. Would she recognize the letter 'R'?

'R for remortant,' she murmured to herself, with a wry smile. 'R for repenful . . .'

Someone had brought her own skirt, bodice, and petticoat down and laid them over one of the boxes. Quickly she snatched up the skirt and reached into the pocket. Her head was aching badly, now, and her mouth felt sour and dry.

Her fingers reached deeper . . . scrabbling in the empty space.

It wasn't there. Her laudanum. It had gone.

CHAPTER 19

Concerning idle gossip and lurid speculation

T rying hard not to panic, Ivy patted the skirt all over, checking every fold and crease. Had she forgotten to bring it? No. She would never have forgotten something she had come to rely upon to get her through most days. It must have fallen out . . . somehow . . . somewhere . . .

Oh no, oh no.

Sinking down on a trunk marked 'Cloaks' she pressed the fingers of both hands, hard, against the sides of her skull.

Breathe, she told herself. *And think. Breathe and think. Or maybe don't think. Thinking 'urts. Just breathe. You can get some more. Later . . . Aunt Pamela'll 'ave some. Tell 'er the painter man's pleased . . . that he could look at you forever . . . then maybe she'll let you 'ave a few drops of 'ers . . .*

A light tapping at the door made her jump and then cringe. 'Are you ready, my dear?' trilled Oscar. 'May I escort you through to supper?'

'No . . .' Ivy replied quickly. 'That is . . . I ain't quite ready . . . yet.'

'Mother says do you have everything you need?'

Ivy hesitated. *Think. Think. Mrs Frosdick probably meant pins or face powder—ladylike stuff, anyway, to do with gettin, ready for supper in a wealthy 'ouse.*

120

'Can I 'ave a glass of water?' she asked after a moment.

'Of course! How thoughtless of me. You are bound to be thirsty after posing for so long . . .'

'And . . . um . . .' She cleared her dry throat and licked her lips. 'Are you still there . . . sir?'

'Yes, yes. I'm still here. Is there anything else that you need? Anything at all?'

Ivy took a deep breath. It was important, she instinctively knew, not to sound desperate.

'I 'ave a slight 'eadache,' she said. 'So if you've got anything . . . some laudanum, per'aps . . . for me to take with the water . . .'

'I will go and ask mother this very instant.'

When he had gone, Ivy took off the blue robe and put her own clothes back on. She couldn't face rummaging through trunks, to see which one contained robes, so simply folded the one she had been wearing and slid it on top of the chest of drawers.

Blue: a fashionable colour. Good quality cloth and plenty of it. It would make a couple of skirts, that robe would, with enough left over for a few cravats.

Ivy winced. Even now . . . even here . . .

Blue had probably gone out of fashion a long time ago, but the habit she had picked up from Carroty Kate, of seeing potential in any large swathe of material, had yet to leave her. A Union Jack draped from a window could make her think: *fancy waistcoats: at least four* before she had passed it by. And the sight of a boat's sails, slapping and straining in the wind, would set her off on a similar calculation for trousers.

One day, she hoped, she would be able to look at a flag and just think '*flag*' or watch a boat sailing along the Thames without reckoning more than: '*how fine that boat looks.*' And then she would know that the past had become a vague and distant thing that could no longer disturb her, or matter. A lot like the present, in fact. Or how the present usually was, so long as . . .

Another knock-knock sent her hurrying back across the room, not caring that she banged and hurt bits of herself against boxes and trunks as she ran. Flinging open the door she was taken aback to see, not Oscar standing there, but his mother.

'Your water, my dear,' Mrs Frosdick said.

'Thank you.'

Ivy took the proffered glass with shaking fingers and waited to be left alone.

Mrs Frosdick, however, stayed right where she was.

'I'm much obliged,' Ivy added. 'Me poor 'ead's pounding.' And since the woman still didn't go, she retreated back into the room, raised the glass to her lips, and drank. Alone, she would have gulped that water down and maybe even spilled some in her haste to feel the calming, numbing sensation that laudanum induced.

But with Mrs Frosdick's eyes upon her she forced herself to sip . . . and sip . . . and sip . . .

'Better now?' Mrs Frosdick held out her hand for the empty glass.

Ivy nodded, as she handed the glass over. But she didn't feel better. She didn't feel any different at all.

'Supper is ready,' Mrs Frosdick added. 'If you would care to follow me.'

The dining room was a fussy place: red walls covered in portraits (mostly male Frosdicks judging by the pink-faced bald-headed look of them); two sideboards loaded with decanters and silverware and a table that could have seated twenty but was set for only three.

Oscar had changed from his painter's smock into a suit and used scented lotion to smarm what was left of his hair into anchovy-like strands over the top of his head. 'Allow me,' he said, pulling a chair out and motioning Ivy to sit.

Ivy sat.

A big silver dome covered the plate in front of her and there appeared to be several choices of cutlery.

Oscar sprinted away to the head of the table. His mother was already seated. Between the three of them was so much space that they might as well have been dining in separate rooms. The tablecloth was so vast and white it put Ivy in mind of a courtyard after snow. *Good linen though. Starched too. Four decent-sized petticoats, at least.*

'We don't stand on ceremony in this house,' Mrs Frosdick was saying. 'Nor do we say grace. Do start, my dear. *Oscar*—the wine.'

Slowly, Ivy lifted the silver dome from her plate.

'I say!' exclaimed Oscar, popping up behind her with a decanter of wine. 'Mother, you have surpassed yourself. Those colours are magnificent—the green of the beans against the white of the china, and the way the meat juices swirl around . . . Why . . .'

'Sit down, dear boy,' his mother ordered. 'You're gabbling.'

Ivy looked, in horror, at the slab of creature under her nose. Creature so lightly cooked that it was still bleeding.

123

'I do hope, young lady, that you are not a *faddy* type.' Something in Mrs Frosdick's tone made Ivy nervous. Reluctantly, she picked up her knife and fork, speared a green bean and raised it to her mouth. The cutlery was so heavy she thought she might drop it and crack the plate.

'Because faddy gals,' Mrs Frosdick continued, 'are quite insufferable; always fainting and fretting and not at all suited to life as a model—or to life in general, come to that. Our Italian neighbour—an artist of some repute, whose name you are doubtless familiar with—was married to just such a type. Dead and gone she is now. An accident, the coroner said, and one can only suppose he knew what he was talking about . . .'

'Now, mother,' Oscar dabbed a fleck of beefsteak from his mouth with a pristine napkin. 'I'm sure our young lady has no interest whatsoever in idle gossip and lurid speculation. Let us change the subject. I have an idea for my next painting. It is rather ambitious but . . .'

Mrs Frosdick waved his idea aside. Leaning forward, over the great expanse of tablecloth, she fixed Ivy in her sights and said:

'He had her exhumed, you know.'

'Now, mother . . .'

'He did. Just over a year ago, in the dead of night. They *say* it was to get his poems back—love poems he'd written for her and then slipped into her coffin, thinking never to want them again. He let seven years go by, he did, before suddenly deciding he wanted those poems published after all. Rather *odd* that, don't you think? I mean, if the man's *half* the genius he's made out to be, why didn't he just write some more? The Lord knows, there were enough other pretty gals trotting in and out of his studio by then to inspire a whole *trunk*ful of sonnets and swoonery . . .'

Ivy set down her knife and fork, hoping it looked like the right thing to do in order to listen better. She felt sick as well as faint, and would have welcomed any excuse to stop eating the green beans that were swimming, now, in creature juice. Mrs Frosdick's face was flushed and her eyes extremely bright. She had finished her wine and was beckoning Oscar to hurry over with more.

'They say,' she continued, 'that when the coffin lid was raised, she was perfectly preserved. *Perfectly* preserved. And that her hair—she had red hair, dear, like you—had continued to grow and that it glinted, bright as a copper penny still, in the light of their lanterns.'

'Mother, that is quite enough. You are putting our guest off her food.' Oscar's own plate was empty. He was ready for his treacle tart and custard, and worried that his beautiful young model appeared to have less appetite than an earwig.

'I am merely making the point,' Mrs Frosdick remarked, 'that the Italian's wife, for all her looks, was too spineless to either get by in this world or remain in it. An accident, my eye . . . Eat your beefsteak, my dear. You are clearly in need of the nourishment, and we are waiting for you.'

Ivy lifted her knife. Her slab of creature had grown cold and was congealing in a puddle of its own liquids. Cutting into it would be like stabbing a human being. It was a long time, she realized, since she had felt as strongly as this about the food on her plate. At home, in Paradise Row, she had stopped fussing on the subject a long time ago. It had become easier, as she grew older, to avoid mealtimes altogether and simply fend for herself. And if that wasn't always possible . . . well, there was usually so little meat in the pot that she had trained herself to keep what few stringy bits she was given in her mouth long enough to get away, and spit.

This though . . . this piece of flesh was almost as big as her own shoulder.

Averting her eyes, she began to press into it with her knife. It was either that or explain. And she was too tired to talk to these people. Too tired and too unwell. There had been no laudanum in that glass of water, she was certain of it. So the sooner she ate this the sooner she would be allowed to go home, to Aunt Pamela's supply.

She would pretend this poor creature was a new kind of vegetable. Something from a faraway land . . . something that grew on a bush under blazing skies, or in soil watered by rain as warm as gravy.

'Now who can that be?' grumbled Mrs Frosdick as a knocking on the front door echoed down the hall. 'Aha!' she remembered. 'I know. *Oscar*—stay! I know who it will be. Pray excuse me while I ask him to wait. You may wish to apologize to him later, dear girl, for being such a slow eater.'

The second she left the room Ivy put down her cutlery and slumped against the narrow back of her chair. It was no good. Her half-hearted attempts at dividing the creature into smaller, more manageable pieces had left it bleeding twice as much and looking not just lightly cooked but tortured.

She was aware of Oscar's eyes upon her but did not

dare to meet them. Instead, she focused on a patch of the tablecloth, just in front of her plate, and tried to think. If she could only get Oscar to leave the room as well, just for a minute, she might be able to hide the contents of her plate somewhere. In a vase, perhaps, or behind one of those big sideboards.

Think, think . . .

When the point of Oscar's own knife came slicing down in front of her, she jumped so abruptly that her chair almost toppled. She hadn't noticed him standing up, or leaning her way, and yet there he was, looming over the salt and pepper pots as intently as a vulture.

It was quite a stretch, and for a few wobbly seconds it looked to Ivy as if he might lose his balance and crash face-down on the table-top. But he did it. He got the meat on the point of his knife, hoisted it clear, and landed it, all frayed and cold and dripping, on his own empty plate.

Then he ate it. Every scrap.

'Our . . . (*gulp*) . . . little . . . (*gulp, gulp*) . . . secret . . .' he said, reaching for a toothpick.

And so elated was he to have pulled such a fast one on his mother that he overcame his bashfulness enough to tip his stunner a joyous and companionable wink.

Meanwhile, out in the shrubbery, an armadillo woke up in a cloud of forget-me-nots and sniffed. Moving fast for such a cumbersome creature, it scuttled from the flower bed and went trotting across the lawn.

Round the plum tree it went, still sniffing, and on to a rougher piece of ground where grass cuttings and dead flowers had been thrown in piles, to rot. And there it found its own piece of beefsteak, laid out on a stone like a proper little supper.

And it ate it. Every scrap.

CHAPTER 20

In which Alfred is obliged to run and Oscar can barely move

It was, as Alfred had already realized, a fair old step to Lambeth. But the second he set eyes on Oscar Frosdick's stunner he stopped minding about how far it was and whether or not he would be home before midnight. Not because she was beautiful—although he supposed she was, in that red-haired big-eyed way that the Pre-Raphaelites seemed to favour—but because she looked so forlorn that he just wanted to look after her.

He had expected to be introduced to a haughty girl, like the ones who came most often to pose for his master. He had been imagining someone who would look down her perfect nose at him, like a duchess contemplating a stain on the carpet, and say something snipey. So when she smiled, in a sincere and friendly manner, and whispered, '*I'm so glad you're takin' me 'ome,*' he knew he would have walked with her, and protected her, as far as . . . oh . . . the very edge of England. Every night. For the rest of his life. Without once complaining about blisters, or the passing of time.

'You're looking very . . . um . . . *dapper* . . . this evening, Freddie,' Mrs Frosdick said, her mouth twitching spitefully as she led the way along the hall towards the front door. And Alfred felt a stab of panic, in case she was about to

129

ridicule, publicly, the lengths he had gone to in order to spruce himself up.

Mrs Frosdick, however, turned immediately to her son's new model: 'And you, my dear,' she observed, loudly, 'are looking quite deathly, if you don't mind me saying so. I do *hope* you aren't about to fall prey to some protracted illness or other, for Oscar would be *so* sorry to lose you. Goodnight.'

Left to get on with the business of being an escort, Alfred wasn't sure how to behave. Should he offer the girl his arm? Was that the proper thing to do, or would she consider it a liberty?

Ivy solved that particular dilemma by hurrying down the steps, and moving so fast down the path that he had to run to catch her up.

'Are . . . are you all right, Miss Ivy?' he asked, as she fumbled with the latch on the gate.

'No, I ain't,' she told him. 'I'm sick. I need to get 'ome.'

Alfred took over the job of opening the gate. She certainly looked pale. And skinny enough to slip down a grating. 'Are you well enough to walk?' he wondered. 'Because if you're not . . .'

'I can walk,' Ivy insisted. 'I can run, even. Running's fun. Let's run. It'll be quicker.' And she was off. Away towards Battersea Bridge, leaving Alfred to follow or not, as he chose.

There were a lot of people out that evening, taking the air, for it was not yet hot enough for the Thames to smell truly poisonous and the magnolia trees along Cheyne Walk were starting to look exotic.

Everyone, it seemed, turned to stare at Ivy as she tore

along the embankment, her bright hair streaming behind her and her shawl lifting like the wings of a turtle dove. Alfred, pounding along in her wake, could only hope that no one imagined she was running away from *him*.

He wasn't used to running and was glad when Ivy stopped at the bridge, and waited. He was panting like a puppy when he reached her, and the sweat was dripping off him.

'Can . . . can we . . . slow down . . . now?' he gasped. '. . . Please?'

Ivy looked at him.

'What's the matter with your face?' she said.

'Mother,' mumbled Oscar, putting down a half-smoked cigar and rising, unsteadily, from his chair. 'You will have to excuse me. I'm feeling a little . . . indisposed . . . all of a sudden. I think I might need to lie down.'

Mrs Frosdick continued to poke a needle into something. She wasn't unduly worried. After all, she had no idea that her precious son had taken it upon himself to relieve his stunner of her unwanted beefsteak.

'Bowels or belly, dear boy?' she asked, without looking up.

'Both,' he declared, grimly, before leaving the parlour with as much dignity as he could muster.

Too much wine at supper, Mrs Frosdick assumed. The dear boy simply hasn't the constitution for it. His father was the same . . .

Meanwhile, out beneath the plum tree, the armadillo had stopped moving. For good.

* * *

'My face?'

Alfred had forgotten. About what he had done to spruce himself up. So entranced had he become, by the sight of this girl, that his own appearance had ceased to matter. This was strange, he realized, for it ought, really, to matter more than ever.

'It's dribblin',' Ivy told him. 'Onto yer shirt.'

Alarmed, Alfred lifted both hands to his perspiring cheeks and dabbed, cautiously, with the tips of his fingers. They came away flesh coloured and he felt himself blushing for shame.

'Oh dear,' he muttered, fumbling in his pocket for a handkerchief. 'I see what you mean.'

' 'Ere.'

Ivy may have lost her laudanum but her handkerchief was still to hand. And quickly, to save time, she shook it out, spat on it twice, and began cleaning paint from Alfred's nose.

Alfred heard himself squeak, like a rodent, as she clasped the back of his head and tipped it gently to one side, the better to get to his face. She was taller than him and clearly stronger than she looked. He felt like a child having tears wiped away. He felt happy and confused and hideously embarrassed. He felt hotter than ever, even though he had stopped running.

'There,' Ivy said, giving the side of his mouth one final swipe. 'All gone.'

He didn't know what to say. What could he say? That he had borrowed his master's paints and spent all after-

132

noon getting the proportions of cadmium red, titanium white, chrome yellow, and yellow ochre exactly right, as a match for his own skin tone? And that it had taken five attempts, with three different brushes, to paint over his freckles so that they didn't show through?

She would think him mad. Or ridiculous. Or both.

But Ivy wasn't thinking of anything except her urgent need to beg, borrow, or steal some laudanum from her aunt. 'Come on,' she said, thrusting the paint-stained handkerchief into her pocket as if nothing much had happened. 'I'll race you over the bridge.'

'Dear boy?'

Mrs Frosdick tapped a second time on Oscar's bedroom door.

The faint groan he emitted, by way of an answer, was barely audible.

'Oscar, are you there? Is there anything you need?'

Had Oscar been capable of speech he would have rattled off quite a list. But he was having problems swallowing, never mind talking, so his needs were going to have to go unmet. And as another vicious cramp twisted his innards, he couldn't help but wonder what it was that he needed the most: a good dose of Epsom Salts or a priest, to administer last rites.

'Well then, I will say goodnight. And Oscar? I have arranged for a carriage to go to Lambeth first thing in the morning, as you requested, but don't be surprised if that gal lets you down. For I have a suspicion—a very strong suspicion—that she is unreliable, as well as faddy, and really not up to the rigours of modelling. To be honest, dear boy, I doubt very much we shall see her face again.'

Oscar opened his mouth, to protest, but all that came out was a belch that tasted of metal.

'So goodnight, dear boy. Sweet dreams.'

As her footsteps went away Oscar struggled to raise himself into a sitting position. Water. That's what he needed the most. A big jug of water to slake his thirst and quell the awful sickness rising up in him.

Little did he realize that milk would have been a better option. For milk (along with burnt toast and cod-liver oil) was what was usually recommended—albeit to no avail, most of the time—as an antidote to arsenic poisoning.

Clocks were chiming midnight as Alfred strolled back along Cheyne Walk. He could have returned sooner but had dawdled, savouring his role as Ivy's escort even though she was safely home and probably not thinking of him at all.

The front door of number sixteen stuck, as he tried to push it open. *I really must get that seen to*, he reminded himself, giving the damp wood a good shove with his left shoulder.

On the mat lay a calling card. Alfred picked it up. It was from a poet friend of his master's, who lived nearby and sometimes visited in the evenings to smoke cigars and debate the existence of God, true love, and the monster in Loch Ness.

'*Where are you?*' read the message on the back of the

card. *'Or did you say the twenty-sixth, not the twenty-fifth? In which case, my mistake and I will see you for supper tomorrow.'*

Tomorrow? So Alfred's master was due back tomorrow, then, was he? It was typical of him, Alfred thought, to let his friends know, but neglect to inform his servants. What would he be expecting to eat at such short notice? Magnolia petals? The peacock?

Ordinarily, Alfred would have been delighted at the prospect of returning to normal—or to what passed for normality in this curious household. Now, though, all he could think was *Will I still be able to escort Miss Ivy home? Will he allow it?*

First thing in the morning, he decided, he would get the other servants back. What else? The house was spotless, he had seen to that. And the animals had been well looked after. *Surely*, he thought, *I have earned some time off in the evenings. For I have fulfilled all my duties admirably while left here all alone.*

Or almost all, he corrected himself. *All, except one . . .*

It had been three days, at least, since Alfred had visited the upstairs room to check for strange sounds, objects out of place, or anything else unusual.

It was late now, and very dark. All he wanted to do was go to bed, and maybe dream a beautiful dream about Miss Ivy. He would look into the room as soon as he woke up. *No you won't*, his conscience said. *You'll go now. Otherwise you won't deserve any time off. Nor will you sleep easy.*

There was an oil lamp on the hallstand and matches in a tin box. The lamp had a red shade that cast a rosy glow as Alfred crept up the stairs. On the top landing, he hes-itated. But it was silly, he knew, to think things happened after dark, just *because* it was dark. And it was more than silly—it was unmanly—to be afraid of entering a locked and empty room.

His fingers found the key and turned it.

Oh . . .

It looked—it *felt*—as if someone was already there. Someone holding up a lantern, the better to gaze upon the painting above the mantelshelf. But it was only moonlight, he realized, a brilliant shaft of moonlight, shining through a gap in the curtains directly onto the painting, and illuminating the woman's face.

He took a deep breath and waited for his heart to slow down. And while he breathed he listened . . . *nothing* . . . and peered quickly all around, raising and swinging the oil lamp so that shadows and moonlight were rendered less spooky by more familiar beams.

Nothing. Really, nothing.

He was ready to leave—more than ready—but his eyes were drawn back, as they always were, to the face in the painting. And maybe it was a trick of the moon. Or maybe he was feeling particularly sensitive, just then, towards red-haired models who didn't look well. But, whatever the reason, he could have sworn—*on his life*—that the woman's eyelids trembled. And as he stared at her, in pity and in wonder, it seemed blindingly obvious to him, all of a sudden, that the thing she was yearning for . . . reaching for . . . striving for . . . was to wake up.

To live.

A conjuring of the light, that's all.

And Alfred, satisfied that he had completed this final duty, and there was nothing to report, went thoughtfully off to his bed.

CHAPTER 21

Concerning a case of mistaken identity

Ivy was ready and waiting when the carriage arrived the next morning, to take her back to Chelsea.

'Remember, Ive,' Cousin Jared told her, before she left, 'keep stringin' that painter man along. Let 'im think 'e'll get special treatment, by and by, so long as 'e continues generous wiv 'is payments—but push 'im off if 'e gets too fruity. This is a nice little earner, this is.' And he had thrown her an apple, to eat for her breakfast.

It was funny, Ivy thought, as the carriage rattled along, how much nicer certain members of the family were being, now that she had become its main breadwinner. Aunt Pamela had made none of the expected fuss last night when badgered for more laudanum. And this morning Cyn had offered to do her hair.

'It'll clog up yer brush,' Ivy had reminded her.

The older girl had shrugged. 'You gotter look decent for the painter man though ain'tyer?' she'd said. 'Or 'e won't shower yer with wealth.'

Ivy had expected Cyn to be both quick and vicious with that brush, for she had never been pleasant—not even after Hor and Mad left Paradise Row to be with their men, when she might have tried harder to be friends.

Surprisingly, though, Cyn brushed carefully. Gently, even. And such thoughtfulness made a pleasant change, even if, as Ivy suspected, Cyn was only being nice in the hope of benefiting personally from any 'shower of wealth' that fell.

Only Orlando seemed just the same—withdrawn and preoccupied, hunched over his writings. Poor Orly. Through choice he wrote love poems and whole plays in rhyming verse. Through necessity he wrote rubbish. On a 'good' week he got paid several shillings by a printer who didn't want anything 'fancy' but bought ballads about hangings, murders, and unfortunate accidents to sell on the streets. On a *really* good week he got a commission to write someone's epitaph.

It was a long, long time since Ivy had felt close to Orlando. Still, some lingering sensitivity towards him told her that he wasn't exactly thrilled about her nice little earner. She decided not to fret about it. Why should she? Orlando behaved as if being able to read and write made him saintly, or royal—a lot better, anyway, than anybody else in Paradise Row.

It was another sunny day. Leaning back in the carriage, Ivy suddenly felt glad to be heading out of Lambeth towards a prettier part of London. Modelling was all right, she'd decided, for it required little of her. And she didn't mind Oscar Frosdick all that much, for he seemed too ridiculous to pose much of a threat. Mrs Frosdick was a mean-spirited person, of that there was no doubt. But she could probably be avoided from now on. So could supper.

By the time the carriage rolled into Cheyne Walk Ivy was feeling quite buoyant. It was such a strange sensation, compared to her usual inertia, that she instantly mistrusted it. Stepping from the carriage she refused to take pleasure in anything, from further thoughts of her nice little earner, to the wonderful scent of wallflowers beyond the Frosdicks' gate. For the trouble, she knew, with feeling good about something was you felt ten times worse when you lost it.

When nobody replied to her knockings at the front door she assumed, with only the smallest pang of regret, that she had been right not to trust her good mood. *They don't want me no more*, she chided herself. *Me face ain't right after all.*

But why, then, had they sent the carriage? Which, she now noticed, hadn't waited. Resigned to the long walk home, Ivy turned away from the Frosdicks' house. It was just as well, she told herself, that she hadn't much liked either it or them and that she'd only spent a day here and not a year and a half.

Might she dream about this place, though? Would the memory of a blue robe, a ticking clock, and dining room walls the colour of blood haunt her sleep the way other things did ... things from longer ago?

She doubted it.

Absorbed in her thoughts, and the beginnings of a headache, she didn't see Alfred come prowling up the path until she almost bumped into him.

'Oh,' Alfred exclaimed, jumping guiltily away. 'Good morning, miss.' He felt himself blushing and hurried to explain his presence. 'I was looking in the hedges. For a big armadillo. They haven't said anything, have they? Mrs and Mr Frosdick, I mean. About findin' one somewhere? In the back garden perhaps?'

Ivy hadn't the faintest idea what he was talking about. 'Armadillo' sounded, to her, like one of the colours Oscar Frosdick mixed on his palette. He had told her the paint names yesterday, by way of conversation: *raw umber, cobalt blue, cadmium red, burnt sienna*. Nice-sounding, she'd thought, but nonsense.

Armadillo orange.

Frosdick-faced pink.

Waste of time white.

There. She could invent paint-names that sounded just as daft. But the painter man and his stupid colours were in the past now, along with his mean old mother, the blue robe, and the ticking clock. She could forget them all. Easily.

'There ain't no one in,' she said to Alfred. 'Not even a servant to answer the blessed door and give me me marchin' orders.'

Alfred looked up at the brass door-knocker shaped like a lion's head. 'The Frosdicks don't keep servants,' he said. 'Only a cook, part-time, and a laundrymaid on Mondays. Mrs Frosdick finds the presence of strangers irksome— even those strangers who would keep the grate blackened and cobwebs off the ceiling.'

'I see,' said Ivy, although, really, she didn't give a cat's scratch.

'She does most of the chores herself,' continued Alfred. 'And Mr Frosdick, he lights the range and buffs his own boots. A strange set-up, if you asks me, but that's arty types for you, miss, and it ain't my place to question it.'

He looked at Ivy, hesitated, and then added: 'If you'd care to step next door, miss, and wait a while, I'm sure Mr Frosdick will be home by and by. I'd offer to escort you over the river, right this very minute, but my own master is returning from Oxford today, and I must be here when he arrives.'

Ivy was not looking forward to breaking the news, back at Paradise Row, that her nice little earner had been scuppered. So she walked with Alfred round to number sixteen, to wait in the sitting room while he got on with his duties.

'If you hear a knocking sound,' Alfred said, opening the shutters for her. 'Let me know. It might be the armadillo, stuck somewhere.'

Ivy gathered her skirt closer about her and glanced, suspiciously, all around. There were plenty of chairs and screens and cabinets in here, behind which a strange-sounding thing might hide. She had to ask. 'What's a harmydill-o when it's at 'ome?'

Alfred smiled. 'A nuisance,' he said. 'That's what an armadillo is. A wretched nuisance. And ugly. The ugliest living creature you ever saw.'

Ivy felt her own face breaking into a grin. 'Really?' she said. 'As ugly as that Mrs Frosdick?'

Alfred chuckled. He couldn't help it. 'Same big nose,' he said. 'Always sticking itself where it's not wanted. Always sniffing around for trouble.'

Ivy laughed out loud. She was starting to like this boy. This Alfred. He reminded her, a little, of Orlando—or of how Orlando might have turned out if he hadn't taken education quite so seriously.

142

Her laughter delighted Alfred. She hadn't been like this last night—so easy to be with. He shouldn't be insulting Mrs Frosdick though. It wasn't his place.

'Can I get you anything, miss?' he said, in his more formal voice. 'For while you're waiting? We've had a delivery, this morning, so there's a ham in the pantry, and potted shrimps.'

'Some water, please,' Ivy replied. 'And you don't 'ave to call me "miss". Just Ivy. Plain Ivy.'

Alfred looked at her. At the real her, and at the dozens of reflections of her in the mirrors around the room. Each reflection, he realized, would make a perfect work of art. Even the back of her head was lovely.

'Not "plain",' he said, huskily. 'No one could ever c-call you plain.' And away he scurried, kicking himself, as he went, for being a clumsy stuttering stupid idiot. With freckles.

Left alone, Ivy sat down in a wooden chair that rocked as she leaned back in it. In the mirrors, her face moved backwards and forwards, as pale as a china doll's, and her hair looked very bright. She didn't like being surrounded by so many fragments of herself, so she closed her eyes.

That's strange, she thought, as she began to relax and to drift. *Me 'eadache. It ain't got no worse. In fact . . . I do believe . . . it's gone.*

She didn't think she had slept. Not deeply, anyway, or for very long. But when she opened her eyes, and saw the glass of water on a low table by her side, she guessed that Alfred had returned, without her noticing, and placed it there.

Seeing the water made her think, immediately, about taking a few drops of laudanum. Her head was clear, and she felt surprisingly well, but since she usually took a dose at around this time, she felt compelled to do so now even if it was more through habit than necessity.

Taking the bottle from her skirt pocket, she sat up very straight, so as not to spill the contents while she removed the stopper. *Two drops or three?* She didn't feel bad enough for it to be a three-drop day. Or even a two-drop day. *Will one drop be enough to see me through though?* she wondered. *Will one drop keep me 'ead from hurtin', and stop me from gettin' in a tizzy?*

And as she hesitated, holding the laudanum bottle over the glass, something made her look up. Sunlight, streaming in between the opened shutters, burnished the weight of her hair and dazzled her eyes. She blinked.

Was that Alfred, standing there? Looking for all the world as if he had just seen a ghost?

But no. The man in the doorway was not Alfred. Nor was it Oscar Frosdick, or anyone else Ivy recognized. He was a tall big-boned man—no longer young—with a broad face, weary from travelling, and hair inclined to wildness.

Whatever he had expected to see, as he entered his sitting room, it could not, of all things, have been a red-haired girl preparing to dose herself with laudanum. And to Ivy's consternation, his initial look of surprise changed, in two blinks, to one of such raw hope, and delight, that it scared her.

She couldn't move. Not a finger. Not a muscle. For the stranger's eyes seemed to pin her to the chair, her body turned, still, and the hand holding the laudanum frozen in mid-air.

His voice, when he finally found it, seemed too faint a thing for a man of his height and weight—a tremulous sound, part cry, part whisper, as if he feared anything louder would cause the whole room to cave in.

'Lizzie! My Lizzie! You've come back.'

And the way he put it . . . It wasn't a question. It was a statement of fact.

CHAPTER 22

Concerning interesting developments in Battersea

Alfred did his best to explain things. He had been given permission to walk Ivy home. Immediately. Straight away. And his heart had leapt even though it would mean leaving his master alone, and in a bit of a shaky state, for most of the afternoon.

'It's a good few years since she died,' he said as they paid the tollman their ha'pennies and stepped onto Battersea Bridge. 'So I never saw her, except in paintings. But I know he loved her very much and ain't never stopped thinking of her or wishing she were with him still. He broods a lot, miss. I mean—Ivy. And sometimes he imagines things, like she's close by in spirit, twitching curtains and stuff.'

Ivy looked away to where the river rippled, muddy-blue, like a rumpled skein of silk. 'Mrs Frosdick said 'e 'ad 'er coffin dug up,' she announced. 'To get 'is poems out.'

Alfred looked uncomfortable. 'It was all done proper and legal,' he said. 'I know that much. And they put her straight back again, no harm done.'

They walked quietly on for a while, the sun hot on their shoulders.

Then: 'You don't look *that* much like her, miss . . . I mean, Ivy,' Alfred blurted out. 'It was probably just the shock of it made him think so—of seeing you sat in her chair, when he weren't expecting it. That and the red hair. And the other thing . . . the thing you were doing . . .'

His voice trailed away, embarrassed.

Ivy frowned and walked faster.

'I 'ad an 'eadache,' she snapped. 'So I was takin' something for it. That's all. I weren't stealin' nothin', nor wipin' me nose on 'is blessed cushion covers. I weren't doin' *nothin'* for anyone to 'ave twenty fits over. So there.'

Mortified, Alfred quickened his own pace. 'You don't understand,' he said. 'About . . . what happened to her. To my master's wife. About . . . how she died.'

Ivy stomped on without answering. She didn't want to understand. She didn't want to know *another single thing* about the woman she had been mistaken for. What had Mrs Frosdick called that woman? Spineless. That was it. Completely unsuited to life as a model, or to any kind of living at all.

An accident, the coroner said, and one can only suppose he knew what he was talking about . . .

Beneath her hurrying feet a bargee, making his tricky way downstream, let loose a volley of curses. His anger, and his filthy words, filled Ivy with a kind of despair. Beside her, Alfred was still trying to explain.

'Save yer breath,' she yelled at him. 'I ain't interested. Your painter man's a lunatic, just like old baldy Frosdick. He'd've pounced on me, I reckon, if you 'adn't come in. Yes, that's it. He'd've pounced on me good and proper, and then made out he'd every right to, seein' as how I was his own wedded wife come back for a cuddle from beyond the blessed grave!'

147

Exhausted by such an outburst, she stopped walking and leaned against the side of the bridge. 'Wretched painter men,' she muttered. 'Dirty old arty types. I'm best off sellin' violets.'

Alfred's head was in a whirl. How had they gone from death to seduction, in the space of a few sentences? And what could he say to calm her down? Her fury, although aimed at the two artists, seemed to encompass every man and boy alive. It made Alfred feel guilty, and then cross with Ivy because he didn't think he deserved to feel that way. His master, too, was being unjustly maligned and he wasn't having that.

'My master is a true gentleman,' he declared. 'He would never make improper advances, not to you or any girl. Not without knowing they'd be welcome, he wouldn't.'

Ivy sniffed.

'But I promise you this,' Alfred went on, 'if Mr Frosdick has *dared* so much as . . . Well, I'll . . . I'll . . .'

With his fists clenched, and his shoulders squared, he looked like a boxer about to punch a hole through the bridge, or knock a passing gull clean out of the air. He looked like a knight in less-than-shining armour. Saint George without a dragon.

'All right, all right, keep yer 'air on.' Calmer, now, Ivy found herself touched by this small display of chivalry on her behalf. And she couldn't help but notice, in an almost-fond way, how a bright flush of anger made Alfred's freckles disappear almost as effectively as three layers of paint had done. ''E didn't do nothin', old baldy didn't,' she added, kindly. ''E never got the chance. And 'e never will now, will 'e? Cos it don't look like I'm goin' to be 'is model no more, does it? Come on—let's go.'

They were off the bridge and onto Battersea Park Road before Alfred dared to say, 'But you'll come back to Cheyne Walk, Ivy, won't you? Surely Mr Frosdick will want to finish his painting of you? Surely he will?'

Ivy shrugged. The closer they got to Lambeth, the more dream-like her encounters in Chelsea were beginning to seem. It would take only a small effort of will, she knew, to forget everything—even the sweetness of this boy—once she was back, for good, in Paradise Row.

To distract him she nodded towards a group of people huddled outside a vast building close to the arches of the London and South Eastern Railway line. A man in their midst was reading from a handbill, turning occasionally to shake his fist at the building as if it had done something terrible.

'Troublemakers,' said Alfred. 'Don't get involved.'

The women in the group were agreeing with the man and eyeing the entrance to the building with great trepidation. 'I durn't care how needy they are,' said one. 'I won't be passin' by this place no more, once they're in residence. Not likely I won't. I values me fingers and toes too much.'

'Me neither,' another woman declared, with a shudder. 'They say the worst ones foam at the mouth . . .'

'A new lunatic asylum,' said Alfred. 'That's what it'll be. People hate having loonies on their doorsteps. Or a big jail, which they'll hate even more cos the wretches in there will be mad *and* wicked. Murderers, some of 'em, waitin' to be hanged.'

Ivy, who had already turned away from the building, didn't bother looking back or breaking her stride as she told him: 'I knew someone that 'appened to. But she weren't mad and she weren't wicked. Not really.'

'Pardon?' said Alfred, 'I didn't hear what . . .'

He was interrupted by a girl. A girl with rosy cheeks and stout boots who thrust a handbill at him and hurried away. He read slowly, as Ivy stalked ahead, picking up speed as if she intended, once again, to run.

'Hey!' he called. 'Hey, Miss Ivy, slow down. Listen to this!' But his words were drowned by the clatter and shriek of a passing train.

When the train had gone, slicing so close that both the building's windows and the protestors' teeth rattled, Alfred returned his attention to the handbill. It had a picture to go with the words. A picture of exactly the kind of newcomer people didn't seem to want in Battersea. He—for Alfred assumed it was a 'he'—looked utterly wretched. You could count every rib in his body, and his eyes, as big and round as wheels, were pleading for scraps or just not to be kicked.

Alfred smiled.

He had been wrong about the lunatic asylum. And the jail. The bleak-looking building next to the arches was about to become a Temporary Home for Lost and Starving Dogs.

Ivy was out of his sight now. He hurried to catch her up. He wanted to tell her about the lost and starving dogs. He thought it might amuse her. But when she didn't so much as glance his way, when he finally reached her side, he decided not to bother.

CHAPTER 23

*In which Ivy ignores a warning and receives
a rude awakening*

By the time Alfred and Ivy reached Paradise Row the silence between them had lasted eighteen minutes and twenty-six seconds. It wasn't bothering Ivy because silence never did. And anyway, she had retreated into something of a trance, astonished at herself for speaking so casually about something she hated to even think about.

Alfred, however, was miserable, for he was taking the silence personally. *Will she say goodbye?* he wondered. *Will she at least do that before she disappears up them stairs? Maybe she's sorry for slighting me. Maybe the thought of us never meeting again is grieving her like it's grieving me. Maybe she can't speak in case she cries or the words come out wrong.*

'Goodbye,' said Ivy.

And she stepped out of the alleyway without looking back.

Alfred gawped after her. The hallway she had entered was dark and smelt of all the bones and cabbage stalks being boiled up for dinners in the various rooms off the landings. Ivy, in her pale clothes, looked like a wraith as she hurried up the first flight of stairs, turned a corner, and disappeared.

Alfred opened his mouth to call after her. He didn't

know what to say. 'Goodbye' seemed too final . . . too cruel . . . even though she'd said it first.

Alfred thought of his master . . . of how his master never said 'goodbye' any more but left those closest to him with a riddle to solve, a task to fulfil, or a piece of good advice that they would do well to follow. 'Let me know how you get on,' he would say, earnestly. 'Send word to me tomorrow.' That way no one ever went into a void, so far as he was concerned. No one ceased to exist.

So what Alfred meant when he began calling after Ivy, up the dark and smelly stairs was *'Don't go. Don't vanish. I care too much about you for you to simply disappear.'* But the words that came out of his mouth were: *'It was the laudanum that killed her. My master's wife. She took too much of it and never woke up. You should stop using that stuff, Ivy. It's like poison. Didn't you know? You'll stop taking it now, won't you? Now that you know?'*

And all Ivy heard—and she heard every word—was an unwanted lecture from someone who had no right, no right at all, to tell her what to do.

Good job I never told 'im, she thought. *About the Mighty Grand Plan and what 'appened to Kate. Good job 'e got distracted.*

Wearily she rounded the final bend in the stairs. With luck Cyn and Jared would still be out, selling flowers and plumped-up oranges, Orlando would be lost in his writings, and Aunt Pamela would be asleep. With luck she wouldn't have to explain the sudden reversal of their fortunes until she too had slept a while.

Only, first . . .

152

'*Let me know how you get on,*' Alfred begged. '*Send word to me . . .*'

The first door on the top landing clicked shut.

'*. . . sometime.*'

'*Zzzschneerzzz . . . shnoik, shnoik . . . Zzzzz.*'

Aunt Pamela was asleep all right; sprawled on the chaise longue with her mouth wide open and her rat-coloured bonnet all askew. There was no sign of the others. Even Orlando had gone out.

Looking round, Ivy tried to imagine this room with nice things in it. A comfortable chair beside the fireplace, with an embroidered cushion for your back. A little table, with legs like barley sugar twists, to put a drink of water on. A big mirror, in a frame of gilded petals and leaves, for Cyn and Jared to preen themselves in.

But her imagination soon failed her. This room, she knew, was never going to change, not while her aunt and the cousins were in residence. Aunt Pamela would probably die here one day—although this was as difficult to imagine as portraits on the walls and silk drapes at the windows—and then Cousin Jared would simply shove the chaise longue out of the way. Or sell it.

Sleep, she thought, reaching for her laudanum. *That's what I need.* And if Alfred's words of warning were echoing, still, in her ears they certainly didn't cause her a second's hesitation, or stop her deciding, as she opened up the bottle, that it was a three-drop day after all.

Sleep . . .

Going to sleep is like falling down a deep, dark well. Other times it can be like fleeing down a tunnel. Or slipping down a hillside, going faster and faster and faster. Whichever way she

153

goes, the dream is just the same. Or almost the same, in the way that certain stories, like jiggled kaleidoscopes, have the same elements but a different pattern with each successive telling.

Always, though, that one person waiting. At the bottom of the well. At the mouth of the tunnel. At the foot of the hill. Waiting impatiently, because Ivy is late and the plan—the Mighty Grand Plan—does not allow for tardiness.

And always, just beyond the well, the tunnel, or the hill, the same little girl out walking with her nursemaid. Walking slowly round the park that was a pebble's throw from her home. Walking so early in the morning that even the ducks at the pond are asleep still, with their heads tucked under their wings. Walking slowly and chattering nineteen to the dozen, because that was the kind of little girl she had been. A little girl who never slept more than two hours a night, and would scream and kick and bite her poor nursemaid if she didn't get attention the minute she woke up.

A little girl who insisted on dressing like a lady for her five a.m. visits to the park and on taking a carpet bag of real money and special things with which to play shops.

Sometimes, in Ivy's dreams, the Crow is in the park. For he was the one who, on his way home from a dodge, had clocked the sleepy young woman and the shrill little girl and doubted, momentarily, the sharpness of his eyes. In her dreams Ivy ignores the Crow. It wasn't him she had tried to warn.

In her dreams, Ivy follows Carroty Kate all around the park. Sometimes she catches up with her and they share something— a potato, a joke, the contents of a blue and orange bag. Sometimes—and more often than not, as months and years pass—Kate eludes her completely. In these dreams, when she cannot find Kate, Ivy always tries to hide somewhere until the sky turns navy blue, and fills up with stars that weren't really stars, but shapes made from sequins and tin.

No matter where she hides, though, it is always the girl who finds her. The little girl wearing a white lace dress (Italian, with plenty of flounces. Excellent.) and blue satin slippers (a good fashionable colour) under a coat with a velvet collar. Nice clothes. Lovely clothes. But not what they had been after. Not that time.

'Ivy. Wake up. Wotyer doin' here? Why ain'tyer workin'?'

Ivy opened her eyes. Her breathing was quick and shallow. The face of Cousin Cyn was peering down the well. Round as the moon. As greasy as a dish. And the echo of her voice was so harsh and unwelcome that it hurt.

'You'd better not 'ave skived off, like a useless slug-a-bed. You'd better not 'ave done, Cousin Ive. Jared and mama'll swing for yer if you've gone and done that. They will. Are yer listenin'? Oh, what's the use . . .'

Cyn's face disappeared. Her voice went grumbling away. Relieved, Ivy closed her eyes and sank.

The little girl is still waiting. In the bushes where Ivy had lured her with promises of peppermint for her make-believe shop. And the pin on her coat—the pin of real diamonds—twinkles and flashes in what bit of light there is.

The bag isn't there. The carpet bag full of money and special things. It is out on the bench with the nursemaid. This is right. Even in her dream, Ivy knows this is correct. For the bag had been the Crow's responsibility, not hers and Kate's. It was

155

enough, the Crow had said, that he trusted them enough to get that diamond pin.

The little girl had been a talker. A right little chatterbox.

'You should be asleep,' Ivy tells her, in the dream. 'You should be dead to the world. Have you tried laudanum?'

And then, while she waits and wonders where Carroty Kate has got to, the dream shifts, the pattern changes, and there stands Alfred shaking his head at Ivy as if he dotes on and despairs of her in equal measure.

'Get away from me!' Ivy shouts. 'Go on, you stupid boy. You shouldn't be here. Scram!'

But he just stares . . . devouring her face with his eyes as if her nose were made of sugar and he would help himself to it, if only he dared. And then the dream takes an even more peculiar turn, as Ivy realizes that the bush she was in has become a tree, and she is up in its branches. Stuck.

In her dream, Ivy tries to move. To get to Carroty Kate and tell her that things are about to go horribly wrong. That the Mighty Grand Plan is doomed. And so is Kate. Doomed for ever if she doesn't listen . . . doesn't run . . . doesn't leave the park at once.

But when she points her toes they hit a barrier. And when she stretches up, she strikes her head. Reaching out with her right hand she touches a third obstacle. With her left hand she encounters a fourth.

A frame. Ivy is stuck in a frame. And Alfred is still gawping at her. And the child is staring as well. And the Crow is there too. And the nursemaid. And the bluebottle who, unfortunately for Ivy, Kate, and the Crow, had been in the park at first light hoping to nab whoever had been poaching ducks from the pond.

And now Oscar Frosdick is among them, mixing a new colour

156

on his palette. Only it isn't paint he's mixing, it's gravy.
'Creature brown,' he drools. 'Delicious.'

And Ivy cannot say a word. Not to any of them. She can only
perch where she has found herself—in a tree, in a frame, in a
dream—looking beautiful.

Until the petals on the tree turn to snow.

No.

Rain.

Until the petals on the tree turn to rain.

'Ivy! Wake up, gal! Shake a leg! You've got some
explainin' to do.'

Jared was tired. Jared was hoarse. Jared was fed up to
the back teeth with extolling, day after day, the plump-
ness and juiciness of duff oranges. If all Cousin Ivy had to
do, to improve this family's circumstances, was sit around
all day and be sweet to a painter man, then strike him,
she had better have a damned good reason for being back
here instead, spark out on the best mattress and sleeping
like a babby.

Trickling water onto her face wasn't having much
effect. Was she ill, then? He hoped not. It was bad enough
having an invalid mother to support. A malingering
cousin was the last thing he needed.

'Cousin Ive! Rouse yerself, for cryin' out loud, before I
loses me composure and belts yer one.'

'Oh, let 'er be,' his mother called, from her place in the
middle of the room. 'The tiresome gal. She'll come round
soon enough. Let 'er be, I say.'

The door swung open and in came Orlando.

And if Jared was fed up with selling fruit, Orlando was fit to weep over his lot in life. For two of his poems had just been rejected for not being 'dramatic' enough. And by 'dramatic', Orlando knew, that sniffy little back-street publisher had meant not lewd, crude, or bloodthirsty enough. So it was back to the drawing board for Orlando until he had twisted his precious prose into something more corrupt.

'Orly, me darlin' boy! Let's 'ave a pot o' tea. And crumpets. Surely there are crumpets?'

Orlando ignored his mother. 'Stop it!' he called, sharply, across the room. 'What are you doing? Leave her alone.' There were times, just lately, when Orlando could have slapped Cousin Ivy himself. Slapped her hard, and more than once, because she was doing well in the world and he wasn't. It was a sour way to think, he knew that, which was why he felt compelled to help her now.

Jared lowered his fist and scowled. 'She's pretendin',' he muttered. 'To be asleep. So she don't 'ave to explain why she ain't across the river, earnin' a bob or two.'

Wearily, Orlando laid his poems down on the table.

'Ivy,' he called, softly. 'Ivy, wake up. Wake up, please.'

And Ivy heard him and opened her eyes.

'Right!' Jared thumped the mattress. 'What's 'appened? Why ain't yer off posin' for the painter man?'

Ivy yawned. She had been dreaming. She couldn't remember the precise details, but waking up felt like returning from a journey so long and exhausting that it made the walk from Chelsea to Lambeth look like a hop across the room.

'The painter man's changed 'is mind,' she said, leaning back against the wall.

'Changed 'is mind? Whaddyer mean? And keep yer eyes open, blast yer. No more dozin' off.'

Ivy sighed.

'They never let me in,' she said. 'When I got there this mornin'. So that's that, ain't it? 'E's changed 'is mind.'

Jared leapt to his feet. 'Well, 'e can change it right back again, swelp me 'e can,' he growled. 'Orly? Where's the contract? What's it say in our contract about breakin' the arrangement?'

Orlando had begun toasting crumpets. Without a word he laid aside the toasting fork and went to the battered box where all his writings were kept. Family documents were at the bottom, a thick piece of cardboard dividing them from his poems, as if to prevent contamination. The contract Mrs Frosdick had signed, on behalf of her son, was right on top of the family pile.

Orlando slid it out.

'If this binding arrangement,' he read, 'between Mr Jared Roderick Montague Jackson (guardian to Miss Ivy Jackson) and Mr Oscar Aretino Frosdick (painter) should be terminated without at least a month's notice and a very good reason, Mr Frosdick will pay Mr Jared Roderick Montague Jackson the sum of five pounds by way of compensation.'

Jared nodded, his face brightening. Then he threw the rag he had been using to drip water on Ivy's face up into the air and caught it again, triumphantly.

'We're sorted then,' he crowed. 'That painter man's got till the end of the week to settle 'is account. Till the end of the week 'e's got and not a minute more.'

Mrs Jackson clapped her hands, claw-like in a pair of lace mittens. 'There's my smart lads!' she chuckled. 'There's my bright sons. Now let's 'ave those crumpets. With butter, I think, by way of a celebration.'

Ivy closed her eyes. Her head was beginning to throb. She should have known it wouldn't be easy, coming back here. Not again. Not this time. She should have realized they wouldn't just let her sleep, and forget, like they'd done when she was only seven and had turned up out of the blue.

For this time they knew exactly where fortune had taken her. This time there was a contract.

Cousin Jared was buttering the crumpets. A big wodge of butter for himself and a tiny scrape for everyone else. He was whistling a happy tune.

'What'll we do,' Ivy asked him, 'if Friday comes and the painter man ain't settled?'

'Same as we always do,' Jared told her, stabbing through a muffin with the point of his knife. 'We'll send the boys round.'

CHAPTER 24

Concerning the power of the written word

For the rest of the day, and the day after that, Ivy tried very hard not to think about Oscar Aretino Frosdick. In particular, she tried not to think about what he was going to look like if he didn't hurry up and send five pounds to Cousin Jared.

On the Wednesday afternoon, she was troubled by a sudden realization. In order to send the five pounds Oscar needed to know they were expecting it. And since he hadn't signed the contract himself—his mother had done that—he would only be aware of the penalty for breaking it if Mrs Frosdick had seen fit to inform him.

Ivy kept telling herself that she didn't give a worm's wriggle whether old baldy knew about the contract or not. *Serves him right if he gets 'is face bashed in*, she thought. *Leavin' me on the step like that—it weren't polite. And 'e won't look no uglier, anyway, wiv 'is nose rearranged and a few teeth missin'.*

Still, it continued to niggle her that a man who wasn't really wicked—only bad-mannered and ignorant—was about to get a good hiding. *If only I'd learned me letters*, she fretted. *I could send word to 'is 'ouse, and warn 'im.*

She considered asking Orlando to write the warning for her. But Orlando was looking particularly grim as he brought the language, tone, and themes of his poems right down to gutter level. *'Eek! Eek!'* he wrote, to rhyme with *'Ghastly freak'*. And *'Aaaaaaaaagh!'* to rhyme with *'grabbed her hair'*. Orlando had no time to spare for a real-life moral dilemma. Ivy could see that.

By late Wednesday evening she had made up her mind. She would go back to Cheyne Walk in the morning, just as soon as she could slip away. And she would enlighten Oscar Frosdick as to what usually happened to people who broke a contract with her family. If he had any sense in that balding head of his, he would give her the five pounds right there on the spot; then Cousin Jared would be happy, the boys needn't bruise their knuckles, and everything would be sorted.

That's the answer, she told herself. *That's exactly what I'll do.*

The letter arrived first thing. A single sheet of paper in a thick cream-coloured envelope marked for the attention of Miss Ivy Jackson.

Since Jared was out Orlando was the one who took charge and opened it.

The money that fell into his hands, and then onto the table, did not add up to five pounds. But it was a reasonable sum, all the same.

Quickly, Orlando unfolded the single sheet of paper and read it.

'Well?' piped up his mother. 'Wot's it say? Wot's 'is excuse and 'ow much 'as 'e sent us?'

Orlando waved a hand for silence. He read the letter again and frowned.

It wasn't from Oscar Frosdick.

Across the room, Ivy stopped lacing her boots. She had emptied the chamber pots, rolled up all the bedding, swept the floor, made porridge for her aunt, and run out for a twist of tea and an onion. She had been about to slip away, as planned. Now, as she waited for Orlando to disclose the contents of the letter, she resigned herself to staying put. And the little spark of interest she had felt, over having a day with some private purpose to it, flickered and died.

She wouldn't be going anywhere.

Orlando put the letter down. He considered his cousin, sitting quietly beneath the window on an upturned basket that had once contained cabbages. *Was* she beautiful? he wondered. Was she really so lovely that her face might one day be seen in galleries all across Europe? Across the world, even?

He himself would not have called her beautiful. But there was something . . . a certain grace, perhaps, in the way she sat . . . a kind of purity to her face . . .

'Orly, dear boy. The suspense is givin' me heartburn! It ain't good for an invalid woman to be suspended for so long wiv 'er poor heart racin' like a hound. Wot's it say?'

Ivy looked up then. Straight at her cousin. But she spoke not a word, which made it easier for Orlando to pretend that she didn't really mind what happened.

I'll write a poem about her, he promised himself. *One day I'll write a poem about Ivy that will be read all over Europe and right across the world. A remarkable poem that will last and be admired for as long as any painting would have been. Even a painting by a man such as this . . .*

He glanced back, in genuine awe, at the signature on the letter.

The truth was, he didn't want his cousin to start modelling for this person. This luminary of the arts world. He didn't want her bettering herself, simply for being looked at, while he—the one with the education—remained stuck here in Paradise Row writing trash for a pittance. The other artist—that Frosdick—hadn't mattered. No one had heard of him and likely never would. But *this* man . . .

'Orly!'

He cleared his throat, picked the letter up again, and pretended to read: 'Mr Frosdick says he's very sorry,' he lied, 'but for reasons beyond his control he's had to let Ivy go. He sends a guinea towards what's owed, on account of 'im breakin' his contract, and will settle the balance in due course.'

'Due course?' sniffed Mrs Jackson. 'Our Jared won't like the sound of no "due course" . . .'

'. . . very soon,' Orlando improvised. 'He will pay the balance very soon.'

Mrs Jackson sniffed again. 'Write back,' she ordered. 'Tell 'im we want our balance by return or there'll be trouble. 'E's tryin' to pull a fast one, that painter man is. 'Im and 'is uppity mama. Go on, Orly, do it now. And, Ive—put the kettle on. Frettin' over our circumstances 'as given me a beast of an 'eadache and the Devil's own thirst.'

Ivy did as she was told. So did Orlando—after a fashion.

'Dear Sir,' he wrote. '*I am writing on behalf of my cousin, Miss Ivy Jackson, with regards to your generous offer.*

Unfortunately, my cousin has taken sick and will be unable to model for anyone in the foreseeable future. Should she recover the use of her limbs I will let you know. In the meantime she has asked me to express her eternal and undying gratitude for the sum of a guinea which will go some way towards paying the doctor's fee and other medical expenses, which at present—and much to her widowed aunt's grave concern—amount to five pounds, two shillings, and sixpence.

It behoves me to add, Sir, that I am a great admirer of your art, in all its forms. Your poetry, in my opinion, is far better than Mr Browning's, and your paintings are sublime.

I remain your most humble and obedient servant,
Orlando Bartholomew Montague Jackson.

He read the words through twice. Would they do? Would this artist let them keep the guinea even though Ivy wouldn't be earning it? And, more important still, would he be moved to send four pounds one shilling and sixpence by return? Orlando trusted that he would. Italians were a generous breed, after all, and reputedly sentimental where young women were concerned.

Satisfied, Orlando folded and sealed the letter and set about addressing it. Just printing the great man's name gave him a lift. He noted the address 16 Cheyne Walk—and determined not to forget it. Later, when the dust had settled on this other business, he would send this important man some of his own poems to read. Orlando had long wished for a benefactor—someone to introduce him into the literary world. This could well be the answer to all his prayers.

* * *

The second letter arrived the next day.

'That was quick,' Mrs Jackson observed, slurping spilled tea from a chipped saucer. 'Whatever you wrote to 'im, Orl, must've frightened the piss out of 'im.'

One glance at the writing on the envelope, however, caused Orlando to suspect that this piece of correspondence was *not* from the great poet and artist at 16 Cheyne Walk.

He was right.

It was from Oscar Frosdick.

'Well—'as 'e sent the balance?'

There were ten shillings in the envelope. That and a short note, penned by a hand that had clearly been shaking.

Dear Miss Jackson, said the note. *Pray forgive my silence. I have been severely indisposed. However, my strength is returning, and I am eager to begin a new painting. I will write again as soon as I am fully recovered. In the meantime I enclose the sum of ten shillings, as a retainer for your services. Rest assured, my dear Miss Jackson, that I grow stronger by the day and remain your most respectful and admiring servant,*

Oscar Aretino Frosdick

'Part of the balance,' Orlando said. 'He has enclosed part of the balance.'

'Hah!' Mrs Jackson took another loud slurp of tea. 'Our Jared won't like that. Not one bit, 'e won't. 'E'll be sendin' the boys round, our Jared will.'

Orlando did not want Jared sending the boys to Cheyne Walk. He did not want any rough stuff going on

166

which might compromise his own position, one day, with Frosdick's illustrious neighbour.

'The rest of the money is on its way,' he hedged. 'So I say we wait.'

'Write back,' his mother snapped. 'Put the frighteners on 'im.'

'There is no need for that,' Orlando replied, folding Oscar's note to make a firelighter. 'Not yet anyway.'

The third letter arrived on the Monday.

'In the nick of time,' Mrs Jackson observed. 'Them boys are primed and ready to go. Them boys'll knock ten bells out o' that painter man tonight if 'e ain't paid 'is debt in full.'

Orlando opened the thick cream-coloured envelope, his heartbeat quickening. What if this particular Italian was neither generous or sentimental? What if he turned out to be a tight-fisted cynic who wanted his guinea back? What if he had boys of his own to send round to Paradise Row?

Thank you, he breathed as four guineas slid into his hand.

And then there was a fourth letter. One that arrived while Mrs Jackson was asleep and Orlando out at a stationer's shop, spending part of his profit on pens and ink.

Ivy, sitting glumly on the upturned cabbage basket, and thinking of nothing much at all, was the one who answered the door and took the letter in her own hands.

She was about to put it on the table, where Orlando would see it later, when something about the writing on the envelope made her pause.

The word she was looking at—the name of the person this message was for—began with the letter that looked like a stick.

'I' for 'inattentive'.

'I' for Ivy.

That's me, she realized. *This letter is for me.*

And because it was hers, and nobody else's, she squirrelled it away in the pocket of her skirt, and resolved to tell no one it had come. The fact that she couldn't read it didn't bother her at all. Nor was she curious to know what it said. For it was doubtless more drivel from the painter man and since he had already proved he had no further use for her, by paying off his debt, nothing he had to say to her now was of the slightest bit of interest.

An unopened letter and a bottle of laudanum. These were now the two things Ivy kept with her all the time.

CHAPTER 25

In which Oscar's physical well-being is once again at risk

I vy was sitting on a doorstep in Paradise Row, watching a group of small boys playing leapfrog, when she heard her name being called.

At first she failed to recognize the figure tottering towards her, beyond the leaping, tussling boys. For Oscar Frosdick had lost so much weight he looked gaunt.

'Gi's a penny, sir!'

'Jus' a few coppers, sir. Go on, be a gent.'

Swatting children away like flies, Oscar continued to pick his way along the alley. He felt a touch light-headed, still, and just a little queasy here in this rather *unsavoury* neighbourhood, but his face as he drew closer to Ivy was pink with delight and lit by a smile.

'Thank you,' he said to her, as his gangly shadow fell across her lap. 'For being ready. I have a coach waiting in New Cut. Shall we go?'

'Go where?' Ivy replied. 'And why?'

Oscar looked puzzled. His shadow twitched. 'Did you not receive my letters?' he said. 'The first informing you of my—ahem—painfully slow recovery from a serious indisposition and another giving notice of our rendezvous today?'

Ivy thought back. There had been several letters,

hadn't there. But Cousin Orlando had said nothing to her about any indisposition, serious or otherwise. She pictured the one letter Orlando hadn't seen—the one tucked, unopened still, in her skirt pocket. Maybe that was the one about the rondy-whatever. Not that she would have recognized the word, or known what it meant if she had.

'We got the readies,' she told him. 'I know that much and that's all I know.'

'Well . . . good-oh,' said Oscar, warily. 'So . . . will you come with me? Shall we go?'

Ivy shrugged her shoulders. 'Don't see no purpose in it,' she said. 'Not if I ain't yer model no more.'

Oscar looked even more baffled. 'But you are,' he said. 'That's the whole point. We need to go and buy clothes, for the new painting. And an animal—a very *special* animal—for you to pose with. That's why I'm here. Didn't you know? Didn't you . . . ah.'

He stopped. Embarrassed. Clearly she hadn't. Couldn't. And whichever member of her family had opened his letters and pocketed his money was clearly illiterate too otherwise he—or she—would surely have explained things. How *very* disconcerting. And how lucky he was, under the circumstances, to have found Ivy at home and at his disposal.

'I'm going to paint you as Eve,' he said, proudly. 'In the Garden of Eden. Just after the Fall.'

'Oi! You! Wot's your game? Step away from me cousin this instant!'

Ivy waited until Jared was close enough for her not to have to shout. Then she said: 'It's the painter man. 'E

170

wants to paint me as Eve. After she fell.'

Puffing, Jared stopped in his tracks and lowered his fist. 'Does 'e indeed,' he said. 'Well, there's a thing. Thought twice, 'ave yer, sir, about our Ive? Decided to give 'er another try?'

He looked Oscar Frosdick up and down. *My, my*. The man had certainly lost a lot of weight since that day at Lambeth market, when he'd come looking for a bird and found Ivy instead. Why, the daft toff was practically a shadow of his former self. Perhaps, Jared mused, he had been pining for Ivy. Wasting away for the want of her. And now he was going to keep pushing his luck, was he? Ha-ha!

'Eve, is it?' he said. 'Jolly good. Starkers, is she?'

Oscar looked shocked.

'I b-beg your pardon?' he stuttered.

'Starkers. In the buff. Naked as a pup.'

Oscar's face went from pink to puce.

'My dear sir,' he blustered. 'What can you be suggesting?'

Jared gave him a prod in the chest. Just a light one, so as not to push him over. 'Don't play the innocent wiv me, Frosdick,' he growled. 'You know full well wot I'm drivin' at. Are you plannin' to paint me cousin Ive in the nuddy?'

'*No* indeed!' Oscar was genuinely appalled. 'On my honour, I . . .'

'Cos if you are,' continued Jared, 'that's double the fee. Oh, and an extra five shillin's danger money in case she catches cold or gets stung on 'er unmentionables by a wasp.'

Ivy, who had yet to budge from the doorstep, had to cough three times, very loudly, for attention.

The two men looked down at her as if startled by her presence.

''E ain't paintin' me at all,' Ivy declared. 'Not in the nuddy, not in a blue robe, not in a coat as thick as a bloomin' eiderdown, 'e ain't. Cos I ain't interested in bein' a model no more. I've 'ad enough.'

'But . . .' Oscar Frosdick would have leaned against the alley wall, for support, if it hadn't looked so filthy. 'But . . . I paid you a retainer.'

Jared told him to pipe down. 'I'll 'andle this,' he said. Then he snatched his cousin by the wrists and yanked her to her feet.

'I say . . .' Oscar yelped, leaping clumsily to Ivy's defence. 'There is no need for . . .'

'Shut it!' Jared roared. And, with his free hand, he grabbed a fistful of Oscar's shirt front, twisted it into a knot, and fair whisked the man off his feet as he shoved him back against the alley wall, well out of the way.

'Now then,' he said, turning his full attention to Ivy while Oscar, released, slid down the wall, gasping and spluttering and plucking at the front of his mangled shirt. 'You will go and pose for this painter man, whichever way 'e fancies. You got that? Cos if you don't, I'm disownin' yer. It'll be the streets for you, Cousin Ive, strike me if it won't. Now—get goin'!'

Ivy turned away from him and waited, expressionless, while Oscar rose, inelegantly, to his feet. Her mind was blank. Empty. She was refusing, absolutely, to think.

'So . . . you'll come with me . . . then?' Oscar panted at her.

The nod Ivy gave was so brief, and so lacking in

172

enthusiasm, that only a man with the sensitivity of a cobblestone would have taken it as a gesture of willing assent.

'Good-oh . . . that's wonderful . . .' sighed Oscar, happily. 'Our carriage awaits.' He had decided to ignore the assault upon his person, on the grounds that he was clearly no physical match for this Jackson brute and would only be reduced to pulp if he demanded an apology. He still had the services of his gorgeous stunner, and that was what mattered the most.

Ivy was already walking along the alley, in the direction of New Cut and the awaiting carriage. Oscar gave the front of his clothing a final, ineffectual, brushing down with his hands, and set off after her.

'Oi! Painter man!'

Oscar cringed. *What now?* He turned round slowly, half expecting a belated punch on the nose.

Jared was grinning broadly. There was something in his hands which he was preparing to . . . no . . . he *was* throwing; throwing hard and fast, like a cricketer at Lord's.

Oscar braced himself as whatever it was came flying straight at him. He cupped his hands and swallowed a whimper, for this unidentified missile might hurt, or bite, or splatter his front with some noxious substance.

The thing hit his chest like a small cannon ball and he closed his eyes as his fingers fastened round it. No squishing, no smell, and no pain. His relief was palpable.

'Well caught!' chuckled Jared. 'Don't bruise it now. And no takin' bites neither. Cos you'll be needin' it, won'tyer, for this paintin' of Eve.'

Oscar opened his eyes. An apple. He was holding an apple—a big crimson one, polished like glass to an unnatural shine.

Jared snapped his fingers and held out a demanding hand. 'That's a shillin' to you,' he said. 'Sir.'

CHAPTER 26

In which a shock awaits Ivy, down Rosemary Lane

I vy and Oscar sat in silence for a while, as the carriage lurched across London. The apple had been placed between them, and whenever the carriage turned a corner it rolled against their legs like a very small and very drunk fellow passenger. Eventually Oscar picked it up and put it in his pocket.

'I was thinking of off-white or a flesh-tone,' he said. 'And of something close-fitting, to give the *impression* of—*ahem*—Eve's natural state, with minimum embarrassment to yourself. A sheath-like garment, perhaps. Or the kind of body stocking worn by acrobats.'

Ivy sniffed. She didn't care. She didn't give a pig's sneeze.

'And our garden will, again, provide the perfect setting,' continued Oscar, with growing enthusiasm. 'For mother's roses are all out, and it will be easier for the snake.'

Snake? Ivy asked herself. *Did he really say 'snake'?*

Still, she refused to speak, and after a few more minutes the carriage rattled to a halt.

'Will you permit me to take your arm, while we peruse the stalls and barrows hereabouts?' Oscar asked, as they stepped down into the street. 'For this is a rough area, for all its pretensions at honest trading.'

Ivy shook him away. 'I'm used to rough,' she snapped. 'You've met me Cousin Jared, ain't yer? You 'ad a good snoop along Paradise Row, didn't yer?'

'Well . . . Just don't go wandering off, there's a dear girl,' Oscar replied, faintly. 'There are wonderful garments to be found in this vicinity, for an absolute song, but the types who lodge in the off-streets . . . well, let us just say that even your big strong cousin would be intimidated.'

Ivy was no longer listening. She had turned from the carriage and was gazing down the opposite street with a peculiar look on her face. *So many garments . . . so very many garments . . . flung over clothes horses, heaped in piles, displayed in rows, or strung up on lines . . . dress coats, frock coats, greatcoats, and game-keeper's coats . . . trousers and knee-breeches, jackets and capes, dull brown, black, or grey like the pelts of dogs and weasels . . . women's skirts, spotted and striped . . . here the bold scarlet and green flash of some-thing tartan . . . there the wing-like flutter of a dozen lace handkerchiefs.*

'Are you familiar with this place, Miss Jackson?' Oscar asked. 'Have you been here before?'

'No,' Ivy murmured. 'I don't . . . I ain't . . . Where are we? It ain't . . . it ain't Petticoat Lane . . . is it?'

Oscar placed one hand, hesitantly, on her elbow to guide her across the busy road. She let him do it; her eyes on all the clothes, still, as she walked closer and closer towards them.

'No,' Oscar said. 'This is Rosemary Lane. Near the docks. Down there are Blue Anchor Yard, Glasshouse Street, Hairbrine Court, and Sparrow Corner—truly ghastly places, so I'm told, inhabited by the very lowest of the low—dredgers, slop workers, common thieves, and the Irish, to name but a motley few . . .'

They had reached the entrance to Rosemary Lane. Ivy could pick out the smaller items for sale now—limp feathers, bent hatpins, and tangles of ribbon and braid, all jumbled up on squares of old matting. The larger displays, stretching away along both sides of the Lane, looked dingier closer to; all ragged hems, missing buttons, and stained fronts.

Ivy's thoughts went spooling back into the past. She couldn't stop them. *Kate wouldn't 'ave given tuppence for this lot. She would've stitched that hem, replaced all them buttons so they matched, and got the grease spots off of that shirt with a sprinkle of magnesia powder, rubbed well in and allowed to dry. 'Girly,' she would've said, 'we gotter 'ave standards. There ain't no way the Grand Plan'll ever work out if we lets our standards slip.'*

'You get a lower class of trader here, compared to Petticoat Lane,' Oscar declared, rather loudly. 'But you also get more bargains, so it's worth slumming it awhile. Now, my dear Miss Jackson. Think off-white or flesh-coloured. Think Eve just after the Fall! Let us enter the fray!'

The fray consisted of buyers and traders as scruffy and stained as the clothes. Nearly everyone, it seemed, was managing to do two things at once—barter and smoke, barter and eat, or barter and drink. Ivy was used to markets and the way they worked, but she was a stranger at this one so very soon attracted attention.

'A ribbon for the lady's 'air, sir? Such a lot of 'air . . . and such a bold colour too!'

'Your sweetheart'll be needin' a parasol, sir. A fine parasol

like this one 'ere, to keep the sun from burnin' that milk-white skin.'

'Lost your bonnet, dearie? We've bonnets that'd frame that sweet face o' yours a treat . . .'

It was no different, really, to the kind of banter that went on at the markets around Lambeth. Hor and Mad and Cyn were experts at it. Hor, Mad, and Cyn, Uncle Elmer used to joke, could have sold violets to a blind man with no nose. Ivy, though, could barely bring herself to smile whenever she too had been sent out on the streets with a tray of posies round her neck. Uncle Elmer had despaired of her. *You should've seen me out skinnin'*, she had felt like telling him, aged—what—eight, nine? *I 'ad the gift of the gab for that, all right. Never mind sellin' posies to all an' sundry. I could wheedle a child from its nurse or its mama quicker than you could throw a turnip in the air an' catch it again.*

Here in Rosemary Lane, every single trader had the gift of the gab, along with a bonnet, shawl, gown, or coat that 'could've been run up especially for yer, dearie, it'd suit yer so fine.'

Oscar kept his hand on Ivy's elbow as they made their slow way along. He was enjoying the attention his stunner was attracting—enjoying it so much that he was practically strutting. *Who would have thought*, he marvelled to himself, *that this time last month I could barely lift my rear end off the WC.* Every now and then he spied a fold of material that was off-white or flesh-coloured and made a little dart towards it. But nothing was quite right. 'I am an artist,' he told the vendors as they tried to palm whatever it was off on him anyway. 'I know precisely what I'm looking for and will settle for nothing less.'

They were almost halfway along the three-quarter mile stretch of the Lane when Oscar spied the garment of his dreams. It wasn't white and it wasn't flesh-coloured. In fact it wasn't remotely suitable, by any stretch of the imagination, for the picture he was planning.

'It's purple,' said Ivy. 'And it's got leaves an' things all over it.'

'It's lavender,' Oscar breathed. 'And it is divine.'

'Lookin' at the royal gown are we, sir? Belonged to Mary Queen of Scots that did, 'afore she parted company wiv 'er 'ead. See them thistles embroideried round the hem? A Scottish flower, sir. She 'ad the same emblem on 'er 'andkerchiefs, Queen Mary did.'

'Stuff and nonsense,' sniffed Oscar. 'The style is quite wrong, and the brocade too complete for the age you would pin to it.'

'Well, it's bin updated, sir, ain't it? Cut about a bit by a good seamstress. And kept carefully folded in a trunk these many years so the moth couldn't get to it. Passed down the generations, it was, sir, by Queen Mary's maidservant Mary Beaton, wot was me late wife's great-great-great-great grandmama, Lord rest 'em both.'

Oscar lifted the material in his hands. The embroidery was exquisite. As well as thistles there were poppies and daisies, pansies, violets, and forget-me-nots stitched in swags and single blooms all over the skirt and bodice. Floral symbols of vain love, chastity, death, and remembrance. Ophelia's flowers.

It was a long time since old Millais had painted his vision of Shakespeare's Ophelia. And Ivy, in this dress, would be the perfect model for a fresh interpretation.

'How much?' he said.

The vendor named his price.

'That,' Oscar said, 'is absurd and you know it.'

Ivy was bored. The dress—purple, lavender, whatever it was—was too big for her, she could tell. And it wasn't right either, not unless Eve fell tripping over a hem, it wasn't.

Oscar and the vendor were haggling in earnest now. Ivy raised a hand to push the hair from her eyes. She wanted to go. Being around so many clothes was bringing on a bad headache. All those dangling sleeves and piles of petticoats . . . they were like ghosts pressing in on her from all sides. Making her think. And remember.

'I am an artist!' Oscar was declaring. 'A member of the Pre-Raphaelite elite! I have an eye for these things, sir, and I'm telling you Mary Queen of Scots would no more have worn this garment than caught a train to Waterloo.'

Ivy took a step away. Then another and another until she was several stalls along. She could still hear Oscar Frosdick making an idiot of himself, but at least he was no longer bellowing in her ear.

It wouldn't be wise, though, she realized, to walk any further without him. She had no money with her and only a little laudanum. She didn't want to get lost. Not in this neck of the woods. Not with a bad headache coming on.

'That is absolute piffle, my good man! Just because a chap lives in Chelsea and moves in the highest circles doesn't mean he is made of money. I have a widowed mother to support, sir. Now lower your price!'

'*Chelsea, is it, sir? Well, la-di-da.*'

180

'Keep a good wine cellar do yer, sir? I'm partial to a nice drop o' port meself.'

Ivy, still waiting quietly for an end to this foolish charade, lowered her gaze. Close by her feet was a display of cheap brooches: flower sprays, initials, lucky horse-shoes, bluebirds, and butterflies. They were all made of tin, or worthless bits of coloured glass. One of the bluebirds was missing its pretend-sapphire eye, and the butterflies were starting to rust. Still, someone had gone to a lot of trouble pinning each brooch onto a pad of black velvet, the better to show them off.

One of the initials looked like a stick. It was fashioned from green stones, with only one missing, and set in a circlet of leaves. Ivy leaves.

Slowly Ivy bent low enough to reach out and touch . . . just to touch that one special brooch, with the tip of her finger. *I for 'Ivy'.*

'Take it.'

The voice was close . . . right above her head . . . but so low that it was only just audible above the din of passing trade, and the continuing squeal of Oscar Frosdick's bartering.

'Take it. Go on.'

Quickly, Ivy pulled her hand away from the brooches. *Who on earth?*

'I ain't no thief!' she snapped, jumping to her feet and whirling round to confront whoever this was, trying to lead her astray.

Her first thought, before the shock hit her, was that the man she found herself face to face with—the man who had spoken—had shrunk. But of course he hadn't shrunk at all. It was her . . . she had grown. Her next thought, as the shock sent a shiver running right the way through her, was that the years had not been kind to him. And, in that respect, she was right.

''Ello, girly,' said Fing Nolan. 'Fancy meetin' you 'ere.'

CHAPTER 27

*Concerning foolish revelations and
dangerous creatures*

O scar was delighted. Oscar was cock-a-hoop. He came bounding towards Ivy with a triumphant grin, the lavender dress clutched as lovingly as a bride in his arms. 'There you are,' he scolded. 'I thought I'd lost you.'

Ivy had yet to find her voice. Fing Nolan, however, was having no trouble with his.

'Chelsea, is it, sir?' he said. 'Couldn't 'elp over-'earin'. Nice part of London, Chelsea is. Luvverly gardens. What particular part of that fine borough would you be from then, sir?'

'Cheyne Walk,' Oscar replied. 'Now if you will excuse me . . .' He turned his back on Fing and beamed, pinkly, at Ivy. 'Ophelia!' he said to her. 'We will do Eve After the Fall and then we will do Ophelia. I have a long-standing invitation to visit Kelmscott Manor, near Oxford. We will go the third weekend in August and I will paint you in the river that runs close by. We will all go. Mother, too, if I can persuade her to leave our house empty for a while.'

Ivy blinked. *Get me away from here*, she begged, silently. *Please. Take me away.*

Fing Nolan's face, although thinner and greyer, still had the look of a bulldog chewing a wasp. But as he pretended to be busy, re-arranging things on his stall, he appeared, for once, to be chomping on something rather sweet.

Cheyne Walk, he told himself. *Third weekend in August . . . Cheyne Walk, third weekend in August . . .*

'Can we go now—please?'

Ivy's voice came out faint, like a little girl's.

Oscar looked at her, only vaguely concerned. 'If you wish,' he said. 'I haven't the readies now, anyway, for Eve's costume, so we will make do with whatever we can find back at Cheyne Walk. I cannot think what, but there is bound to be just the thing at number sixteen, in some cupboard or trunk or other. I will ask Alfred to search. Now—allow me, if you will, to purchase some buttons and then we will take the carriage to Jamrach's Animal Emporium.'

Number sixteen Cheyne Walk, Fing repeated, silently.

He reached out a hand and caught Ivy by the sleeve as she tried to follow Oscar to the button stall.

'Don't holler,' he said, quickly. 'Ain't no need for hollerin'.'

Ivy stood very still, and trembled. 'L-let me go,' she managed to stammer, through gritted teeth. 'I . . . I ain't got nothin' to say to you . . .'

'Really?' Fing said. 'And you such a noisy little mite too, once upon a time . . . An artist's model, eh? You've done all right for yerself, ain'tyer? Live wiv 'im, do yer? At 'is big 'ouse in Cheyne Walk.'

'No,' Ivy snapped back. 'I don't.' She tugged her arm, but Fing's grip was tight.

'Take the brooch,' he said.

Startled, Ivy took a deep breath and swung round to face him '*What?*'

'It's mine—mine to sell for sixpence or give away as I fancy. 'Oos didjer think it was? This is where me and the lads 'as our stall now, see? Gone down in the world, ain't we, girly? Not like you . . .'

He let go of Ivy's sleeve and stooped to detach the initial 'I' in its circlet of leaves from the careful arrangement of brooches. Ivy could have run then, but she didn't. Fing's hair, she noticed, had turned white. But it wasn't stubbled so he was either living straight, nowadays, or just hadn't been jailed for a while. His hands, as they fiddled with the clasp of the brooch, had an old person's tremor and he wheezed as he straightened up.

This man had been a tailor, once. And Carroty Kate had loved him.

Do you still say a prayer before supper? Ivy wanted to ask. *And do you still make the best 'taters and sauce in the world?*

But she said nothing. '*Go 'ome, girly!*' Kate had shouted, fighting to be heard as the bluebottle wrestled her to the ground the better to tie her wrists. '*Run. As fast as you can. Go on. But not to Fing's place. Not there. 'E won't want yer— not wivout me. Go 'ome, girly. You know where, don'tyer? You ain't forgot, 'ave yer? I know you ain't. Run—run away!*'

'Old Carroty. If she was 'ere, she'd want you to 'ave a little present,' Fing said. And he placed the brooch in Ivy's hand and closed her fingers around it. 'She was very fond of you, old Carroty was. She'd've liked the chance to see yer, all grown up.'

Ivy felt her throat tighten. Just hearing Kate's name, being spoken aloud, made her desolate. Tears though . . .

when was the last time she had cried? She couldn't remember.

Fing Nolan patted her clenched fingers. 'There, there,' he growled. 'No need for any blubbin'.'

'I say! Unhand the young lady, sir! Unhand her this instant!'

Oscar Frosdick came lolloping towards them. The lavender dress was still in his arms but the skirt had unfurled and was hampering his stride with swathes of flowers.

'You don't know me,' Fing muttered. 'You ain't never seen me before.' And he turned his back on Ivy, and on the ludicrous gent from sixteen Cheyne Walk, and began folding stockings.

Ivy swallowed and cleared her throat. Then she slipped the brooch with her initial on it into her skirt pocket and turned to face old baldy.

'Keep yer 'air on,' she told him. 'And let's get goin', shall we, like I asked yer.'

Then, without another glance or word for Fing Nolan, she began to walk away.

'I would have knocked him from here to Kingdom Come, by Jove I would,' declared Oscar, folding the lavender dress into a more manageable bundle as they hastened towards the waiting carriage. 'I would have punched him into the middle of next week, if you hadn't prevented me.'

Ivy ignored him. She could sense Fing watching their backs. Part of her felt as if it couldn't get away fast enough; the rest of her wanted to linger. *Did she die brave?* she wanted to ask. *When they 'anged 'er? Did Carroty Kate stay strong right to the end? And what 'appened to the Crow?*

It was a relief, none the less, to reach the carriage and to know that, if she really wanted to, she could make herself forget that she had crossed paths with Fing Nolan today. The brooch though . . . that was a reminder. As soon as she could, she would throw that brooch away.

'Jamrach has set aside the ideal reptile for us,' Oscar was saying. 'A male python—fairly elderly but with enough life left in it, still, to coil.'

Ah, yes, thought Ivy. *The snake*. There was nothing quite like the prospect of meeting a snake, she realized, to distract a person very nicely from any previous encounter. ''Ow big is it?' she wondered.

'I'm not sure,' said Oscar. 'We will have to wait and see. Big enough, so I've been told, to coil at least twice round your legs and stay there, looking tempting. Jamrach says it's both docile and biddable and will twist itself around just about anything without posing a threat.'

Ivy thought about this.

'Wot if I don't want no snake around me legs?' she said. 'Wot if I'm scared?'

Oscar seemed surprised. 'But according to mother, you would happily pose with a snake,' he said. 'She says it was one of the things she specifically asked you, before you agreed to be my model.'

Ivy thought some more. She could remember no such conversation.

'I don't know about that,' she said, carefully. 'I ain't sure about that at all.'

'*Jamrach's*,' shouted the coachman, pulling the carriage to a halt.

'My dear girl,' Oscar protested, preparing to leap out.

187

'I simply cannot paint Eve After the Fall without a snake. Once you have met the reptile in question, and seen for yourself how tame it is, you will, I am sure, be completely reconciled.'

Jamrach's Animal Emporium stank the way Noah's Ark must have done. From the outside, it looked scarcely big enough to house a litter of kittens. Inside it was a veritable warren, with whole rooms turned into aviaries, and recessed passageways given over to row upon row of clouded tanks, wire cages, and slatted wooden crates.

The arrival of Ivy and Oscar set off an alarming chorus of shrieks and screams. Monkeys stamped and rattled bars. Birds rose up in a flurry of seed husks and tiny feathers. Some distance ahead, out in a yard, something howled.

Ivy sneezed. Holding her breath, to avoid swallowing feathers, she skirted a suspicious looking puddle and stubbed her toe on a big stone.

'*Oh . . .*' she breathed as the big stone pulled its head and feet in. She had never seen a tortoise before.

Charles Jamrach was deep in the bowels of his Emporium, doing what he was obliged to spend most of his time doing, given the large number of beasts and birds he kept here.

'Ah,' he said, setting aside his shovel and a bucket of excrement. 'It's young Mr Frosdick, ain't it?' His voice had a foreign rasp to it. 'I 'ave your python, all ready an' waitin, sir. This way . . . this way . . .'

Following the two men along yet another passage, Ivy was so acutely aware of the presence of creatures that it seemed rude to pass them by without some form of acknowledgement. Slowing down, she began to take notice. A barn owl, tethered by one claw to a mouldy branch, regarded her wearily. Parrots, crowded thick as flies against a wall of mesh, inclined their heads as if summing her up. *''Ello,'* she said softly. *''Ello, dearie!'* they shrieked back in ear-splitting unison. *'Givusa kiss, you old tart!'*

Up ahead, Jamrach chuckled. 'I 'ave no idea,' he said, raising his voice so that Ivy would hear, 'which bird it was that came in 'ere with that line lodged in 'is 'ead, for the others picked it up within 'alf a day. If I knew which one it was, that started 'em all off, I would wring 'is wretched neck, for there ain't many will give 'ouse room to birds that speak ill of the ladies.'

Ivy looked back at the parrots. Their beaks and claws clattered on the mesh as they shifted sideways towards her. *I'd give 'em 'ouse room*, she realized. *I'd look after 'em, every single one, whatever stuff they said. They need lookin' after better. They ain't 'appy.*

She thought of the birds young Salvador and his father sold in the streets, and of how she had never really considered the welfare of those. They had simply been things for sale, like Jared's oranges or Cyn's violets. Objects, nothing more. Thinking about them now made her feel guilty. Had she really been so wrapped up in herself all these years that she had been blind to the distress of those creatures?

The men had stepped from the passageway into the room where Jamrach did business with customers and kept his accounts. There were no animals living in there, but it stank just the same.

Ivy was about to go in after them when she saw the wolf.

What a beautiful dog, she thought, for wolves, like tortoises and underclothes, were an alien concept.

The wolf looked at Ivy with eyes the colour of rain. It was tied up in the yard and if Jamrach hadn't left the back door open, for a little fresh air, Ivy would not have seen it.

''Ello,' she said, moving towards it.

The wolf's whole body stiffened and its hackles rose. It had been landed at the docks that very morning, maddened after many weeks at sea. Somewhere in its wolf-brain was the memory of another place . . . of freedom and of light . . . of other creatures that were wolves . . . And it was this awareness of change and loss which, more than anything else, was driving it mad.

'Well now,' said Ivy. 'Ain't you a fine one. Ain't you a special creature.'

And without a single thought for her own safety she reached out both hands to stroke it.

CHAPTER 28

In which a trap is carefully baited

'What on earth possessed you? What were you thinking of? How *could* you have been so foolish?'

Oscar Frosdick gazed, in utter bewilderment, at his model's perfect profile as the carriage hurried them away from what could so easily have been a scene of bloody carnage.

'That beast could have ripped your throat out. It could have . . . *mauled your face* . . .' He shuddered and closed his eyes. A stunner with scars? It didn't bear thinking about.

Ivy's chin tilted, stubbornly. 'Well, 'e didn't though, did 'e,' she said. ''E were glad of a bit o' kindness I reckon, the poor creature.'

'Kindness? *Kindness?*' Oscar shook his head in despair. 'My dear girl, it was a *wolf*. Where, pray, would it have picked up any appreciation of "kindness"? Not in the forests of Transylvania, that's for certain. Not in its lair, which was doubtless littered with the bones of far stronger mortals than yourself. No . . . you have had a lucky escape, Miss Jackson. A *very* lucky escape.'

Ivy's expression remained obstinate. 'What'll 'appen to 'im?' she wanted to know. 'Where will 'e end up?'

'At an estate in the north of England,' Oscar told her.

'A Lord somebody-or-other has a penchant for wolves and paid Jamrach a great deal of money to get one snared and imported. Had we been obliged to kill that wolf, to retrieve you from its jaws, neither Jamrach nor the lord in question would have been very pleased.'

He shook his head again. The image of Ivy petting the wolf—tickling it behind the ears and calling it a good boy—was so vivid he could have sketched it from memory.

'At least,' he said, 'I can be satisfied that you will have no fear of Valentine.'

Ivy looked sideways at him. ' 'Oo's Valentine when 'e's at 'ome?'

Oscar indicated the pillowcase on the seat between them, within which his newly-acquired python was curled up, fast asleep.

'Valentine,' he said. 'So-called by Jamrach because when it sleeps it forms the shape of a perfect heart.'

Ivy had nothing to say in reply to that. But her hand moved to rest upon the python's scales, through the grubby cotton of the pillowcase.

'*Ello, Valentine*, she communed, sensing through her fingertips that the snake was as confused and unhappy as the wolf had been. '*Ello, old creature. You'll be all right. Old baldy won't 'urt yer. And if it ain't comfy coilin' round me legs for hours on end you won't 'ave to. Don't worry.*

The following day dawned cool, for July, with a sky that threatened showers. But a carriage came for Ivy anyway, so she resigned herself to a lengthy session posing as Eve After the Fall.

Crossing the river, she wondered, vaguely, how Alfred was and whether she would see him later. But she was actually far more interested in finding out how Valentine the snake had settled in at his new abode.

Fastened to her shawl was the brooch that said 'I' for Ivy. She hadn't thrown it away after all. On the contrary, she had waited for the carriage to roll several streets from Paradise Row before taking it out of her pocket and pinning it on. Never in her life before had she owned a piece of jewellery and it seemed, after all, a shame to deliberately lose it. Her fingers kept moving upwards, to trace the letter 'I', and as they did so she thought about Kate, and about seeing Fing Nolan again, and was astonished to discover that she could actually think those thoughts without too much dismay.

Old Carroty . . . She'd want you to 'ave a little present.

From the carriage window she noticed a barge, sliding along the Thames. It was gaudily painted and on its deck stood a woman, shaking a sheet into the breeze while seagulls swooped low hoping for crumbs. The sheet was blue and big enough to billow.

A good fashionable colour. Two petticoats and a couple of 'andkerchiefs. Ivy patted her letter 'I', and smiled.

The big houses along Cheyne Walk were almost completely screened by lime trees in full leaf and flower. The path leading up to the Frosdicks' front door had nasturtiums tumbling over it and a lot of ants marching in a purposeful line in the opposite direction to Ivy.

Oscar answered the door wearing his painting smock, a resolute expression, and a smudge of purple carmine on his nose. Everything was fine, he said, only Valentine was still digesting a mouse so might not be inclined to coil around anything much for a while.

'But he's perfectly content and will oblige us by and by, I am certain,' he said.

The costume he had chosen for Ivy to pose in as Eve was laid out across a trunk in the little dressing room. Ivy looked at it and tried to see the point. 'It's a tablecloth,' she said. 'And it's filthy.'

'I know,' replied Oscar, happily. 'That stain is goose grease. Those are gravy and that yellowy one is egg. It was mother's idea. It represents defilement.'

Ivy looked blank.

'Impurity,' he elaborated. 'Filth. Debasement. Eve defiled herself, you know, by consorting with the serpent and bringing sin into the world. Just wrap the cloth around yourself, there's a good girl, so that only your head, shoulders, arms, and feet are uncovered, and come into the garden. There is a box of pins over there by the window. If you need any help, mother is around and will be pleased to do the honours.'

Off he bounded, to prepare his palette, leaving Ivy to get undressed and drape herself, as fetchingly as possible, in something so heavily defiled with spilled wine, meat juice, and bits of old egg that some of the patches were still wet.

Shuddering, as a particularly nasty stain stuck to her bare skin, Ivy reached for the pins. At least the tablecloth was big enough to protect her modesty, and thick enough not be seen through. Pinning it, however, wasn't easy. She could have done with another pair of hands but had no intention of summoning the awful Mrs Frosdick.

Satisfied, eventually, that this revolting costume would not fall off so long as she moved slowly, Ivy set off for the garden. She took with her a handkerchief, carefully folded and knotted around her possessions—the 'I' for 'Ivy' brooch, the phial of laudanum, and the unopened letter. This she placed under a rose bush, where she knew it would be safe. She was taking no chances, this time, on losing the contents of her pocket.

If Oscar noticed what she was doing, he didn't pry.

'You look wonderful,' he sighed, reverently. 'Stand there, beside the pink roses, and do your best, if you will, to look sorry. For I'm sure Eve was very sorry indeed once she realized what she had done. And oh—here's the apple. Hold it in your left hand, close to your mouth . . . that's it. That's perfect. Now . . . let's see if our Valentine is ready to coil . . .'

It was hard for Ivy to watch, and to hold her own pose. But by lowering the apple, just a little, she was able to observe as Oscar whipped the lid off a wooden box and lifted out a giant python.

'Steady, boy,' he said, as the thick tail lashed sideways. 'Steady now.'

He continued to hold the snake, the way Charles Jamrach had shown him, until it gave up the fight and stopped writhing.

'There,' he said, bending to his knees and depositing the whole reptile at Ivy's feet. 'Off you go, old chap. Coil away!'

Peering down, Ivy could see that Valentine was in no mood to coil. There he lay, all five foot of him, as thick as a bell pull and perfectly still.

''E don't want to,' she said to Oscar. 'You'll 'ave to start wivout 'im.'

Oscar ignored her. He had picked up a stick and was preparing to prod, poke, or, if necessary, lift the beast into action.

'I wouldn't do that,' Ivy warned. 'I really wouldn't do that . . .'

At the first prod, the python reared up, hissing. And before Oscar could jump clear it had struck.

'I warned yer . . .' said Ivy. 'I told yer not to.'

Oscar dropped the stick as if it had suddenly turned white hot.

'I d-don't understand,' he spluttered. 'Jamrach swore blind the thing was docile.'

''E probably is,' said Ivy. 'Unless someone jabs at 'im wiv a whopping great stick.'

Oscar glared belligerently down at the snake where it lay on the grass in a spent and quivering tangle. A few inches up and the thing would have bitten into his hand instead of the stick. His *painting* hand as well, by Jove.

'Would . . . would you care to move away?' he whispered to Ivy. 'In case it strikes again?'

Practically on cue the python moved, uncoiling just enough to cover Ivy's toes. Then, with infinite slowness, it slithered all the way round her feet to form, upon the warm grass, the rough but unmistakable shape of a heart.

''E's all right now,' Ivy said. 'Just leave 'im alone. Look. The sun's comin' out. Don't you want to start paintin'?'

'All right,' Oscar agreed, backing away. 'But only if you're sure. What . . . what if the wretched creature turns nasty again?'

''E won't,' Ivy said. 'Cos I ain't about to attack 'im, am I?'

'Very well, very well,' Oscar muttered, retreating behind his easel and picking up a brush. 'But I am not a happy man, by thunder I am not. And I shall tell Charles Jamrach so at the earliest opportunity . . .'

Half an hour passed. An hour. An hour and a half. The sun grew warmer, intensifying the scent of roses . . . the tang of cut grass . . . the stench of food stains heating up nicely right under Ivy's nose.

This ain't comfy, she thought. *This ain't pleasant.* She considered speaking out, but Oscar was dabbing away so intently, behind his easel, that she didn't like to disturb him.

A pulsing movement at her feet was the first indication she had that the snake had woken up. *So, you're a coiler after all, are yer?* she thought, as the whole scaly weight of it began spiralling up her ankles.

'Hurrah!' cried Oscar, from his safe distance. 'About time too!'

From an even safer distance, inside the glass conservatory, Mrs Frosdick watched and silently applauded. She had started to think her dear boy's python was either too stupid, or too full of mouse, to respond to the smells emanating from her tablecloth. Her very *best* tablecloth.

But snakes, as Mrs Frosdick had made it her business to find out, would have to be very stupid or very full indeed to ignore the tempting aromas of animal fat and hard boiled egg. And anyone who happened to be *wearing* those smells when the snake in question drew back its head and opened wide its jaws—well, how very foolish was *that*?

197

CHAPTER 29

*In which Ivy struggles to release herself from
a potentially fatal embrace*

rs Frosdick was not the only person watching Ivy being entwined by an egg-and-meat-loving reptile that had finished digesting its mouse. Alfred had been looking down on the scene for almost an hour, trying to decide how he felt. He hadn't noticed the snake, until it began to move. He had only had eyes for Ivy, standing so calm and still beside the roses, with sunshine blazing in her hair and her bare shoulders and arms as pale and as lovely as marble.

The last he had heard, she had been in no fit state to pose for *anyone*. According to his master, she had been taken quite seriously ill—with the same terrible sickness, he assumed, that had afflicted Mr Frosdick.

At first, Alfred had been desperate to go to her, to the point of almost abandoning his duties. But his master had advised caution. 'She may not wish to see you,' was what he had said. 'In which case, to go would only break your heart. Leave it awhile, dear boy, until we learn how she fares. You will see her soon enough, depend upon it. For as soon as she gets better she is to pose for *me*.'

The idea of Ivy posing for his master had not pleased Alfred very much. For although he longed to see her again, and prayed she would get well, he did not want to share her with a man whose charm, fame, and extraordinary talent made so many young women swoon.

Most disturbing of all, Ivy clearly reminded his master of the wife he had loved and lost, which meant he was bound to fall for her, and maybe already had.

No. Alfred did not want Ivy working at number sixteen. Not under any circumstances. Ever. And now . . . why, here she was, fully recovered from whatever had ailed her and posing, once again, for Oscar Frosdick.

My master won't like that, Alfred realized. *He won't like that one little bit.*

When the snake began to move, he thought, at first, it was a detail on the hem of Ivy's less-than-flattering costume—a cream flounce, with brown markings, rippling in a sudden breeze. Then he saw the head, with the forked tongue beginning to flick, and he froze.

Alfred had a horror of snakes. Had his master kept one he would have refused, point blank, to feed it. 'Hurrah!' he heard Oscar Frosdick shout. 'About time too!' Was the man mad? Didn't he understand that his precious stunner was in mortal danger? Alfred would have flung open the window but it had been sealed long ago, when this room was a children's nursery, and barred too to prevent little ones tumbling out and smashing their heads on the ground.

'Help her, you fool!' he cried, reaching through the bars and beating at the window with his fists. *'Kill the thing, before it bites her, or crushes her to death!'*

Oscar didn't hear him. He had grabbed a slim piece of charcoal and was applying it to his canvas in swift curling strokes. 'Don't move,' he called excitedly to Ivy. 'Stay exactly as you are. This is perfect.'

Ivy was in no position to move. Valentine's coils were around her kneecaps now, and slithering steadily upwards. She wasn't scared, just uncomfortable, and heartily sick of the hot smell of egg. She heard the rapping sound coming from the house next door and was surprised to see Alfred leaping up and down at an upstairs window, as if bees had discovered his bottom.

She looked around—so far as she could without moving her head—in case the cause of his agitation lay outside. But Oscar was painting. The sun was shining. Valentine—*bless 'im*—had started to coil. All seemed well.

The python's embrace grew tighter as it slipped round Ivy's thighs. Beneath its scales, the tablecloth was twisting out of shape, straining at the pins. At this rate, Ivy realized, the whole costume was going to slip, leaving her naked after all and every bit as mortified about that as Eve in the Garden of Eden.

She looked down at Valentine's head, moving with blunt determination towards a particularly pungent gravy stain, stretched flat against her stomach. He was a good chap—a dear creature—but enough was enough.

She thought back. How had Oscar Frosdick held him? About a hand's width from the head and around four times that, from the tip of the tail. Well, if he could do it, so could she. So could *any*one. Slowly, so as not to startle or annoy, she raised her right hand—just a tiny distance—so that it hovered behind Valentine's head. Then, quick as lightning, she grabbed him.

'Ouch!' she yelped as the coils around her legs gripped harder. 'Valentine—that hurts.' The python's forked tongue began flicking like fury. Instinctively Ivy turned its head away, breaking eye contact. This wasn't going to be easy. For some reason she had expected this creature to realize she was uncomfortable and oblige her at once by untwizzling. Well, she knew better now, didn't she. She had learned her lesson there, all right.

'What's the matter?' Oscar cried, throwing down his charcoal and jumping to his feet. 'Why are you spoiling the pose? That snake's not hurting you, is it? It won't, you know, if you keep still.'

'Don't shout,' Ivy ordered him, uncomfortably aware that she was having to raise her own voice, to be heard. ''E don't like it. Stay there—right there. *I mean it*.' She could hardly feel her legs now. It was a good job, she told herself, that there were no coils around her ribs. At least she could still breathe. Just.

Oscar sat back on his stool. Poised, though. He was poised, just as any true gentleman would be, to make a heroic dash to his stunner's rescue. He was beginning to wonder whether this snake had been a bad idea after all. Perhaps he should have improvised, with his dressing gown cord or a length of rope.

Ivy was holding Valentine's head straight out, at arm's length. The constriction of her legs was making her dizzy and she wasn't at all sure what to do next. Her left hand was free—she had ditched the stupid apple—but what good was it? She could neither reach the tip of the snake's tail, nor unwind coils single-handed.

Glancing up, she saw that Alfred had stopped jumping around at the window. He was standing very still, with his mouth wide open in a silly-looking way. He wasn't going to help, she could tell. He was too scared—too scared, and too grateful for the lawns, wall, and thick pane of glass separating him from the Frosdicks' reptile.

Old baldy she had already dismissed, as being next to blinking useless.

And there was no one . . . no one else around.

Think . . . think . . .

Her right arm was beginning to ache, stuck out at such an unnatural angle, and the fingers around the python's throat were cramping. This was one pose, she knew, that she would not be able to hold for very long.

When the snake began to shiver, she assumed, at first, it was from fury. He had been thwarted, after all, in his urge to continue coiling until there was no more of her left to wrap up. But then she began to wonder—was he *frightened*? Could it be that he was as fearful of her as she was of him? She had her fist around his throat after all, and the possibility of being choked was doubtless as distressing, for a snake, as the thought of being crushed was to a human being.

'*It's all right, Valentine,*' she murmured, loosening her hold as much as she dared. '*I ain't tryin' to 'urt yer. I'm yer friend. I don't mean yer no 'arm.*'

The python just thought this was dinner talking and didn't understand. What it did perceive, however, was that dinner wasn't throttling it any more so, in response, it generously loosened its own grip a little. In its younger days it would have kept right on squeezing, determined to win this battle and eat. But it was old, now, and all for an easy life. This dinner was causing unexpected problems. This dinner wasn't worth a fight.

'*That's better,*' Ivy crooned. '*Good creature. Good boy.*'

The coils around her legs loosened again, just a tiny bit more.

'Good boy,' Ivy repeated.

Again. They had loosened again. Only the merest fraction, but all the same . . .

It's me voice, Ivy realized. If I don't move . . . if I just keep talkin' . . . 'e might . . . 'e just might . . . let me go.

And so, Ivy held her pose and talked.

'Good boy. Good creature. That's the way. That's better. No one's goin' to 'urt yer, are they now? Course they're not . . . 'Oo would dream of 'urtin' a lovely creature like you?' And after a while she stopped using coherent sentences because she realized it was probably just the *sound* of the words that was soothing him—through his ears, if he had any, or as some kind of feeling through his skin. It was an interesting noise she made then: a cross between a babble and a hum. And although it was complete and utter gibberish it was so perfectly pitched that, really, it could have been patented as the perfect lullaby for tired old pythons.

Oscar Frosdick, still seated on his stool, and young Alfred, still up at the window, watched with total incredulity, and growing relief, as the snake began to let Ivy go. Not quickly, or immediately, but in small slips and slithers as if it had been glued to her body and was gradually coming unstuck.

At what point should I dash to the rescue? Oscar wondered. *When, exactly, would it be wise for me to intervene?*

In the conservatory, and un-noticed by everyone, Mrs Frosdick had turned a definite and particularly livid shade of Frosdick-pink. This wretched, *wretched* gal was clearly not as spineless as she looked. *How was she doing that? Divesting herself of that snake as if it was no more lethal, and barely more troublesome, than a badly twisted maypole ribbon?* For two pins, and to get that reptile biting, Mrs Frosdick would have run screaming into the garden. But what if the nasty thing fell to the ground and turned its venom on *her*? It was practically dangling now, with just one more coil left to unwind. Dropped, it would be off in a flash—up somebody else's petticoats or trouser leg, probably.

No. It was too late for intervention. Too late for Mrs Frosdick to do very much at all except watch and seethe and eventually admit—as Ivy lifted the unresisting python in both hands and carried it gently to its box—that a perfectly good tablecloth had been ruined for nothing.

CHAPTER 30

In which Ivy is lulled into a false sense of security

For several days, after what he insisted on calling 'the rather unfortunate snake incident' Oscar Frosdick treated his stunner with a little bit more respect. After that, it was business as usual.

'Do you think,' he said, having tried, without much enthusiasm and even less success, to paint his dressing gown cord as a substitute, 'that we might give Valentine a second chance? He might be more settled now, and therefore better behaved.'

'No,' Ivy told him, emphatically. 'I ain't riskin' it.'

So Valentine stayed in his box and got thrown the occasional mouse, until Oscar found time to return him to Jamrach's Animal Emporium where he swapped him for a racoon and three green lizards.

'May I see the picture?' Ivy asked when, after six days as Eve After the Fall, her costume had stopped smelling, the red apple was getting wizened, and she herself was extremely bored.

'Absolutely not!' Oscar could not have been more shocked if she had asked him to dance a jig in the nude. 'It's . . . it's not finished yet. Nowhere near.'

'All right,' said Ivy, striking the required pose (sorry-looking face, apple raised in left hand, dressing gown cord pinned loosely round her shins). 'Keep yer 'air on.'

At around four o'clock Mrs Frosdick appeared, carrying a tray of dishes and plates which she proceeded to set out on a table beneath the plum tree. She had made it her business to find out what kind of food Ivy actually liked and was providing it promptly and cheerfully at a point in the afternoon when Ivy was more than ready to abandon her apple, stretch her limbs, and sit down.

To start with, Ivy had been wary of this sudden display of kindness. Approaching, for the first time, the table under the tree she had half-expected to find kidneys or a slice of tongue on her plate, even though she had expressed no liking for those things. To her amazement, however, the food was so good, and so completely to her taste, that she found herself looking forward to it.

As for Mrs Frosdick—she was actually being pleasant. *Really* pleasant.

Today there were cold baked tomatoes, stuffed with breadcrumbs and cheese; a salad of green leaves, sprinkled with lemon juice; bread rolls with walnuts in them; and a gooseberry tart with cream.

'Come along, my dears,' cooed Mrs Frosdick. 'Eat up.'

'Mother, you are an angel!' Oscar declared, plopping tomatoes onto his plate so fast that they squished. 'An absolute angel.'

Ivy had to admit that Mrs Frosdick, if not precisely angelic, seemed a completely different person to the one who had ranted on about faddiness and practically forced her to eat meat.

Before long, she had completely accepted this sudden change in character. The woman was simply odd, that was all. Some women, according to Aunt Pamela, did act a little odd as they got older—snapping your head off one minute, nice as pie the next. Aunt Pamela called it being two pecks short of a bushel. And it was sometimes understandable, Aunt Pamela said—forgivable, even—for women of a certain age to go two pecks short of a bushel, especially if the only things they had left to look forward to in life were saggy jowls and the grave.

Today, however, it seemed that Mrs Frosdick had plenty to look forward to. In particular, she was getting very excited about the impending trip to Kelmscott Manor.

'Such a wonderful place,' she said. 'So tranquil. And dear Janey Morris and her little girls . . . such delightful company, all of them. Although I understand the Italian will also be there, blast him.'

'Most definitely,' Oscar replied. 'Try keeping him away, now that old Will Morris is off on his tour of Iceland.'

Mrs Frosdick sniffed.

'And young Alfred is going too, I believe?'

'He is,' said Oscar. 'He has family near Kelmscott—a widowed mother and some sisters—with whom he wishes to spend his annual leave.'

Mrs Frosdick picked up a pair of silver salad servers and helped herself to lettuce. *Rabbit food*, she thought, scornfully. *No wonder the wretched gal is as thin as string and paler than a milk junket.*

She chewed the leaves and then stopped, as if struck, suddenly, by a marvellous idea.

'Have you ever travelled on the Great Western Railway, Miss Jackson?' she asked.

'No, Mrs Frosdick,' Ivy said. 'I never 'ave.'

'Then you and I will take the train from Paddington to Oxford, and have a carriage take us on to the Manor. My treat. I simply *adore* train travel. Brunel was a genius, an absolute genius.'

Ivy waved a wasp away from the gooseberry tart. *'Oo was Broo-Nell when 'e was at 'ome?* Her Uncle Elmer used to say it wasn't safe for young girls to go on railway trains. He said the speed made their brains boil, and rattled up their innards so bad it stopped them having babies in later life.

Oscar opened his mouth to say that he too would travel by train if that was the ladies' preference.

'You will go up by carriage a day or two ahead of us,' his mother informed him, briskly. 'It will do you good, dear boy, to do nothing but rest, and enjoy the country air, before starting a new painting.'

Oscar closed his mouth.

'That's settled then,' Mrs Frosdick said. 'I'm so glad we all agree.'

That night, when Ivy told Cousin Jared she would shortly be going to a manor house near Oxford, with the painter man and his mama, he immediately upped the fee. 'They never said nothin' about takin' yer outer London,' he said. 'That's extra that is, for the anxiety it'll cause yer, bein' so far away from yer nearest an' dearest.'

Cousin Cyn was deeply envious. 'A manor 'ouse,' she sighed. 'You lucky beggar.' She looked critically at Ivy's faded frock. 'You can borrer me red flannel petticoat if yer like,' she said. *'And* you can take the brush. You'll wanter look particularly decent, won't yer, for goin' away? Cos 'e's bound to pounce in this manor 'ouse, ain't 'e, the painter man?'

Aunt Pamela said the pouncing was inevitable and probably the only reason Ivy was being taken away in the first place.

'No, it ain't,' Ivy told her, indignantly. ''E's paintin' me by the river. As "Oh, Feelier".'

'I bet 'e is,' Jared snorted. 'Since it's a feel of yer 'e'll be wantin', that's for sure! You might 'ave to relent this time, Cousin Ive, and let 'im 'ave 'is wicked way.'

Cyn cried out that her brother had a filthy mind and that she, for one, would give anything—*anything*—to be taken from Paradise Row to a beautiful manor 'ouse, and wooed properly, under a starry sky, by a *gentleman*.

'Wooed, my elbow,' Jared scoffed. 'Wooed, my ears and whiskers. Now where's me supper? Orlando—clear the table or I'll be usin' yer scribbles t'wipe me gob on.'

Quietly, Orlando did as he was told. He would finish his new ballad later, when everyone else had gone to sleep. For weeks, after Oscar Frosdick came and got Ivy back, he had been unable to write, so great had been his anxiety over possible repercussions. Now though, he was starting to relax. Clearly, Frosdick had little, if anything, to do with his more famous neighbour for nothing appeared to have been said about any exchange of correspondence, nor about the readies each painter man had sent to Paradise Row, to secure Cousin Ivy's services.

With continuing luck, Orlando told himself, nothing *would* be said. Gentlemen were a peculiar breed, after all, with a strange sense of honour where money and women were concerned.

'Are you eatin', Cousin Ive?' called Jared. 'Gotter keep yer strength up, ready for all that courtin' under the stars. Ha-ha!'

'You . . . you BEAST!' shrieked Cyn, hurling a spoon at her brother's back.

'My dears, my dears,' cried Mrs Jackson. 'Remember, if you will, my poor aching head . . .'

Ivy ignored them all. She had slipped behind the screen and was lying down. She hadn't taken any laudanum today, she realized, or yesterday either. Had she really not felt the need? Normally, by now, she would be in a terrible tizzy and desperate for some relief. Oddly enough, she didn't feel too bad. *Take a few drops anyway*, said the voice in her head. *Just to be sure.*

She began to move, but then stopped. In order to take her laudanum, she needed a glass of water . . . only . . . she didn't want Cousin Jared to see her fetching one, and start bullying her to eat. For one thing, she was still too full of Mrs Frosdick's delicious lunch. For another, the family's circumstances were so much improved lately, thanks to her, that there was bound to be meat in the pot.

Slowly, she lay back down. But without her usual bedtime drink it was hard to relax and impossible to go straight to sleep.

At first her thoughts skittered around, but then they settled on the memory of Fing Nolan unpinning the 'I' for 'Ivy' brooch down Rosemary Lane. Was he still living in the house with the Secret Place, Ivy wondered? And were the others still there too—the Muck Snipe, Dan-of-the-Ditch, and Bludger McNab? And what *had* become of the Crow, after that terrible morning in the park?

Remembering the park—going back there consciously and deliberately—felt like pressing a bruise. It still hurt, but not as much as it might have done once upon a time.

There had been so much blood. That was her most vivid and immediate recollection. Great gouts of it, all over Carroty Kate's hands and down the front of her dress. And on the nursemaid's throat . . . and on the blue-bottle too as he manhandled Kate to the ground.

Go 'ome, girly. Run!

The nursemaid had been on the ground already, lying very still and at a most peculiar angle. There had been ducks waddling around her body, Ivy remembered that . . . waddling around as if they seriously expected her to sit up and throw them a crust.

Of the Crow there had been no sign. Evidently he had scarpered, taking the bag of jewels and money with him.

As fast as you can. Go on!

The little girl, left alone in the bushes where Ivy had lured her, had begun to scream and cry out for her mama. And Ivy had wanted to scream too. But most of all she had wanted to go to Kate. To stick to her like spit because they were in this together, however horribly wrong it had all suddenly gone.

But the little girl's shrieks had jangled up her head . . . and the sight of the blood had made her feel sick . . . and the bluebottle, struggling to make his arrest, had begun pulling Kate's hair . . . her long red hair . . . *and something odd had happened to that hair.*

211

Run . . . Run away! I'll come and find yer, girly. As soon as I can. I promise.

And Ivy had run. Oh yes she had. As fast as she could, away from the screams and the blood and as far away as possible from the nursemaid's body with the stupid, stupid ducks all around it. But most of all she had run from Kate. From the sight of Carroty Kate, who she had come to love, like a mother, fighting like . . . like a *wrestler* . . . while her hair got tugged so hard . . . so very hard . . . that it . . . *it had slipped.*

' 'Ere you go, Cousin Ive.'

Startled, Ivy sat up to find Cyn passing her a bowl of raspberries.

'Eat 'em in bed if y'want,' Cyn whispered, round the screen. 'It's what a lady in a manor 'ouse'd do, ain't it, if she chose? Only she'd 'ave a nicer dish and a silver spoon. I've sugared 'em for yer, but there ain't no cream. That fat pig Jared finished it all.'

Ivy took the bowl. 'Thank you,' she whispered, taken aback by such kindness.

The raspberries were from the market; small and sweet. Ivy ate one, then another and another. When she had finished she tried, once again, to fall asleep but it was no good—she simply wasn't tired.

I could've asked Cyn to fetch me some water, she realized. *For me laudanum.*

After a while she heard Jared go out. Then Orlando started reading to his mother, as he did every evening, before the light faded. Tonight it was poetry, even though Mrs Jackson complained that a nice simple tale about murder would have been more to her fancy.

Since she was so very wide awake, Ivy moved closer to the screen and listened:

I have been here before,
  But when or how I cannot tell:
I know the grass beyond the door,
  The sweet keen smell,
The sighing sound, the lights around the shore.

You have been mine before,
  How long ago I may not know:
But just when at that swallow's soar
  Your neck turned so,
Some veil did fall—I knew it all of yore.

Has this been thus before?
  And shall not thus time's eddying flight
Still with our lives our love restore
  In death's despite,
And day and night yield one delight once more?

Zzzzzz . . . schnoik, schnoik . . . .Zzzzzz . . .

Mrs Jackson had gone from bored, to very bored, to fast asleep.

Orlando let his shoulders sag. Across the room, Cyn began sluicing the supper dishes in a bowl of scummy water. 'I could wallop that Jared,' she muttered. 'Scoffin' all the cream like that . . . the pig . . . . the greedy, fat pig . . .'

Then Ivy's face appeared round the screen, making Orlando jump.

'That was nice,' she said. 'I liked the bits about lights on the shore and the birds soarin'. You should write more poems like that, Orly. It's lovely.'

Orlando swallowed, hard, and stared at her. *Yes*, he thought to himself. *I didn't see it before, but I see it now. I see what it is about her that artists want to capture . . . to immortalize.*

'It's . . . it's not one of mine,' he admitted.

'Oh,' said Ivy. 'Sorry.' And she disappeared again, behind the screen.

'It's by one of our greatest living poets,' Orlando continued after a while, as if she was still there—still there and still interested.

Ivy didn't answer. She had lain down again and was managing, this time, to drift, gently and naturally, towards sleep. Cyn wasn't listening either. She had propped a piece of mirror in the window with the best remaining light, and was using the last raspberry from supper to colour her lips and cheeks before going out.

'A magnificent poet,' Orlando added, reaching for his own unfinished ballad—the one that Jared had threatened to use as a mouth-wipe. 'And a great artist too. If I tell you his name, Cousin Ive, you will know who he is. You will definitely know.'

No answer.

Orlando picked up his pen.

'I wish I 'ad some proper rouge,' Cyn grumbled, loudly. 'The juice in this blinkin' raspberry 'is 'urtin me boils.'

CHAPTER 31

In which Ivy finds a friend

T he last week in July was viciously hot. So hot that Oscar, in order to protect his bald patch, tied his mother's parasol to a broom handle, and sat under it while he worked. Ivy, however, was obliged to continue posing as Eve in the full glare of the sun.

Mrs Frosdick appeared in the garden at regular intervals with jugs of iced tea. 'Miss Jackson must be allowed frequent rest and refreshment,' she scolded Oscar. 'Otherwise she will get one of her sick headaches. She is a delicate flower, dear boy, or hadn't you realized?'

Such unexpected concern for her health and comfort rather pleased Ivy, although the truth was that, despite the heat, she hadn't suffered with a headache for—oh—ages. In actual fact she felt surprisingly well. Bored though... she was bored rigid by now, with standing still.

A delicate flower... Was that another way of saying she was spineless? She certainly felt spineless, holding this stupid pose for hours on end. Cousin Jared's red apple had long since rotted and been tossed on the compost heap, so now she stood with her left hand curved around nothing. It didn't matter, Oscar said, because he had finished with the apple. The apple had been easy. It was trying to paint the snake, with only his dressing gown cord for inspiration, that he was having trouble with.

To pass the time, Ivy invented more paint-names. *By-Joveian* (a deep pink), *Wolf brown*, *Scorcher yellow*, and greens that ranged from *Spinach* (dark) to *Lettuce* (pale) with a shade in-between that she was thinking could be either *Sage* or *Pea Pod*.

By the end of the week she had invented enough colours, in her head, to paint rainbows of varying intensity and landscapes in all four seasonal hues.

Browned off, she grumbled to herself. *I am truly browned off, I am*.

She thought of the wolf and of poor old Valentine (now back at Jamrach's Animal Emporium) and hoped they were not too unhappy.

'Come along, my dears,' Mrs Frosdick called. 'Time for refreshments.'

Today there were cucumber sandwiches, cut thin, mushroom tarts, and a chocolate cake sprinkled all over with violets dipped in sugar.

'You're looking rather flushed, Miss Jackson,' Mrs Frosdick said, as Ivy bit into a sandwich. 'Is your head aching? Do you need to take your laudanum?'

Ivy almost choked.

'Me 'ead's fine, thank you,' she managed to reply.

'Because you do *take* laudanum, don't you, dear? And in quite large quantities too, am I correct?'

'*Mother!*' Oscar protested, turning bright with indignation on his stunner's behalf. 'I hardly think Miss Jackson's personal...'

'The Italian's wife was an habitual user,' Mrs Frosdick

pressed on. 'And it did for her in the end. You should be careful, my dear. Too much of the stuff can put you into the sleep of all sleeps, if you take my meaning.'

'*Mother!*'

'But it's true! Although...' she lowered her voice to a theatrical whisper and leaned a little closer towards Ivy, 'it is entirely possible that dear Lizzie didn't *want* to wake up. That she was sick, literally to death, of her husband's philandering ways and yearned, therefore, for complete forgetfulness—for *oblivion*.'

'*Mother, that is quite enough!*'

Ivy put down her sandwich and lowered her gaze. She no longer had much of an appetite and, now that it had been mentioned, was indeed craving her laudanum. Not much. Just a drop. Just enough to stave off the headache that would surely start to grow behind her eyes, as a result of Mrs Frosdick's stupid chitter-chatter.

And how, Ivy wondered, had the woman known of her reliance upon laudanum? Had she been talking to Alfred?

'Me 'ead's fine,' she said again, aware that she sounded less convinced this time.

'Well, that's all right then,' Mrs Frosdick declared, brightly, 'isn't it? Eat up!'

The early evening brought thunder clouds, piling up over the Thames. There was a carriage waiting in the street when Ivy unlatched the Frosdicks' front gate (she was sent home by carriage every evening now and had assumed, without really giving a duck's quack, that Alfred was either too busy to escort her or no longer wished to bother).

Usually, she welcomed the luxury of being driven back to Lambeth. This evening, however, she sent the carriage away. All that talk about the Italian's wife had left her out of sorts and she was loath to return to Paradise Row where the Jacksons' own brand of contemptuous chatter would do little, she knew, to soothe her nerves.

She had taken some laudanum. Not much—only one drop—but enough to deaden any concern she might have had about walking, unescorted, all the way to Lambeth. She knew the route. She had a halfpenny for the bridge. It was still daylight. She had legs. Why *not* walk?

The distant thunder clouds didn't bother her either. Indeed, their colour, as she crossed over Battersea Bridge, gave her ideas for a new shade in her imaginary palette. *Thunder grey.* Or was it more of a blue? And what about the tinges of red and that hint of yellow round the clouds' edges where the sun was still trying to shine. *Bruise*, she decided. *It's the colour Bruise.*

By the time she reached Battersea Park Road, the sky above was one great whopper of a bruise and rain had started to fall. *It'll pass*, Ivy thought. But it didn't. It got worse. Then it turned into hail—great chunks of ice that pelted down so hard and fast that Ivy feared they might cut her scalp.

Most other people caught in this vicious downpour had umbrellas with them, or enough money to leap into an omnibus, or a newspaper, at the very least, to hold over their heads. Ivy had nothing except a couple of half-pennies, which wouldn't have got her far, a handkerchief too small and thin to protect her head, her 'I' for 'Ivy' brooch, a bottle of laudanum, and her unopened letter.

'*Quick!*' somebody shouted. '*In here!*'

And before she could protest this somebody had grabbed

her hand and was pulling her towards the building next to the railway arches. Ivy recognized the place at once. And the girl—the girl tugging her along—she recognized her, too.

'*Phew!*' the girl exclaimed, dragging Ivy into the building and slamming the door. 'Hail in July—do you think it's a bad omen?' She was holding something—a wad of paper—under one arm which she fished out, now, and gently and anxiously squeezed.

'Look at that!' she wailed as a trickle of coloured water ran around her fingers and down her raised arm. 'The Committee's handbills. They're ruined!'

Ivy stood with her back to the door, her long hair dripping, and tried to look sorry about whatever it was that was ruined. A faint but unmistakable smell was reminding her of Jamrach's Animal Emporium. If there were prisoners or lunatics here, she thought, they were not being kept very clean.

The short hallway was bleak—no carpet on the floor, no tall clock, like the one at the Frosdicks', and no feathery plants in big china pots. Not a single thing to suggest that this was somewhere people lived comfortably or well.

Close by, a dog began to bark. Then another, and another. *Guard dogs*, Ivy thought, *to stop them prisoners or lunatics escapin'*.

'My name is Rosa,' the girl with the handful of sodden paper was saying to her. 'Rosa Pavitt. My father is the keeper here. I've seen you before, walking past with your young man. What's your name?'

'Ivy,' Ivy said. 'Ivy J-Jackson. And he's n-not my young m-man.' She was starting to shiver inside her sodden dress.

'You're soaked right through,' the girl called Rosa said. 'How far have you got to go, to wherever it is you were going?'

'L-Lambeth,' Ivy told her, through chattering teeth. 'N-not v-very far.'

Rosa deposited her ruined handbills on a scarred wooden bench beside the door. Her clothes, too, were wet through, but she seemed impervious to the chill. She shook her plaits, sending droplets of water all over the floor.

'It's far enough away, Lambeth is,' she said. 'And the hail has turned to heavy rain. Just hark at it hammering against the door! Come in—into the in-comers and out-goers room—and get dried off. There's a flask of beef tea in there somewhere, which may still be warm. We can have some of that. And biscuits...I believe there are biscuits, unless father fed them all to the little tyke with foot rot that was brought in this morning.'

Ivy followed her, cautiously. The dogs outside were making quite a din, now, and she could hear a sort of scraping sound, followed by clangs, as if the doors to prison cells were being opened, and then almost immediately banged shut.

'Feeding time,' said Rosa. 'It's always a scramble out there at feeding time. The bigger ones fight the little ones, given half a chance. And father and I have to be careful not to get bitten. Not because of rabies, you understand, but because it just plain hurts!'

She passed Ivy a towel. 'For your hair,' she said. 'It's amazing, your hair is. We had a spaniel once, with hair that colour. Excuse the towel—it's perfectly clean but everything gets a bit whiffy in here after a while.'

Ivy took the towel. *Biting...rabies...whiffy...* She was more than a little uneasy now.

'Beef tea?' asked Rosa.

Ivy shook her head. 'No...thank you.'

'Oops!' Rosa moved a ledger, before it could topple, then a big pile of papers, and sat herself up on a table. The mug of beef tea she had poured herself smelt not unlike the towel. There was a tray right next to her, Ivy noticed, full of tin tickets that had marks on them. She thought she recognized 'I' for 'Ivy' although it was actually the number '1'.

'We tag them when they first arrive,' Rosa said, following Ivy's gaze. 'We name them too—that's always fun. Then they go into cages, boxes, or baskets depending on their health, size, and temper.'

Ivy had to struggle not to look appalled; for it seemed to her unnecessarily cruel to cram prisoners or lunatics into boxes or baskets, however bad or mad they were. 'What...what happens to them after that?' she dared to ask.

Rosa took a sip of tea. 'We keep them for about a week,' she said, cheerfully. 'And then, if they've not been claimed, and aren't too ill or ancient, we sell them.'

Quickly, Ivy carried on towelling her hair. This was not somewhere she wanted to linger.

'One thing we don't do is turn them back out on the streets,' Rosa continued. 'It's one of the committee's rules: "a dog, once housed at the Home, will never again be set at liberty with no better prospect than starvation before it."'

221

Ivy stopped towelling. 'Dog?' she said. 'Did you say "dog"?'

'Of course.' Rosa put her cup down on the ledger and looked at Ivy in surprise. 'This is the Temporary Home for Lost and Starving Dogs. Didn't you *know*? We opened last month. I thought everyone who passed this way knew about us. There's been quite a fuss.'

Dogs . . . why, of course . . .

Ivy smiled. So much for Alfred, thinking he knew what was what. If she ever got to speak to that boy again she would tell him he had been wrong about this place. *Dogs* . . . *a Home for Lost and Starving Dogs*. Well, fancy that.

Rosa jumped down from the table. 'I must go and help father,' she said. 'Stay here if you like, until the rain stops. I'm sorry there are no biscuits. Father is too soft by half, sometimes, particularly with the little ones.'

Ivy draped the wet and whiffy towel over the back of a chair. 'Thank you,' she said. 'But I don't mind the rain.'

'Take this then.' Rosa lifted a big oilskin coat from a hook behind the door. 'It's all right. We can spare it. Just bring it back next time you're passing.'

The coat was huge, with deep pockets and a hood. Ivy put it on. There was a dog lead made of plaited string in one of the pockets, which she removed and hung over the chair with the towel. It reminded her of Valentine, that lead, so she handled it gently and smiled.

'Do you like dogs?' Rosa asked her. 'Or are you frightened of them?'

'I like all creatures,' Ivy declared. 'I met a wolf the other week. *And* I 'ad to stop a snake from coilin' all the

222

way round me. They were both more frightened of *me*, I reckon, than I was of them.'

'Oh,' said Rosa. 'How extremely...fascinating.'

'It's true,' Ivy mumbled, her pale face beginning to redden. 'It really is.'

Rosa grinned at her. It was a wide, friendly grin—one that clearly didn't believe in the wolf or the snake for a single moment, but expressed a genuine liking for Ivy all the same. 'When you bring the coat back,' she said, 'I could show you round, if you want. If you were interested.'

Ivy stared back at her, uncertain how to respond.

Then: 'Thank you,' she said, shyly. 'I'd like that. Yes...I'd like to meet them dogs.'

CHAPTER 32

In which Rosa has Ivy's best interests at heart—unlike Mrs Frosdick

I t took several days for Ivy to pluck up enough courage to return to the Temporary Home for Lost and Starving Dogs. Not because she was scared of the place—not now that she knew its true purpose—but because she felt more drawn towards it than she had ever been to anywhere. And the magnitude of that—the unexpected thrill of it—scared her.

What if that girl—that Rosa—was just bein' polite? she thought. *What if she was only sayin' that, about showin' me round, to get rid of me double quick? What if she didn't mean it?*

Then she began to feel guilty about keeping the oilskin coat. For it was a good, serviceable coat—albeit rather whiffy—and anyone going out in all weathers, to rescue lost and starving dogs, must be missing a coat like that.

And so, after deliberating the matter for long enough, she dismissed the Frosdicks' carriage for a second time, crossed over Battersea Bridge, and walked up to the door of the Dogs' Home with the coat bundled up in her arms.

'Ivy!' cried Rosa, flinging the door wide open. 'Come in! Father's admitting a lurcher. Wait here for a moment, will you? We won't be long.'

Obediently, Ivy remained in the hall while Rosa dashed back into the room for in-comers and out-goers, grabbed the big heavy ledger in one hand, and the stub of a pencil in the other, and said, 'Right, then, father. What'll we call this one?'

From where she stood, still clutching the oilskin coat, Ivy could see straight into the room. She wondered whether to step back, in case her presence was annoying or unwanted. But Rosa's father nodded amiably at her, so she knew it was all right to stay where she was.

Keeper Pavitt was a tall, burly man, red-cheeked like his daughter, and intent on admitting the Home's latest in-comer as quickly as possible, so that it could get on with the business of eating, sleeping, and recovering its strength. The lost and starving lurcher had been tethered to the table leg where it stood, as obediently as Ivy, but shaking uncontrollably in these unfamiliar surroundings and doing its best not to whine.

Ivy could tell, immediately, that this was a good dog. A noble dog. A dog that would follow a person for miles, on the strength of a kind word or, if kicked, turn away philosophically and wait for better fortune.

The lurcher, sensing her presence, raised its head and stared at her with bloodshot eyes. Then, very slowly, it began to wag its tail.

'Well, just look at that!' Rosa exclaimed. 'This lurcher likes you, Ivy. He truly does. Perhaps *you* should name him. What letter are we up to, father?'

'The letter P,' said Keeper Pavitt, quietly. 'Only, not so boisterous, dear. You're frightening the dog.'

'P,' Rosa whispered, loudly, leaning forward so that she could see Ivy through the doorway. 'What shall we call him Ivy, beginning with P?'

Ivy hung her head. 'I don't know,' she replied. 'I can't think. You name 'im.'

When she looked up, Keeper Pavitt was regarding her kindly over the top of his spectacles. 'He's a very regal dog, isn't he?' he said. 'Despite his condition and present circumstances. A most *princely* dog, don't you think?'

'Yes,' Ivy agreed. ''E *is* like a prince. Just like.'

'Then that will be his name,' Keeper Pavitt said. 'Prince. Thank you, Ivy.'

After that, Ivy dismissed the coach from Cheyne Walk every single evening and went straight to the Dogs' Home, to see how Prince was getting on. By the middle of the second week in August, she was helping to muck out the kennels.

'Are you sure?' Rosa said to her, the first time she volunteered. 'I mean, it's a dirty old job, and we can't afford to pay you.'

'I've already earned me keep today,' Ivy reassured her. 'Standin' still for hours an' hours, pretendin' to be Eve after she fell. I'm doin' this because I want to. *Oi, Queenie, leave Rascal alone. 'E ain't botherin' you!'*

'All right,' Rosa said, above the yipping and yapping of almost ninety dogs. 'We could certainly do with the help. Only, you mustn't walk home unescorted after dark. Father and I would worry.'

'I don't mind the dark,' Ivy told her. 'I'll be all right.'

In the late evenings, after Ivy had returned to Paradise Row, Rosa and her father did their final rounds, then sat in the in-comers and out-goers room to review the day and make final notes in the ledger. 'Fancy Ivy being an artist's model,' Rosa remarked one evening, through a big

226

mouthful of biscuit. 'She has met Rossetti, you know—imagine that!'

Keeper Pavitt raised his shaggy eyebrows but kept his attention on the ledger. 'Humph!' he grunted. 'We must keep a particular eye on that bulldog tomorrow, dear. I don't like the look of his torn ear. It may fester.'

Rosa took another biscuit. 'I get the feeling she hates being a model,' she said between crunches. 'I get the impression she would be much happier working here.'

Keeper Pavitt wrote some figures in a column and added them up before saying, 'She has a wonderful way with animals, that's certain.'

Rosa bounded to the desk, her plaits swinging, and grabbed her father's free hand.

'So shall we ask her, father? To come and work here, with the dogs? Shall we?'

Keeper Pavitt put down his pen, smiled fondly at his daughter and then shook his head. 'We cannot afford to take anyone on,' he said. 'Not at the moment. You know that.'

'Please, father...*please, please, please*...She can't be earning all that much as a model, surely? Her artist isn't even *known*. And she does hate that job so. We would barely have to pay her anything, and it would be *so much nicer* for me, having someone my age here to help.'

'Rosa...' said Keeper Pavitt, shaking his head again. 'Let me think about it.'

'Promise? Promise me you will?'

'I will,' he promised. 'Only, say nothing to Ivy for the moment, please. Not until the Committee has been consulted and we know whether or not it is possible to

227

take on extra staff. And now, dear...no more biscuits. For they, too, cost money.'

At the beginning of the third week in August, Oscar Frosdick dabbed his final daub on *Eve After the Fall*, and declared it finished. 'Hurrah!' he shouted, throwing down his paintbrush and flexing his fingers. 'That's that one out of the way. Now for *Ophelia*.'

Ivy let the hand round the invisible apple fall, gratefully, to her side and breathed a huge sigh of relief. 'Can I see it now?' she asked. 'Can I 'ave a look at this picture, now it's done?'

Oscar flapped both hands at her, to keep her away. 'It has to dry,' he protested. 'No one must come anywhere near it until it is completely dry!'

Over macaroni cheese with steamed asparagus, Mrs Frosdick went over all the plans for their trip to Kelmscott Manor. Oscar was to leave the very next day—Tuesday. Ivy and Mrs Frosdick were to join him towards the end of the week. It was all arranged.

'I will send the carriage for you bright and early on Thursday morning,' Mrs Frosdick told Ivy, briskly. 'You will come here first, as I may have a couple of things to do before we set off. In the meantime...' she patted Ivy's hand '...you have two free days, to enjoy as you please.'

Ivy thanked her. *Two free days*. She wouldn't tell Cousin Jared or any other member of her family. She would let them all think that she was going to Cheyne Walk, as usual, and then she would spend those two days helping out at the Dogs' Home.

'One thing I beg of you, dear girl,' Mrs Frosdick continued, smoothly, 'and that is: pray limit the amount of laudanum you take before we go. We do not want you drooping around Kelmscott Manor like a marionette with its strings cut.'

Irritated, Ivy put down her fork. There was a wasp in Mrs Frosdick's hair but she decided not to tell her. There were wasps everywhere, it seemed, now that the plums above and around their heads were oozing juice and ready to fall.

I don't droop, she thought, indignantly. *I used to, per'aps, but not any more . . .*

'And if the Italian is there,' Mrs Frosdick added, 'as he certainly will be, do not embarrass yourself, dear girl, by getting upset over his—ahem—"friendship" with Janey Morris.'

Both Ivy and Oscar looked at her in complete bewilderment.

'Mother,' Oscar said, 'what *are* you talking about?'

Mrs Frosdick flicked a wasp from the tablecloth— flicked it so hard that it hit the trunk of the plum tree and immediately expired.

'Forgive my bluntness,' she said, 'but I have it on excellent authority, Miss Jackson, that you have been suffering from the pangs of unrequited love. That you have formed a passionate attachment to our widowed neighbour and find his indifference to you hard to bear.'

Ivy could scarcely believe her ears. *That fat old painter man next door? What nonsense was this?*

'Good gracious, Miss Jackson. Is this true?'

Oscar's mouth formed such a big 'O' of surprise that a whole swarm of wasps could easily have gone in there to feast on the bits of macaroni stuck between his teeth.

'No it ain't,' Ivy cried. 'It's a blessed lie. I ain't even met the man. Or...I 'ave, I suppose, but only once. And it was 'im took a fancy to *me*, that time, cos 'e thought I was 'is missis. The one 'e 'ad dug up.'

Mrs Frosdick patted her hand. Ivy snatched it away. *This barmy woman, with her thirst for tittle-tattle. She must have been talking to Alfred again. That was probably it. And Alfred, for whatever reason, had spun this cock-and-bull tale.*

'My dear girl,' cooed Mrs Frosdick, 'there is no need to be ashamed, or to make excuses for yourself. The Italian positively *seeps* charm in the company of the young and the beautiful. I've watched him. He simply cannot help himself. You made too much of it, that is all. You are not to blame.'

Quickly, she began gathering the plates and dishes. 'Oscar,' she commanded, before Ivy could say another single word, 'come with me. We have your packing to do. Miss Jackson, as soon as you are ready you may return home. Allow me to organize the carriage.'

Ivy opened her mouth.

'Or perhaps the carriage does not suit you?' Mrs Frosdick added. 'Are the cushions too hard? Or our driver too surly? For I understand that, just lately, you have chosen to walk.'

'*Walk?*' piped up Oscar. 'What, unescorted? All the way to Lambeth? My dear Miss Jackson, that is quite...'

'I...I prefer to walk,' Ivy stammered. 'I like walkin'. It...it stretches me legs.'

'But...but...'

Mrs Frosdick silenced her son with a single look.

'Miss Jackson clearly knows her own mind,' she said. 'And we must respect that. Not that a gal in the throes of unrequited love is ever of completely *sound* mind. Still...we can *trust* you, I'm sure, Miss Jackson, not to do anything foolish? Not to cast yourself off Battersea Bridge into the chilly embrace of the Thames? Or *take too much of the same mind-numbing drug that did for the Italian's wife*?'

Ivy stood up. It was hard for her to be justifiably out-raged while wrapped in a tablecloth and stooping to avoid getting twigs or wasps or leaves from the plum tree in her hair. It was hard to be anything at all in the face of such peculiar fabrication—such a sad and silly story that had nothing to do with anything that had actually happened.

So: 'I'm goin' now, thank you,' was all she said.

Mrs Frosdick inclined her head. 'Do not forget to pick up your possessions,' she said. 'That is your little bundle of things, is it not, beneath the hedge? There is no need to hide your laudanum from us, dear girl. You are among friends, you know, and we are well aware of your dependence on the stuff.'

Without another word, and doing her best to look dignified, Ivy retrieved the knotted hanky and stalked across the lawn, through the conservatory and into her small changing room. *Mad old witch*, she muttered, as she unpinned the revolting tablecloth for the very last time and flung it over a trunk. *She ain't two pecks short of a bushel at all—she's the whole blessed bushel short of a bushel she is...*

And then, because she was so looking forward to seeing Prince and the other dogs, she hurried back into her own clothes and away out of the house without giving Mrs Frosdick, or her latest piece of tittle-tattle, another thought.

CHAPTER 33

In which a trap is well and truly sprung

'Will there be maids?' asked Cyn. 'To wash yer drawers an' so on?'

'I don't know,' Ivy told her. 'How would I know? I ain't never been to no manor 'ouse before.'

They were packing a bag—a shabby but still serviceable travelling bag that Aunt Pamela had fished out from under her chaise longue. There had been all kinds of oddments in that bag—hairnets and thimbles and little pencils from dance programmes; shoe buckles and valentines and lavender bags smelling only of dust. But Aunt Pamela had said these things would be all right, for a while, in a pan or a sieve. 'After all,' she said, 'you gotter seem respectable, Ive. You gotter have a proper bag for stayin' at a manor 'ouse, or the painter man might go off yer.'

Ivy didn't care. About the bag or the manor house. And she certainly didn't give a rat's twitch about Oscar Aretino Frosdick going off her (indeed, she would have worn her one pair of drawers on her head and carried the rest of her luggage slung over her shoulder in a shrimping net just to keep him at bay).

'Let's see,' said Cyn, her big red hands fluttering over the open bag, 'pale dress, dark dress, flannel petticoat, slippers, shawl...they ain't very fashionable, are they, Cousin Ive? I'm almost glad it ain't me goin' after all. I'd be shamed.'

Ivy yawned. 'I won't be wearin' 'em much though, will I?' she said.

'Har-har!' snorted Jared, who was polishing his boots beside the grate. 'That's the trick! That's the way forward an' no mistake!'

'I mean,' Ivy told him, indignantly, 'that I'll be posin' most of the time. In the river. Floatin' on me back in a purple dress wiv flowers all over it.'

Jared stopped polishing and frowned.

'In the river, is it?' he said. ''Ow queer is *that*? Well, that's definitely a few shillin's extra, that is. In the blessed river indeed...I always knew 'e was an odd fish, that Frosdick.'

'Ha-ha!' chortled Aunt Pamela. 'You wanter watch out, niece. All that cold water might dampen 'is ardour. Ha-ha!'

Ivy turned her back on them. On all of them. On Aunt Pamela and Cousin Jared laughing their heads off. On Orlando bent over his poems, pretending not to hear. On Cousin Cyn buckling the bag and wishing it was her, getting ready to slide into the painter man's arms. In the river. Near the manor. Under the stars.

Sleep.

The sooner she slept, Ivy decided, the sooner tomorrow would come. And the sooner tomorrow came the sooner she would find herself in the countryside, where Oscar Frosdick would get started on the new picture. And the sooner he started the stupid picture the sooner he would finish it. And then she would be able to return to London and go back to the Dogs' Home.

Or would she?

For a long time, now, Ivy had not needed laudanum to help her sleep. A combination of long walks, Mrs Frosdick's healthy meals, and the exertion of looking after lost and starving dogs had been sending her into a deep and dreamless slumber the instant her head touched the mattress.

Tonight, however, she felt agitated and all out of sorts. It had nothing to do with the trip to Kelmscott Manor. Nothing to do with train travel, owning only one pair of drawers, or being expected to pose in a river, without its depths, currents, or temperature having been satisfactorily explored or explained.

No. What worried Ivy was a sinking feeling, in the pit of her stomach, that Keeper Pavitt and his daughter did not want her at the Dogs' Home any more. That her presence there had started to trouble them. Perhaps she had done something wrong—put too much straw in a cage, maybe, or forgotten to feed an in-comer. Why else would they have insisted, today, that she should leave early?

'Really,' Rosa had said, practically tugging the broom from her hands in a manner that brooked no argument. 'Really, Ivy. You have given up enough of your free time. The Committee is meeting here later, and we can manage until then. Go home.'

Perhaps she had shown too much sentiment upon learning that Prince had been sold. She had known it was likely—he had been at the Home for more than a week, after all, without being claimed—but, all the same, it had come as a surprise . . . no, a shock . . . and she had astonished herself by getting tearful.

'Don't *cry*, Ivy,' Rosa had begged, passing her a whiffy towel for her eyes. 'It doesn't do to get too attached. Not here. For all our in-comers get to be out-goers sooner or later. And at least Prince has gone to a good home.'

Ivy knew what Rosa meant. Some unclaimed dogs were considered too vicious, old, or ill to attract new owners. And those, she was aware, were swiftly and gently dispatched with a drop or two of prussic acid on their tongues.

And so she had dried her tears on the whiffy towel and vowed never to weep again over the fate of any creature—not publicly anyway. But maybe the damage had already been done. Maybe Rosa and her father didn't want someone like her around while they were doing important things, like writing in the ledger or adding up money. Or meeting the Committee. Maybe a girl who only swept and wept was more of a hindrance than a help. Maybe they wished she would stay away for good but were too polite to say so.

She didn't want to think about the Dogs' Home any more. So she poured herself some water, went behind the screen, and took the stopper from her bottle of laudanum. Two drops or three? *Four*, said a little voice in her head. *Just to be sure of a good night's rest.*

It had been so long since she had dosed herself that she actually wrinkled her nose as she swallowed. Laudanum tasted nasty. She had never noticed that before.

And as she sank back on the mattress, her limbs and

eyelids already heavy, she found herself wondering, for the first time ever, if staying awake and continuing to think might have been better for her...might even...just possibly...have led to some answers ...

The carriage came early; so early that Ivy was only just conscious and dragging herself, groggily, into her clothes.

'Stick a smile on your face, gal, for pity's sake!' pleaded Aunt Pamela, keeping a beady eye on her niece as she picked up the travelling bag and headed for the door. 'No man does a moper any favours. Remember that. And we're countin' on you, me and Jared are, to keep the readies rollin' in. Particularly with winter just around the corner, and me growin' more and more invalid with every day that passes. Oh, and your cousin Cyn's in the family way, which ain't exactly good for our circumstances.'

In the carriage, Ivy leaned her head back and closed her eyes. She was still half asleep...fuddled by laudanum...What was it Mrs Frosdick had accused her of doing? Drooping. That was it. She opened her eyes immediately and straightened her spine.

Then her thoughts turned to Cyn, who was in the family way. The news had hardly come as a shock, but it was a pity all the same. Ivy wondered who the father was—if Cyn even *knew* who the father was—and whether he would look after Cyn and the baby or leave them to get by as best they could. Cyn, she knew, was the kind of girl who would want the father of her child to marry her and be there always.

I will never have babies, Ivy promised herself. *I would*

sooner share my life with a dog, or maybe a kitty-cat. Creatures would, I'm sure, be easier to care for ... easier to love. And I could look after them, and love them, all by myself if I wanted to.

The path leading up to the Frosdick's front door had been cleared of its trailing nasturtiums. Someone had hacked them right back, and flung the flowers under a hedge. Ivy supposed there had been no point arranging those blooms in a vase, since there would be no one at home for a while to see them. All the same, something about those cheerful petals, scattered like ashes and already dying, made her uncomfortable.

Mrs Frosdick opened the door straight away, as if she had been waiting a long time, right there on the mat. But instead of inviting Ivy into the house, she chivvied her straight back down the path saying:

'We need to call in at the Italian's. Just for a minute. It won't take long.'

At the gate, Ivy was made to wait while Mrs Frosdick checked the street. Then she was hurried—pushed, in fact—the few paces to number sixteen.

'Are we feedin' 'is animals?' she asked, hopefully. For Alfred had told her there was a peacock in the garden, as well as harmy-dillos, and a big black bird in a cage.

'No,' snapped Mrs Frosdick. 'They are boarding at Jamrach's until the end of September—the nasty, smelly things.' Then: '*Hurrumph!*' she grunted, throwing all her weight at the front door. Ivy was alarmed. Of course, there was no one here to let them in. But if Mrs Frosdick had some task to perform here, why hadn't they left her a key?

Turning her back, Mrs Frosdick did something to the

lock—something quick and surreptitious that Ivy didn't see—and then hurled herself at the door a second... third...fourth time.

She'll do 'erself an injury at this rate, Ivy thought. *What's she up to?*

At the fourth hurl the door flew wide open.

'There,' Mrs Frosdick said. 'Come along in, my dear. And don't look at me like that. The damp from the river can play havoc with these old doors. Absolute havoc. The frame around this one is very badly swollen so the wood sticks fast. Alfred keeps meaning to get it seen to, but in the meantime he and the Italian have fallen into the slovenly habit of not always remembering to lock up. Now...follow me, please. We don't have all day.'

With some reluctance, Ivy stepped into the hallway.

'Up here,' Mrs Frosdick ordered, heading for the stairs. 'You may leave your bag.'

Slowly, but without question, Ivy put Aunt Pamela's travelling bag down on the tiled floor. The stairs creaked as she climbed them and the banister beneath her fingers felt as smooth as a bone.

'In here.'

The first thing to strike Ivy, as she stepped into the room, was the complete absence of furniture. No bed, no table—not even a rug on the floor. Then she noticed the painting above the mantelshelf and gasped. Heavy drapes at the window had been looped aside and the canvas, lit by sunshine, seemed as real as a reflection in glass. *It's her*, Ivy realized. *The Italian's wife. It must be.* And although she had learned nothing about art (except that posing for it was incredibly tedious) she felt the skin on her arms turn to goosebumps in response to the painting's strange yet undeniable beauty.

A chinking sound reminded her that Mrs Frosdick was there and in a hurry to do whatever it was they had come here for.

She turned round.

Mrs Frosdick was pouring a glass of water. Pouring it carefully from a bottle which she must have brought in with her, although Ivy hadn't noticed. It looked cloudy, that water, as indeed it would do, for it contained enough laudanum to send whoever swallowed it straight to sleep. For ever.

Ivy watched the brimming glass, as Mrs Frosdick came over and set it down—set it down carefully on the mantelshelf as if it was a candle, new-lit, and this room some kind of chapel.

'What's that for?'

Mrs Frosdick ignored the question.

'Look at her,' she said, waving a hand towards the woman in the painting. 'The spineless little fool. Doped herself up to the eyeballs she did, rather than face her demons. Her baby girl was stillborn. Did you know? And she was pregnant a second time, so rumour has it, when she took that fatal dose.'

Ivy blinked up at the woman in the painting.

'That's sad, that is,' she said, solemnly. 'That's really sad. But—what's the glass of water for?'

Mrs Frosdick looked from the painting to Ivy and then back at the painting again. 'What a lot you two have in common,' she declared, nastily. 'Why men lose their hearts and souls to such spineless young ninnies is

240

beyond my understanding. All that drooping around—it's pathetic.'

Ivy flushed. 'I don't droop,' she mumbled, looking down at her boots. 'And I ain't...I ain't spineless. We've both got red 'air, that's all...me and 'er. That's all that makes us 'like.'

'Pah!' Mrs Frosdick sounded cross enough to spit into the empty grate.

Startled, Ivy looked sideways at her...at the sagging profile...at the mean mouth...at the frizzing bun of hair which, although as dull and as grey as a rat's nest, contained one or two threads that, seen close up, were still a natural and unmistakable shade of...red.

Mrs Frosdick, sensing this close scrutiny, swivelled round. And, for a moment, she and Ivy were face to face—close enough to kiss, or to bite each other's noses off. And in that tiny space of time Ivy understood two things: that Mrs Frosdick was jealous of her—poisonously jealous—and that there was nothing at all to be done about it.

'Do...do you think we should go now?' she asked, as calmly as she could. 'To catch that train?'

Mrs Frosdick continued to look at her. And it was worse—far worse—than being watched by a hungry snake. Then: 'Of course,' she said, sweetly. 'Only, draw the drapes first, there's a dear girl, so that sunlight cannot fade our neighbour's extraordinary tribute to his beloved wife.'

Ivy, eager to be away, did as she was told. The heavy crimson curtains felt hot between her hands, like the pelt of a dark red creature, and she had to tug, hard, to get them to close.

241

When she turned round Mrs Frosdick had gone.

'Wait for me!'

The door was shut. Ivy twisted the knob...twisted it again...and then again. Then she rattled it, furiously, with both her hands.

'Where are you? Come back! Come back and let me out!'

Downstairs: a muffled thud as the front door banged semi-shut in its swollen frame. And after that?

Silence.

CHAPTER 34

*Concerning Oscar's disappointment and
Mrs Frosdick's satisfaction*

O scar Aretino Frosdick was lying on his back, chewing a blade of grass and dreaming of fame, when news arrived that his stunner would not be joining him at Kelmscott Manor.

The news came in a letter signed, *'with great regret but not much surprise,'* by his mother. *'I can only assume,'* the letter told him, *'since no explanation has been forthcoming, that the silly child changed her mind and went home. My personal opinion is that she could not face the Italian and remains mortally embarrassed by her feelings for him. I hate to say "I told you so", dear boy, but there we have it . . .'*

The servant who had brought the letter into the garden stepped back in alarm as Oscar leapt to his feet and began stamping on daisies, as petulantly as a child denied pudding.

'Bad news, sir?' the servant asked.

'I'll say,' Oscar wailed. *'How could she do this to me? How?'*

His bitter lament embarrassed the servant who retreated, hastily, back into the house. But it made two little girls perched on the earth-closet roof, just beyond the garden wall, giggle behind their hands.

'That sounds like OAF,' whispered the younger one, 'OAF in a tizzy.'

'OAF, OAF, bake me a loaf,' chanted her sister, drumming her heels on the warm grey slates. 'Plight me your troth, O darling OAF.'

'Shhhh...don't...he'll *hear* ...'

'Girls, get down. What are you doing up there? You should be at your lessons.'

Stifling chuckles, both girls leaned carefully forward, not minding terribly much that they had been caught playing truant by their mother and her fat painter friend.

The younger girl had the hiccups. But the older one, peering gravely down between her boots said: 'But the blackbirds were stealing gooseberries again, Mama. We could hear them through the window. And it's such a lovely sunny day, and Roman emperors are so *very* boring.'

Her mother sighed but her companion laughed—a deep rumble, like a bear's laugh, that made his belly wobble.

'Yes...hic...and OAF is in a terrible...hic...tizzy,' chimed in the younger child. 'You must have...hic... heard him, Mama, crying "*How...hic...could she do this to me. How?*"'

Even with hiccups, the mimicry was exact.

'Oh dear.'

The sisters watched, bright-eyed, as their mother turned to her fat painter friend and said: 'That means, I suppose, that we won't be meeting Mr Frosdick's lovely muse after all.' Although only nine and ten years old, both girls recognized sarcasm when they heard it.

'Now, now,' murmured the fat painter man, fondly. And the girls nudged one another, gleefully, as he plucked a piece of thistledown from the dark waves of their mother's hair and sent it floating away over the garden wall.

244

Their mother placed a hand, very lightly, on the sleeve of his jacket. She had beautiful lily-white hands and her fingers, resting on the coarse material of the jacket, looked perfect there but somehow dangerous, as if they might tug this man, very suddenly, towards the edge of a cliff or the mouth of a well.

'He will be looking for another model now,' she said. 'To pose for Ophelia. Is there any chance at all, do you think, that his work will ever be accepted by the Academy?'

'None,' the fat painter replied. 'For our affable OAF is so wanting in talent that he might as well throw mud at a canvas and call it art. He cannot paint, my dear, to save his life. These scamps on the roof could do better. Come, girls—let us go in search of lemonade. And then, I'm afraid, it's back to the schoolroom and the Holy Roman Empire for you . . .'

'And let us hope,' he muttered under his breath, as the little girls scrambled and slid back down to earth, 'that this latest come-about means we are also to be spared the presence of OAF's ghastly mother . . .'

And so they were.

For Mrs Frosdick, having done her worst, was out in her own garden at Cheyne Walk, picking plums. Kelmscott Manor? She had never intended going anywhere near the wretched place. This was her home. Hers and darling Oscar's. Why would she ever want to leave it? And Oscar, with no stunner to work with, was bound to be back in a day or two. And then? Why she, Priscilla Joan Frosdick, would be modelling for her dear boy again before you could shout 'palette knife'.

245

Oh yes...Mrs Frosdick was feeling highly satisfied—content even—as she twisted plums from their stems and placed each one in a china bowl. It was a *splendid* crop this season, enough for many a plum duff, plum tart, plum crumble, and plum fritter as well as an ocean of jam. And her dear boy did so love plum jam, particularly with toasted crumpets on a winter's afternoon.

Having stripped the tree bare, she set about gathering windfalls and throwing them in a sack. Wasps rose up in angry battalions but she ignored them. The fallen plums were pulpy and beginning to moulder. When her sack was full, she lugged it to the compost heap where grass cuttings and dead flowers steamed and stank in the late summer sunshine.

It was certainly warm, for the end of August. *Extremely* warm. In a locked and airless room it would be even warmer. Sweltering, in fact.

Emptying the sack, Mrs Frosdick wondered how much longer to wait before unlocking that door. Two days? Three? A week? The girl was bound to have drunk the water by now. Bound to have sunk into the same lethal stupor that saw off the Italian's wife. Thirst alone would have driven her to it. Not that it would look like that, when her body was eventually found. Oh no.

Mrs Frosdick had rehearsed her response to this 'tragedy' most carefully: '*Oh, the poor girl. The poor foolish girl. Of course, we knew she took laudanum. The signs were obvious. But to have taken her own life that way...and in our neighbour's home as well! She must have known that the scandal would ruin him. Shocking, absolutely shocking, don't you agree, for a man to have not one but TWO women's deaths* on his conscience? And both from an overdose of laudanum! How he can sleep at night, with or without the use of drugs, I simply do not understand... Yes, of course, our poor girl was in love with him. Of course he led her on. The man's an absolute disgrace. He should be locked up—deported at the very least.'

Grabbing a rake, she gave the compost heap a bit of a turn. And as she prodded and heaved all that rotting vegetation, thoughts of Oscar's stunner floated clean away. *Ginger*, she mused, happily. *A sprinkling of ginger in this year's batch of jam might be rather pleasant. And perhaps a tiny hint of grated lemon peel.*

Leaning in, for better leverage, her left foot struck something solid. Recognizing the thing immediately she picked it up, brushed off a bit of muck and turned it over in her hands.

Hmmm, she thought, abandoning the rake. *Waste not, want not. Scoured out, I could use this to store onions in. Otherwise, it would certainly make an unusual vase.*

And off she went, back into the house. And the only question troubling her, as she drifted through the conservatory, was whether a large clump of ferns or a subtle arrangement of dried flowers would best suit an armadillo shell as a centrepiece for her table.

CHAPTER 35
In which Ivy fights temptation

A bridge.

There is a bridge in the painting, above the woman's head. And a tower, with a window cut into it shaped like a cross. Two figures—two men—hover at either end of the bridge, but whether they are watching the woman or guarding the tower Ivy cannot tell. These things are very faint, as if swirling in mist...so barely-there that they seem about to disappear, leaving...what? Blue skies? Thunder clouds? Nothing at all?

Clouds.

Ivy dares to imagine clouds...bruise-coloured, plum-coloured, wolf-coloured clouds, massing and multiplying above her own head until...ahhh...rain...She dares to imagine rain, splashing onto her face in big cool drops.

No. Stop.

She licks her lips. Tastes salt. Feels, with the tip of her tongue, the shreds of dry skin peeling from her mouth.

She is lying on the floor, her head turned so that she can see the painting. She has pulled the drapes down to create a pile of bedding but wishes she hadn't now, for the sun is warming the room to a dangerous degree and she is lying right in its glare.

She would like to hang those drapes back up again, but there is no chair to stand on and, even if there was, she is too weak to cross the room.

Above her head, the Italian's wife appears to shimmer, her face sickly in the heat, her neck as vulnerable as a swan's.

I ain't like you, *Ivy tells her.* I ain't nothin' like you at all, so there.

Gazing at this image of the Italian's wife no longer gives her goosebumps, nor does it fill her with awe. Those closed eyes... that pleading countenance...the mouth partly open, as if about to dribble. Had this woman been alive and looking like that, Ivy would have wanted to slap her by now.

No strength left though...not even to raise a hand.

And up on the mantelpiece: the glass. And it is empty.

For the whole of the first day she had raged. Paced the room like a caged animal. Shouted and screamed and rattled the bars at the window. She had needed the privy and been mortified at having to do her business in the empty grate. Now she doesn't care. She doesn't give an owl's toot.

On the second day she had sat very still on the floor, looking... only looking...at the glass of water. One sniff, hours before, had left her in no doubt at all about what it contained, or what was almost certain to become of her if she drank it.

But a long, airless night had left her dizzy and parched. And water was water, wasn't it, whatever else had been added? And she was accustomed to taking laudanum, wasn't she? And quite a lot of it, as well.

Maybe, she had thought, if she just sipped this water—one tiny swallow every hour or so—she would quench her thirst without doing herself any lasting harm. And if it did send her to sleep...well...there were far worse ways of passing time when you'd been imprisoned in an empty house with nothing but a grate to piddle in and a dead woman's portrait for company.

But how long would she sleep for, she had wondered, if she lifted that glass and drank? Even if it was only a tiny sip? Exactly how much laudanum had Mrs Frosdick added? That was the question that stayed her hand ... that had stopped her swallowing so much as a drop of that water.

On the third day she dipped a finger in the glass and sucked it dry. The bitter taste puckered her tongue and the roof of her mouth but the craving persisted. And as minutes and then hours passed, marked only by the shifting of light on the bare boards of the floor, the will to resist seeped out of her, leaving only a burning thirst and the desire to quench it, at any cost.

Standing up with difficulty, and clutching the mantelshelf to keep from falling over, she picked up the glass of water and raised it to her lips. Raised it carefully and very slowly: not to delay the moment, but so that it wouldn't spill.

Ouch!

Her brooch. It must have come undone, for the pin had jabbed her wrist, drawing a tiny dot of blood. Hearing a clatter, she looked giddily down, her right hand still clutching the glass.

'I'. . . 'I' for 'Ivy'.

The tiny circlet of leaves, and the little stick-shaped letter with its two missing stones, was twinkling away so boldly, down there on the floor, that her dry, cracked lips curved in a rueful smile.

That's me, she thought.

'I' for 'Ivy'. That's me, that is.

For just a moment more, she hesitated.

And then, in one quick, sure movement, she flicked her right wrist, splattering the mantel, the wall, and part of the painting with a shower of tepid drops.

Slowly, deliberately, she set the empty glass back down on the mantelshelf. Then she picked up her 'I' for 'Ivy' brooch and pinned it back on, before lying down in the middle of the room, on her nest of crimson velvet.

And for a little while, or it could have been ages, she watched drops of poisoned water sliding down the painting . . . trickling like tears to the bottom of the canvas before plopping off the edge.

Most of the water, it seemed, had struck the bird—the nasty-looking red bird with a white flower in its beak. Why did he paint that? she wondered feverishly. What kind of creature is that when it's at 'ome?

She thinks she has slept since then, but cannot be sure. She has no idea of the time, or of what day it is now. But the sun is burning hot upon her, and her tongue has started to swell. She knows that much.

The empty glass on the mantelshelf reminds her that she has no choice, any more, about swallowing the drink that would have numbed her, and made everything stop.

But the decision she made when she threw it all away still seems like the right one.

You . . . she thinks . . . looking up at the woman in the painting. Did you mean to sleep for ever? Or did you just want to forget, for a bit, about things that were hurtin' you and makin' you sad? Was it a mistake, goin' into oblivion? Was it?

No answer, of course. No clues, either. And, as Ivy's mind grows quieter, it dawns on her that when she looks at the painting above the mantelshelf she isn't seeing the Italian's wife at all. Not really.

You know what I think? she tells the pale, sleepy face that appears, suddenly, to be floating. I think he remembered you all wrong. This ain't you at all, is it, up there lookin' spineless? Not the proper you, anyway.

Lizzie. That was her name.

And as the face in the painting begins to fade . . . floating like a water lily past the tower and under the bridge, it seems to Ivy that the shadowy men standing guard, and the fierce red bird with the flower in its beak, no longer know quite what to do with themselves.

'Serves yer right,' she tells them, before closing her eyes.

CHAPTER 36

Concerning timely arrivals and a shocking discovery

N ever, in the whole of Fing Nolan's career, had a house been so easy to enter. He hadn't needed to jemmy a lock or use any force at all.

'Where's the welcome mat?' he muttered to his accomplices, closing the front door as best he could and setting his redundant jack and chisel quietly down by the hallstand. 'Where's the big plate of cold cuts an' pickles wiv a sign sayin': "Elp yerselves, lads, before robbin' the place"?'

His two accomplices chuckled under their breaths before lighting a single candle and testing the door to the sitting room.

'You certain about this, Fing Nolan?' one of them whispered, as the door swung open into a room full of mirrors. 'What if this place ain't empty after all? What if you 'eard wrong? Them ears of yours ain't as fine-tuned as they used to be, old man.'

'Shut it,' growled Fing. 'I'm certain.'

For a while after that no one spoke. Satisfied that this strange house was empty and that anyone hanging around outside would not be able to see a thing through the shuttered windows, they lit more candles, and a couple of lamps, and got straight down to business.

Fing Nolan was the first to break the silence. 'Remember the rule of thumb, lads,' he said. 'Small is beautiful and easier to carry and big ain't always worth the effort. Use yer loafs. And don't smash nothin'.'

'We should've 'ired a carriage,' one of the lads muttered, eyeing his reflection with bashful interest in the mirror with a frame of gilded passion flowers. 'Some of this bigger stuff must be worth a tidy sum.'

'Junk shop tat,' growled Fing, heading for a display of silverware. 'And we ain't got the space for storin' furniture, nor the contacts for sellin' it on. We gotter stick to the usual—jewellery...snuff boxes...candlesticks and the like.'

'And clothes,' the lad reminded him. 'Good lace in particular. Fine woollen shawls. Anythin' Oriental. Oh, and silk stockin's—we can't sell enough of them down the Lane. Never could.'

'Right,' Fing agreed, grudgingly. 'And clothes. But only fine 'uns. I ain't luggin' no sackfuls of rags 'alfway across London, not for anyone's sake...Aha, what 'ave we 'ere? Bring that lamp over, Muck Snipe.'

By the time they had worked through every ground floor room but one Fing and his lads had half-filled their sacks with an interesting assortment of loot—nothing that was going to make them incredibly rich, or give the Mighty Grand Plan any kind of boost, but enough to have made such a risky adventure just about worthwhile (assuming, of course, that they got away with it).

The last room they entered, before heading upstairs, was clearly an artist's studio. Easels, frames, and great swathes of canvas took up most of the space, along with a green chaise longue, a screen for young ladies to change their clothes behind, and a pot-bellied stove to warm the air in winter. But what really drew the lads' eyes, and set their pulses racing, was a tall lacquered cabinet fitted with dozens of small and beautifully crafted drawers.

'Lads,' said Fing, solemnly, 'either this painter man collects birds' eggs or there's some serious loot in there.'

The cabinet wasn't locked but that meant nothing, given the state of the front door. Hearts bumping, eyes gleaming, the lads craned their thick necks and gawped expectantly as Fing eased each drawer open, one after the other, to reveal pile after glittering pile of jewellery.

'*Ahhhh*,' the lads sighed, and began chattering both at once:

'Them's gotter be rubies. As sure as me jail crop's growin' back ginger, they gotter be real them rubies 'ave.'

'Just look at the size of them diamonds—as big as beetles, the little beauties.'

'Shut it!' growled Fing. For he could tell at a glance that these stones were all fake—shards and blobs of coloured glass, set in metal of the lowest quality.

'Cheap tat,' he spat, sifting a handful of the brooches, necklaces, earrings, and clips that had been worn by a series of stunners in a variety of Pre-Raphaelite poses. 'Not worth a mouse's fart, none of it.'

A massive wardrobe, further along the wall, looked a lot less promising than the cabinet. But, as Fing was quick to point out, a family's valuables weren't always kept in the most obvious places. Why—hadn't he found a gold watch in a teapot once? And a wedding ring stuffed in the toe of a slipper?

The wardrobe opened to reveal mantles, cloaks, and trailing dresses so ancient and moth-eaten that they seemed certain to disintegrate at the first twitch of the hangers.

Quickly, Fing checked pockets and seams for valuables and ran his hands along the wardrobe's insides.

'That gown looks smart,' the lad with the ginger jail crop observed, wistfully. 'The pale orange one, with the blue stitchin' on the sleeve. We could sell a gown like that for at least a guinea, I reckon. It's worth a quick rummage, ain't it, Fing, to see what else is 'angin' up there?'

The pale orange gown was of the finest corded silk and embroidered not only with dragons and sea waves but with the twelve symbols of authority that only a Chinese emperor would have included in the design. This made it one of the most valuable things in the house. But only to someone in the know.

'There ain't time to go rummagin' through a load of old tat,' Fing snapped. 'There's upstairs to do yet and we gotter be well away from 'ere by daybreak.'

On his way out, and behind Fing Nolan's back, the Muck Snipe snaffled a box of charcoal and a handful of coloured chalks. He still drew things occasionally, the Muck Snipe did, even though the other lads ribbed him for it unmercifully. If he could have stuffed an easel down his trousers and smuggled it safely back to the lodging house he would have done it. For a bread board was all right for resting small sketches on, but not so handy for anything ambitious—and no good whatsoever if one of the other lads was fancying a cheese sandwich.

'Right,' Fing muttered, raising a lamp and leading the way to the stairs. 'Let's see what we've got up 'ere then.'

It was the Muck Snipe who discovered the locked door. 'Lads,' he hissed. 'Come 'ere, quick!'

Fing Nolan was there in a trice, followed swiftly by the lad with the ginger jail crop. All three stood for a moment, frowning at the key protruding from the lock. In their experience it wasn't normal to leave a key in something locked. Not if you wanted it to stay locked, it wasn't. But perhaps the same scatty arty type who had neglected the all-important task of securing the front door had forgotten to remove the key from this one. That seemed the most likely explanation.

'Lads,' said Fing, placing one hand reverently on one of the door's wooden panels. 'There could be some serious loot in 'ere. Follow me.'

Turning the key he stepped into the room, his lamp held high.

'It don't smell too good in 'ere,' he said.

His accomplices sniffed, shrugged, and looked around. They had expected to find a safe, at the very least. Or a trunk full of jewels—the real thing this time.

Nothing. There wasn't a single solitary thing to be found in here. Except . . .

The Muck Snipe had the look of a sleepwalker—dazed yet purposeful—as he skirted an untidy heap of rags, and came to a halt in front of the fireplace.

'Oh my,' he whispered, whipping off his cap in an instinctive show of reverence. 'Look at this . . . just *look* at it.'

257

'Tat,' growled Fing, raising his lantern to be sure. 'Let's go.'

The Muck Snipe continued to stare upwards, his own face pale with wonder. 'Ghostly though, ain't it?' he murmured. 'Tat or not, it's givin' me the shivers.'

'Lads! Over 'ere! 'Urry up, for cryin' out loud. And bring the lamp.'

The Muck Snipe took no notice. Whatever else had been discovered was of little interest to him.

Then he heard Fing Nolan gasp.

'What?' he said, tearing his gaze reluctantly from the picture above the mantelshelf. 'What 'ave yer found, lads?'

CHAPTER 37

Concerning revelations of a most disturbing nature

I vy had been dreaming. Hallucinating. Drifting in and out of consciousness for—oh—hours. The word 'ironic' meant sweet Fanny Adams to her but she was aware, all the same, that it was kind of amusing, in a terrible way, that for once in her short life this pull towards deep sleep had nothing to do with laudanum.

After sunset on—what, the third day? Or was it the fourth?—she had grown shivery, and then very cold, so had bundled herself up in one of the red velvet curtains. *Like a shroud*, she had thought, with that grim feeling, again, that came close to being funny.

She didn't hear the key turning in the lock. And when Fing Nolan said what he said about a bad smell it, too, seemed unreal. '*A smell?*' she repeated, in her dream. '*That'll be the lunatics, sir. They live in boxes, you know.*' The sound of boots passing her head became the drumming feet and hammering fists of lunatics, trying to escape. '*Me too,*' she told them, wearily. '*I'm a prisoner too. But there's a bridge over there. Let's cross it. Only, watch out for that red bird.*'

Only when someone pulled the curtain from her face and began calling out for help and a lamp was she jarred into leaving the lunatics behind. *So difficult though... Painful as well. My throat... My throat...*

'Fetch water,' someone shouted. 'Mucks—you go.'

Mucks?...Mucks?

It was horrible, being dragged awake like this. And painful. Her throat hurt. Her head hurt. Every bone in her back hurt. And her eyelids were so heavy...so very sore and heavy...that it seemed like cruelty, self-inflicted, to try and force them open.

Sleep...I'm goin' back to sleep...

'Wake up, girly. Wake up!'

Girly?

Someone had raised her head...raised it gently enough from the curtain's folds and was stroking her hair away from her forehead. *That's quite nice, that is*, Ivy managed to think as she started to slip away. *That's almost comfy...*

'It's her, ain't it? Look! Look at 'er face. It's our Ive. Our Ivy girl!'

The hand supporting her head began to tremble, and the voice...*that voice*...was shaking too as it kept on and on, imploring her to wake up.

'Stay with us, Ive. Open yer eyes. Come on, girly, come on now. I can't believe this, Fing. I can't believe it's 'er!'

Fing?

Footsteps. Loud footsteps, thudding up the stairs and into the room.

''Ere's...the...water,' panted the Muck Snipe.

And from what seemed like a great distance, Ivy felt and heard the hard rim of a glass go 'chink' against her teeth, felt the trickle of liquid flowing into her mouth...down her chin...onto her neck...

'Steady on, man,' she heard. 'Wait while I lift 'er up a bit.'

Splash it in, man... This girl's overwrought.

'No!'

She wasn't having it. Not now. Not after being so strong—strong enough to throw the last lot away anyhow. *How dare they! How dare they!*

'Get that cup o' filth away from me!' she tried to yell, but her voice was an awful rasp and her flailing hands no match for the ones that seemed intent on pouring laudanum down her throat. *'Get away!'* she yelled again managing, this time, to be heard, and to smack someone a fair old wallop in the face.

'Hell's teeth!' cursed Fing Nolan, clutching his nose. 'She's still with us all right...'

'Hush, girly...' came the other voice...closer now, and clearer. 'It's only water. I'll 'old the glass just right—give it 'ere, Mucks—and then yer gotter take a drink. Come on, Ivy girl. Open yer eyes. Open yer eyes and drink.'

Almost awake now...almost there, but unable, for now, to say another single word, Ivy resigned herself to being lifted...felt the rim of the glass against her teeth again, less violently this time...and the blissful slosh of liquid against her parched and peeling mouth.

And so, trusting herself to fate...to the voice...to whatever she was being offered...she gave in completely and drank...and drank...and...

'That's enough,' growled Fing. 'Too much is as bad as none at all to a person 'alf dead of the thirst. I've seen men in the clink writhin' in agony after bein' confined for days wivout a sip and then guzzlin' their fill.'

'I know, I know. I ain't as dim as I look, Fing Nolan.'

The glass was removed. And Ivy, who had yet to open her eyes, slumped backwards against a cradle of hairy arms.

'Is it really 'er?' the Muck Snipe murmured. 'And is she all right? Whadyer reckon, Carroty? Is she gonner live?'

Carroty . . .

Carroty . . . *Kate?*

Nobody spoke. And for what seemed like a very long time Ivy stayed precisely as she was—face waxen, eyelids sealed, her mouth slightly open and drooling water.

Then she opened her eyes.

'Thank the stars! Thank the stars above! She's all right!'

Carroty Kate—big shoulders heaving, cropped head nodding—sniffed and grinned and blinked back salty tears.

And Ivy, dazed and weakened though she was, saw almost immediately what it was about this person that she had never understood . . . hadn't fully grasped, as a little girl . . . not even in the park when the bluebottle had pulled at Kate's long red hair and it had all come away in his hands.

Carroty Kate hadn't been scalped that morning any more than she had been hanged for murder later on.

Quite clearly she was very much alive.

And she was a man.

CHAPTER 38

In which someone has a lot of explaining to do

'It...it's you. Only...it ain't. Cos you're...you're a...' She couldn't finish the sentence. It hurt her throat and tongue to speak, but that wasn't why.

'Hush,' Kate said. 'Don't strain yer voice. You need sugar, Ivy girl—summat ter get yer goin' again. I'm takin' yer downstairs. Then, as soon as you've got the strength, you tell old Carroty 'ow you came to be locked up like this. Fing? 'Old the door.'

Fing scowled. 'We ain't got the time to go rummagin' for no sugar,' he said. 'We gotter scarper. Wiv the loot.'

Carroty Kate scooped Ivy up, crimson curtain and all, and trudged out of the room, saying: 'Sod the loot, Fing Nolan. This girly needs lookin' after. She can't even stand.'

Fing turned to the window...saw the sky beginning to lighten and spat onto the floor. 'Mucks,' he said, 'gather them sacks together. Carroty can do as she bleedin' well likes, but we're off...Oi! Mucks! Did yer 'ear wot I just said?'

'Yep,' the Muck Snipe replied. 'Just gimme a moment.'

'What in the Devil's name...?'

Fing Nolan would have dropped into a chair, had there been one handy. He would have sat himself down, put his head in his hands and despaired. Of the lateness of the

hour. Of the slim pickings in his sacks. But most of all—
oh, definitely most of all—of the mutinous refusal of his
rat-scally accomplices to follow important instructions.

Instead, he made do with standing right where he was,
in the middle of the room, and telling the Muck Snipe, in
no uncertain terms, precisely what would happen to his
face if he didn't leave that miserable piece of tat above the
mantelshelf alone and fetch the loot.

But the Muck Snipe ignored him.

He was busy.

Meanwhile, downstairs, Carroty Kate had found a big
lump of sugar in the pantry and was dissolving a sizeable
chunk of it in a cup of water. She (he) had yet to stop
talking—'I tell yer, Ivy girl, me old ticker well nigh
stopped beatin' when I saw it was you up there in that
room. I never ceased thinkin' of yer, y'know. All them
months in the clink I thought about yer, day and night,
'opin' and prayin' you'd got 'ome safe. And when I came
out, why—I would've 'aunted Lambeth like a big ugly
ghost, until I'd found yer, only Fing told me 'e'd made
enquiries and that you was a goner. Dead of the whoopy
cough. I tell yer, I wept over that like you was me own
flesh and blood...'

'Fing told you a lie,' Ivy said, in her sore, croaky voice.
But somewhere in her being—her heart, her memory,
her soul, she really couldn't tell—something gritty began
to give way. Because, for many years now, she had been
telling herself a similar story. That Carroty Kate was dead.
Hanged for sure, for murdering that nursemaid. Because
to have believed otherwise, as days, then weeks and then
months, dragged by would have been to realize that Kate

didn't care about her one little bit—not enough, anyway, to come searching for her like she'd promised.

But now, Ivy marvelled, here she was. Or rather, here *he* was, fussing with sugar and water and a cup and a spoon like an old mother hen. And if she didn't look too closely at her—at *him*—it was just possible to pretend that this was the old Carroty Kate in front of her. The one she had loved. A big woman with a knobbled face who had simply shaved her long red hair off—because of the lice, maybe—and disguised herself in men's clothes in order to go out robbing.

Carroty Kate carried on mixing, fully aware of the continuing silence and easily guessing the main reason for it. 'I ain't worn me red wig since I gave up skinnin',' she volunteered after a while. 'I still wears me gowns and a dab o' rouge though—in the privacy of me own lodgin' 'ouse, at any rate, where a lad can be 'ooever 'e wants. You gets me drift, don't yer, girly? You're old enough now, ain't yer, to know it takes all different flowers t'make a meadow?'

'That nursemaid,' Ivy said, fixing her gaze, very firmly, on a table top. 'You didn't kill 'er then?'

Carroty Kate stopped stirring. *Fair enough, Ivy-girl,* she thought. *Fair enough.* 'Lord love yer, no,' she said. 'She'd just passed out cold, that one. A splash o' pond water and she was right as rain. Back on 'er feet again and screamin' the odds.'

'But...all that blood. It was everywhere. I...I *saw* it.'

'The Crow's,' said Kate, grimly. 'I broke 'is nose. 'E 'ad 'is 'ands round that nursemaid's throat, see, cos she wouldn't let go of the bag. Well—that weren't on. I wasn't 'avin' that. And 'e wouldn't be told, so I thumped 'im.'

Ivy nodded, dazed.

''Ere,' Kate said, handing her the cup of sugared water. 'Drink this. Slowly, mind. Then we'd better find yer a biscuit, or a bit o' dry bread or summat.'

Nothing had been said, as yet, about Fing Nolan being a liar.

'I saw 'im,' Ivy said, between sips. 'Fing Nolan. I saw 'im, just a little while ago, down Rosemary Lane. 'E didn't tell yer, did 'e? Well, 'e wouldn't, I suppose. Not if 'e'd already said I was a goner.'

Kate said not a word, only brooded on the matter, while Ivy finished her drink. They were in the sitting room, with all the mirrors, and Kate had lit candles.

'Oh very nice,' scoffed Fing, poking his head round the door. 'Like a meetin' of the Chelsea Associayshun of Gentlewomen. Well, me an' Mucks are away now. Watch out for bluebottles, Carroty, on yer way out.'

'Fing Nolan,' Carroty Kate replied, without even turning round. 'I'll be wantin' strong words with you when I gets 'ome. Mighty strong words.'

Fing looked at Kate, then at Ivy, then back at Kate again. And his face, before it disappeared, looked for all the world as if the wasp he had always appeared to be chewing had finally chewed him back.

'Now then,' said Kate, as the front door semi-closed. ''Ow are yer feelin' now, Ive? Now that you've 'ad that sugar?'

'Strange,' Ivy said, her eyes flicking from the table top to a fire screen and then back to the table top. 'But better.'

'So, you know why me and the lads are 'ere. That sort of goes without sayin', don't it. But why are you? This

266

ain't your 'ome, is it? Cos if it is, you don't seem too bothered about a load of your stuff goin' out the front door in sacks.'

'It ain't my 'ome,' Ivy told her. 'I work next door—for the painter man next door. Oscar Aretino Frosdick, 'is name is. I'm 'is model.'

'So—'oo lives 'ere then?' said Kate, quickly.

'Don't worry,' Ivy's voice was chilly. 'They're away. Away for ages. You won't get caught. And before you asks, I ain't gonner tattle on yer neither.'

Carroty Kate went quiet.

I've shamed 'er, Ivy thought. *Good.*

Then: ''Oo locked you up in that room, Ive?' Kate said. 'Tell me 'is name, and I'll sort 'im. 'E'll wish 'e'd never bin born 'e will, once I've finished wiv 'im.'

Oh yes, and what'll yer do? Ivy wondered, silently. *Send the boys round? Oh—I forgot. You* are *a boy, ain't yer. You could send yerself round. Only not in a frock, mind, or you'd just be one big ugly laughin' stock.*

She closed her eyes, weary, suddenly, of all of this.

'I'm glad you came,' she said, politely. 'For if you 'adn't I would've bin a goner for sure. But I'm all right now, so you can go. Goodbye.'

Even with her eyes closed she could tell her icy tone had made Kate wince.

'Ivy girl,' Kate said. 'Look at me. I know you've 'ad a fair few shocks tonight, and that I ain't exactly the smallest of 'em, but I'm worried about yer. And if some evil swine 'as bin keepin' yer captive it does yer no good to keep on protectin' 'im. So you just tell old Carroty 'oo 'e is and I'll be after 'im.'

With a sigh, Ivy opened her eyes and looked Carroty Kate full in the face. This was how Cousin Jared behaved when somebody broke a contract. All fluster and bluster. All clenched fists, dangerous talk, and mean scowls. It was how Alfred had behaved when he'd thought Oscar Frosdick had been making improper advances.

'There ain't no point me tellin' yer,' she said. 'Cos she ain't even in London. She's away at some manor 'ouse for a while.'

Carroty Kate's expression changed from fierce to downright flustered in two ticks of the sitting room clock.

'"She"? Ive, did you say . . . "*she*"?'

Ivy's mouth, cracked and peeling though it was, began to twitch. She couldn't help it. And the giggles that bubbled up in her seemed to be coming from the exact same place where the old gritty feeling had been,

Yes, you daft beggar. You soft lad. You silly old molly-man. I did. I said: 'She'.

The giggles bubbled over.

'Eh?' said Carroty Kate. 'Wotjer laughin' at? This is serious, Ive. Are . . . are yer sure this nasty piece o' work is a woman? A real woman, I mean? Cos a real woman wouldn't do a wicked thing like that to yer . . . would she?'

And all around the room oval mirrors and rectangular ones, mirrors shaped like crescent moons and mirrors shaped like puddles, trapped, for an instant, the lovely reflection of Ivy's mirth as she threw back the tangles of her hair and laughed until her ribs ached.

CHAPTER 39

*In which memories are shared and loot
carefully concealed*

Since there appeared to be no rush, Ivy and Carroty Kate lingered on at number sixteen Cheyne Walk until the middle of the afternoon. Kate got the stove going and heated water, so that Ivy could bathe and wash her hair. Then she raided the pantry and set about making porridge, and a nourishing broth of potatoes and onions. There were eggs, too, but she didn't trust their freshness—'And the last thing you need now, Ivy girl, is to be dancin' the privy jig.'

'Won't Fing and the lads be worryin' about yer?' Ivy wondered.

'Let 'em!' scoffed Kate, throwing salt into the broth. 'Let 'em worry. You and I got some catchin' up to do. And some eatin'. You're skin and bone, girly. You need feedin' up.'

They ate in the sitting room, with the shutters still closed so that no one entering the garden would think anything was amiss. Kate found a bottle of excellent port and opened it.

'Just a drop for you,' she said to Ivy. 'It's food you're in need of, not strong drink.'

'Splash it in,' Ivy answered, pushing her glass forward. 'I'm overwrought.'

By the time that bottle was empty they had pretty much caught up with the course of each other's lives. Kate, Ivy discovered, had spent a regrettably large part of the last eight years in jail. 'I ain't bin lucky, Ive. Or maybe I'm just losin' me knack—gettin' old an' slow and easier to nick.'

The Crow had fled to goodness knew where, after scarpering from the park with the bag full of loot, and had not been heard of since—'But I'll know 'is face in Hell, girly, and the Devil 'imself won't match old Carroty when it comes to tormentin' that sorry cove.'

Otherwise, Kate said, life at the old lodging house went on much the same. ('Where is it, exactly?' Ivy wanted to know. 'Where it's always been,' Kate answered, carefully.) Yes, the Secret Place was still there. And the tin stars in the window. ('Fancy you rememberin' them, girly'.) And the ghoulish picture that made grown men shudder and little girls screech. As for the Grand Plan—the *Mighty* Grand Plan... Well, it weren't quite so mighty nowadays, was it, not since the skinning had stopped and she and the lads had been forced downmarket, to a pitch in Rosemary Lane.

But things could change. You never knew. She and the lads—they might still get lucky one day. And when they did, they'd have a shop the Queen 'erself would be proud to buy 'er frillies in, God save 'er!

And then Ivy told Kate about being a model. And about the dogs who were temporarily lost and starving. And about the Jacksons back at Paradise Row, who were all heavily reliant upon her nice little earner because one was an invalid, one a poor scholar, one a lazy brute, and one in the family way. And then, as the port warmed her through and made her think of sleep, she said: 'You gave me too much laudanum. In me milk. Every night you gave it me, didn't yer, so I would sleep. That were wrong, that was. You could've killed me.'

Kate threw her a look of genuine puzzlement.

'But it didn't, did it?' she said. 'And you're all right now, ain't yer? Earnin' an honest bob or two right as rain. And look at yer...all that lovely 'air. My old wig never looked like that, not even when I sponged it. No...you're doin' fine, Ivy girl. You just make sure that nutter-woman gets 'er come-uppance, promise?'

'Mmmm,' Ivy murmured.

'Get that brute of a cousin to sort 'er out. That Jared. Because it ain't on, what she did to you. It ain't on at all. And if that's the kind of person you're mixin' wiv these days, Ive, you might wanter think twice about this modellin' lark. Now...I know our lodgin' 'ouse ain't best suited to a young lady like yerself—and you're too tall now, anyway, to kip in the Secret Place—but you and I, girly, we was a good team. And we could be again, I reckon.

'Whadyer say, Ive? Nothin' too risky, not like the skinnin'. But we could work summat out, couldn't we? Some smart dodge to start buildin' up a decent stash of clothes and jewels, for sellin' on?

'I mean, you're in with the gentry now, girly, ain't yer? And some of these arty types, they must 'ave some lovely things stashed away in their 'ouses. Not like in this place, mind, cos there ain't nothin' special 'ere. Take all them mirrors—junk shop tat, my Fing said, and 'e should know. Hey...Ive? You awake, girly?

271

'Well...look at that. I'm talkin' to meself as usual, ain't I? Old Carroty, pissin' in the wind and buildin' up hopes out o' spittle and air...'

When Ivy woke up all the candles had been snuffed and she was alone.

'Kate?' she called. 'Where are yer?'

Receiving no answer, she left her chair, crossed the room and stepped into the hall. Food, a few splashes of port, and a healthy snooze had revived her tremendously and although her mouth was chapped, still, and her throat a little sore, she felt pretty much recovered from her ordeal in the locked room.

'Kate?'

'I'm in 'ere, girly. Nearly done...just got the space for one more...There.'

Carroty Kate appeared from the studio. ''Ow do I look?' she said. 'Not too suspicious, I 'ope?'

'Come closer,' Ivy said. 'And turn around. Slowly.'

'I was lookin' for a wig,' Kate said, lumbering a few steps before pirouetting, gravely, on the spot. 'But there ain't any.'

'There wouldn't be,' Ivy told her. 'That's a painter man's studio, ain't it. And a painter man would never ask a girl to pose if she needed a blinkin' wig. 'E wouldn't even look at 'er. Now...there's a sleeve sticking out of yer trousers. You wanter tuck that in. Or, better still, tie yer trousers round yer ankles if you can find a bit o' twine.'

'Ive,' said Kate, 'you're a marvel. Twine it is. There was some in the pantry, next to the mousetraps. You sure nothin' else shows? And that I ain't lookin' too bulky?

272

I'd wear the bigger stuff properly, all layered like, wiv a bonnet on me 'ead and a slap o' rouge on me face, but it wouldn't look right wivout a wig and we don't want people starin'.'

Heaven forbid, thought Ivy. 'I think you're all right,' she said. 'You'll do, I reckon.'

'Good,' said Kate, bending to tuck the sleeve of the Chinese gown back up her trouser leg. 'I'll go and sort me ankles out and then we can scarper. I know it ain't sundown yet but my Fing'll 'ave a fit if I ain't 'ome soon and if anyone clocks us—well, we can spin 'em a good enough yarn between us, I reckon, given all that's 'appened.'

She straightened up and patted her belly. 'Thank the stars for baggy shirts,' she said. 'Although they don't do the job like me crinolines used to. I could've stashed another four outfits under a crinoline and still 'ad room to spare. Couldn't've run as fast though. Them hoops were a blinkin' nightmare.'

And off she waddled towards the pantry, bigger than ever and beginning to sweat from the weight of the Chinese gown, two silk shawls, a yellow brocade bodice, a cream lace mantle, and two blue overdresses stuffed inside her shirt and down both legs of her trousers.

Left alone, Ivy contemplated Aunt Pamela's travelling bag, on the floor where she had left it. Picking it up felt strange, as if its contents had nothing to do with her any more. She would go back to Paradise Row now, and tell Cousin Jared what had happened to her here. Or most of what had happened anyway. The identities of her rescuers would have to be kept secret—for Carroty Kate's sake.

'Right then... are we off?' With her trouser legs tied, and her shirt buttons straining, Kate looked ready to pop. 'I've enough readies for an omnibus, I reckon. Come wiv me, Ive, back to the lodgin' 'ouse. Then we can both give Fing Nolan what for, the lyin' toad.'

Ivy shook her head. 'I can't,' she answered, gently. 'And anyway, I want to walk—to stretch me legs.'

'Then I'll walk wiv yer. At least till we've crossed over the river. Me own legs could do wiv a bit of a stretch as well—so long as me loot don't chafe.'

And before Ivy could protest, the front door had been tugged open and they were away... down the path, out of the gate, and heading towards Battersea Bridge. At first they moved in silence, both intent, although for different reasons, on getting as far away from Cheyne Walk as quickly as they could. And considering Ivy's legs were still weak, and Kate's stride seriously hampered, they did extremely well.

After crossing the river, Kate took hold of Ivy's arm. Not, she said, to be forward, or even gentlemanly, but because she herself was puffed and needed someone to lean on.

'Let's stop,' Ivy said. 'No one saw us leave. We ain't bin followed. Let's stop for a breather.'

'Good idea,' Kate agreed. 'There's a park not far off, ain't there? Let's sit there awhile.'

Battersea Park was reasonably quiet, for it was a weekday with no brass bands playing and no other attractions that might have drawn a crowd. Kate and Ivy sat on a bench, just inside one of the gates, and sighed with the pleasure of resting their feet.

''Ave some more sugar—keep yer strength up.' Delving, with some difficulty, into her trouser pocket, Kate produced two pink and white striped candy canes and passed one to Ivy.

'Old 'abit,' she confessed, as Ivy scowled at the sweet in her hands as if she intended to stamp on it, or throw it in a bush. 'They die 'ard, old 'abits do.'

'Pah!' Ivy snorted, but she broke off a piece of the candy cane and began to eat it. For the sugar.

A man pedalling by on a boneshaker raised his cap in greeting, wobbling dangerously in the process.

'Now that,' observed Kate, 'is a mighty clever way of gettin' around. No good for a woman in a skirt though. No good at all. Any woman ridin' a bicycle'd need a special kind of outfit—practical, so nothin' gets caught up, but modest too so she ain't flashin' 'er ankles at all an' sundry.'

She paused.

'Somethin' like this,' she added, gazing thoughtfully down at her own baggy trousers, tied neatly at the ankles with lengths of twine.

Ivy wasn't listening. Her attention had been caught by an approaching figure . . . a figure running so fast, straight towards their bench, that he looked almost certain to crash into it.

'E's seen me! Ivy realized, her heart leaping in her chest. *'E knows 'oo I am!*

And it was a good thing she had finished her mouthful of candy cane or she would have choked.

CHAPTER 40

In which Ivy is offered the job of her dreams

'Gawblimey, Ive—'e's a lively one, ain't 'e? Get down there. Get down, yer crazy mutt. Well—'e likes you, girly, an' no mistake!'

Ivy had paw marks all over her front, and her face had been licked like a dish. She didn't care though. She didn't give a rabbit's thump.

'Ivy! What are *you* doing here? I thought you were in the country with your artist. When did you get back?'

Ivy turned her face away from the ecstatic creature slobbering all over her and beamed happily up at Rosa Pavitt.

'I never went,' she said. 'There was . . . a problem. But Prince! *Yes, boy, I know, that's you, ain't it?* What are you doin' with Prince? I thought . . .'

'He pined,' said Rosa. 'He howled and whined all day and all night without stopping, so his new owners brought him back. Father said I could keep him as a pet. But it's you he missed, Ivy. It's you who should have him. Would you like to?'

Ivy looked away from her. Prince had calmed down and was panting, adoringly, at her feet. And so hopeful was the light in his eyes it seemed that he, far more than Rosa, was waiting for Ivy to say, 'Yes. Of course I'll have him.'

But... a dog at Paradise Row? Another mouth to feed? Aunt Pamela didn't care for dogs. And Cousin Jared might be cruel. Correction: Cousin Jared would *definitely* be cruel.

'I... I don't know,' she murmured, sadly. 'I'll... I'll 'ave to ask.'

'All right,' said Rosa, distracted, now, by the sight of Carroty Kate—or, rather, by the fact that something blue and silky was hanging from the front of this person's shirt, like a toy's stuffing.

'Sorry—this 'ere's Rosa Pavitt,' Ivy told Kate. 'She and 'er father run the Dogs 'Ome. Rosa, this is... this is Kate.'

'How do you do,' said Rosa, politely. 'I'm delighted to meet you—Kate.'

'My pleasure, Rosie-girl,' beamed Carroty Kate, shifting slightly on the bench to ease the chafing of her loot. 'My pleasure entirely.'

It was bad manners to stare. Even Ivy knew that. But Rosa Pavitt clearly found it hard to tear her gaze away from Carroty Kate as she said, 'There's more, Ivy—more to tell you. And it's so *exciting*! Just wait till you hear. Father has spoken to the Committee and we've been given permission to hire you—to work with us at the Home. Isn't that *wonderful* news?

'Only... oh dear, this hardly seems right... we can't afford to pay you, not for a while, until we are properly established. But... you could live in, if you wanted, and have your meals with us... so your lodgings and food would be covered. Oh, Ivy, it would be bliss! And to bump into you like this, today, here in the park—why, it seems like the very *best* of omens, don't you agree?'

Very faintly, Ivy agreed. About the omen. She had placed a hand on Prince's head and was scratching him, gently, behind one ear. *Don't get yer 'opes up, boy*, she told him, silently. *Don't go settin' any store by this.*

'What do you think, Ivy? Would you like to work with us?'

'More than anythin',' Ivy admitted, quietly. 'But I can't...I can't read. Or write. I'd be 'opeless wiv the ledger. And I'd number the in-comers wrong.'

'Oh, that's easily solved,' Rosa told her. 'I can teach you all of that by and by. What matters most, according to father, is that you're marvellous with the animals. So will you come? Do say you'll come. Father says you'll need to discuss the matter with your family first, but surely, once they know your heart is set, they won't stand in your way, will they?'

Ivy began stroking Prince's head, neck, and back. Slowly and rhythmically she stroked him, as if flattening out wrinkles or smoothing a path. 'I don't know,' she said. 'I'll ask 'em. As soon as I get 'ome, I'll see what they say.'

'Excellent!' declared Rosa. 'Well, I'd better return to father. It'll be feeding time soon. You'll let us know, Ivy, won't you? As soon as you can? You'll let us know when you can start?'

Ivy nodded. She couldn't speak. She could barely bring herself to think about this offer that seemed too good to be true.

Rosa smiled, tentatively, at Carroty Kate who, by now, had tucked her stuffing in. 'Goodbye,' she said. 'It's been... interesting to make your acquaintance.'

'Likewise,' said Kate. 'Nice cape, by the way. Good cloth.'

'Oh,' said Rosa, faintly. 'Well...thank you. That's useful to know...I suppose.' She looked down at her cape as if she hadn't noticed, until now, that she was wearing one. Then she turned and snapped her fingers: 'Come along, Prince. You've had your walk and you'll see Ivy again soon—*very* soon, I hope. Goodbye! Goodbye!'

And off she went, back towards the park gates, with Prince trotting reluctantly at her heels.

'Well,' said Kate, 'there's an offer. As if any girl'd fancy shovellin' dog muck for nothin'. Why, even the wretches 'oo pick it up off the streets and take it to the tanners in Bermondsey get thrown a few coppers for their trouble. You can do better than that, girly. In fact, I was goin' to suggest...'

'But I don't *want* to!'

'Eh?'

'I don't *want* to do better than that. I *love* workin' with them dogs. I love it more than anythin'.'

Carroty Kate sighed. Then she eased the Chinese gown away from her crotch. Then she looked long and hard at Ivy, who had risen from the bench and was gazing after Rosa and Prince as if they had just left the key to all happiness right there at her feet, like a stick. *Bonnet: none. Dress: faded and unfashionable. Shawl: plain, with a matted silk fringe. Boots: old and scuffed with stringy laces. Brooch: three stones missin', not worth tuppence. Face: stubborn as a mule's but lovely...lovely...and them great big eyes shinin' like Christmas at the thought of what might be. Ivy, me long-lost Ivy girl, all grown up now and on her own path.*

'Well,' she said again, clearing her throat, 'if your 'eart's set, you gotter go wiv it, girly. Follow yer dream, whatever it takes.'

'Like William Forternum?' said Ivy, wistfully.

'Yep,' Kate agreed, her own heart lifting from the unexpected sweetness of such a small, shared memory. 'Just exactly like old Will.'

Ivy's face clouded. 'But Aunt Pamela and Cousin Jared will never agree to it,' she fretted. 'They'll stand in me way, I know they will. They're bound to once they know I won't be bringin' 'ome any readies.'

Kate heaved herself to her feet. 'Ive,' she said, 'just wait an' see. You never know, they might surprise yer. And if they don't—well...it's your life, girly. And you'll 'ave bed an' board, don't forget, with them blinkin' dogs, so you won't be dependent on that bully-boy cousin no more for a roof over your 'ead and a blob o' dinner on yer plate.'

'That's true,' said Ivy. 'That's very true.' But although she sounded reassured, she was a mighty long way from feeling it.

And so they left the park and continued on, along Battersea Park Road and into Nine Elms Lane.

'I go this way now,' said Ivy, indicating right as they came into Vauxhall.

'And I go the other,' said Kate. 'Give us an 'ug, Ivy girl.'

Hugging Carroty Kate didn't feel like hugging a man—or a woman, either. It felt like squeezing a bolster...a big comfy bolster that, all of a sudden, you didn't want to let go of.

'Oi—mind me loot,' Kate scolded. But there were tears in her eyes as she broke away, and a quaver in her voice as she placed both her big hands on Ivy's shoulders and said, 'Footpad Alley, down by the docks. That's where the lodgin' 'ouse is, Ive. Right where it's always been. And that's where you'll find me—where you'll always find old Carroty, I reckon. You got that?'

'Yes,' Ivy said. 'Footpad Alley. I'll remember.'

'Good,' Kate said. 'Now scram.'

Tugging a portion of gown from her left sleeve, Carroty Kate trumpeted her nose into it, hard, as Ivy walked away. *Fine cloth, this. Nice an' soft. And clean too, apart from me own blinkin' snot. Blue too. Excellent. Never goes out o' fashion a good shade o' blue doesn't. Two petticoats-worth at least, and a couple of kerchiefs . . . Goodbye, Ivy girl . . . Goodbye.*

CHAPTER 41

In which Ivy and Cyn form an unlikely alliance

'If you think, Cousin Ive, if you *honestly think* I'm swallowin' this bushel o' lies then think again. Now you tell me, and you tell me true—*if you ain't bin wiv the painter man, all this time, then WHERE WERE YER?'*

'Tell 'im, niece, tell us all...before I faint clean away from the pain in me 'ead.'

'You've got a fancy man, ain't yer? Some lowlife's 'ad yer 'apenny, ain't 'e, before the painter man got so much as a look in. *'Oo is 'e, Cousin Ive?* I'll kill 'im...'

Ivy, her back against a wall, stood very straight as she swore, for the umpteenth time, that she had been locked in a room by the painter man's mad mama with no man—fancy or otherwise—anywhere within sight or earshot. 'And then someone came, and unlocked the door. And as soon as I could walk wivout gettin' dizzy I came back 'ere. It's the 'onest truth. I swear.'

It was no good. No good at all. She must have been addled—unhinged by shock and thirst—to assume she would be given a fair hearing. She hadn't thought it through...had been too carried away with the idea of moving to the Dogs' Home, to consider how the truth was going to sound to someone like Cousin Jared...*stupid, stupid.*

'Truth, my arse. Truth, my ears and whiskers. Where'd yer get that brooch? *Answer me that, yer trollop!*'

Ivy's finger flew to the 'I' for 'Ivy'. She had forgotten to take it off. Well—that was it. The final nail in the coffin. It was barely worth the effort, now, of sticking to the truth.

Still she tried: 'Down Rosemary Lane,' she said. 'When I went there wiv the painter man.'

'Liar!' roared Jared. 'You reckon you can play me for a fool, don't yer? Well, I'll show...'

'Stop!'

'*Don't 'urt 'er.*'

Orlando and Cyn both spoke out at once, but it was Cyn, not Orlando, who went racing across the floorboards to fling herself between her cousin and her brother's fist.

'*Get outer the way!*' snarled Jared. 'Shift yerself, Cynthia, or I'll knock three bells outer you an' all.'

Cyn was not tall enough to shield Ivy's face, so she pulled over a rickety chair and clambered onto it, her own face as grim as Monday morning.

'You lay one finger on either of us,' she shrieked, 'and I'll...I'll set the boys on yer.'

'Don't, Cyn...' murmured Ivy. 'Don't nettle 'im further.'

But Jared, although dangerously nettled already, threw back his head and laughed.

'Oh yeah?' he jeered. 'As if the boys are gonner listen to a fat ugly whore like you!'

Cyn clenched her chubby fists and glared.

'Well, one of 'em would, I'll tell yer that for nothin',' she said. 'Seein' as 'ow 'e's the father of me unborn child.'

Jared's mouth fell open, like a purse. Even Orlando looked stunned.

'I was goin' to tell yer, son...and you, Orly...only I was waitin' for the right moment.' Mrs Jackson's voice had a pleading note to it and she was keeping her head well down, behind the slope of her chaise longue.

'The right moment?' quavered Jared. 'The right *moment*? Oh, this is priceless this is...'

Collapsing onto the one remaining chair he placed his elbows on the table and his head in his hands and groaned. Orlando set his ballad aside and reached for a clean sheet of paper. 'Same as for Hor and Mad?' he said. 'The contract, I mean?'

Jared groaned again, louder this time, and ran his hands through his hair.

''Ardly,' he replied, bitterly. 'Not if it's one of the boys—if it really *is* one of the boys...if our dear sister can swear on 'er life that she would actually recognize the right cove's face in the bright light o' day.'

'*Why, you...you...*'

The chair began to wobble. Ivy grabbed it, just in time, and hung on tight as Cyn jumped clumsily down. Then she grabbed Cyn by the elbow, whispering, 'Leave it, Cyn. Come away. It ain't good to get all agitated. Come an' rest awhile.'

'That's right. Get outer me sight, both of yer. I need to think. Only...which of the boys is it, Cyn? Not Soup-Eyed Stan? Please tell me it ain't that blundering waste o' skin...'

Cyn tugged herself away from Ivy's grip.

'*Don't...*' Ivy breathed.

But her cousin stayed still and her voice remained calm as she said: 'Stanley's all right, 'e 'is. And don't you dare go sayin' otherwise.'

'Oh, my giddy aunt...Soup-Eyed Stan...Lord love us, Cyn, that sorry cove can't even punch straight any more! Oh, this is the worst this is...the very worst...Orly, you're gonner need all yer wits about yer for scriptin' this one.'

Cyn was weeping now. Quietly. Furiously. Ivy began steering her towards the far end of the room where a modicum of privacy would enable her cousin to stifle her sobs against a bolster.

'Don't think I'm done with you, Cousin Ive,' Jared called after them. 'Cos I ain't. The painter man—Frosdick—where is 'e?'

Ivy stopped dead in her tracks. ''E's at the manor 'ouse,' she said, thinking only of protecting old baldy from harm. Of keeping his shiny pink nose intact. 'Frettin' 'imself silly probably cos I ain't shown up. 'E ain't done nothin', Jared, and 'e ain't broke the contract. 'E's bin at Kelmscott Manor all this time, so you just leave 'im be.'

'Oh, I intend to,' Jared replied. 'I ain't got no quibbles wiv that pathetic streak o' pump water. Not so long as 'e keeps payin' 'is dues. Which 'e won't, will 'e, while you're not earnin' 'em, you idle tart. Now get to bed—me and Orly, we got a lot o' sortin' out to do. Or I 'ave, anyway, cos the trouble you two trollops 'ave caused this family ain't the kind, I reckon, that gets sorted by no written words. Now *get out of me sight* so I can think.'

By now it was Cyn pulling at Ivy's dress, while Ivy hesitated, words spinning in her head.

'Come on, Ivy,' Cyn sniffed. ''E ain't gonner listen. 'E never does.'

Reluctantly Ivy turned her back on Jared and Orlando, bent purposefully over Cyn's contract, and on her aunt, feigning sleep in the centre of the room. This was not the moment, she realized, to mention the lost and starving dogs or her hard and fast intention of looking after them—for nothing.

Lying on the mattress next to Cyn—who was soon out for the count and snoring fitfully—she stretched out a hand and felt the shape of Aunt Pamela's travelling bag. It was still packed, ready for her trip to the manor house.

What shall I do? What CAN I do?

Her bottle of laudanum was well within reach, folded in a petticoat at the very bottom of the bag. She was tired. She was agitated. She couldn't sleep.

Take some, said the voice in her head. *Go on. Just a drop or two.*

Tempted though she was, she made the voice go away. Like Cousin Jared, she needed to think.

Oh!

She must have slept, after all, for the sound of the door banging shut brought her back from somewhere too deep and silent to resemble any kind of thought process. It was dark—the room pitch black, on both sides of the screen—and there were snores whistling from Jared and Orlando's mattress a few yards away.

That's Orly, snorin', Ivy told herself. *Which means Jared must've just come in. Or gone out. One or the other...*

For a moment or two she strained her ears and listened—listened so hard she stopped breathing.

Nothing.

No throwing of a boot across the room. No muffled curse as her cousin bumped his knee against his mother's chaise longue. No belching or muttering as he stumbled his way towards his bit of the mattress.

Out. He must have gone out.

Good.

She was wide awake now. Wide awake and thinking fast.

What was it Carroty Kate had said? *'They might surprise yer.'* Well, they hadn't. Only Cyn. Poor Cyn had surprised her—and heartened her, too—by leaping to her aid. *'And if they don't? Well...it's your life, girly...'*

Turning on her right side she reached out, in the darkness, for Aunt Pamela's travelling bag. It would be so easy to pick it up and walk out of the door. It would be the easiest thing in the world. She could be well on her way to the Dogs' Home before Jared returned and he wouldn't have a clue where to start looking for her. It would mean leaving Cyn to face her troubles alone, but maybe Soup-Eyed Stan would do the right thing by her, with or without a contract. And if not, well...

Go! Go now! Leave while you've got the chance!

I don't know...I don't know...What if I bump into Jared, comin' up the stairs? What if Keeper Pavitt 'as changed 'is mind about me livin' in? What if Aunt Pamela wakes up and starts shriekin' the odds? What if...what if?

Oh...go back to sleep, grumbled the voice in her head. *Go on...it's what you do best, with or without laudanum.*

Laudanum. Just a drop. After everything she had been through she surely deserved a drop. A little drop would calm her. And then later on ... or maybe tomorrow ... she would decide what to do.

There was water, already, in a glass next to the mattress. One drop was what she'd promised herself, so one drop was all she took.

It was enough.

When the door banged again she only half heard it. She was dreaming about the Italian's wife—conversing with her about the evil-looking red bird in the painting. The Italian's wife was saying she would have preferred a sparrow, or a cheeky little robin, hovering above her lap for all eternity. 'I know,' Ivy told her. 'I know just what you mean.'

Then she woke up. And because it was not yet light and she hadn't fully registered the banging of the door, she assumed that Cousin Jared was making a merry night of it, wherever it was he had gone, and would not be back now until long after cockcrow.

Go. As quick as you can. Don't start worryin' all over again, or gettin' scared. And don't take any more laudanum. Just go. Go on.

And so, very quietly, she stood up and smoothed down her clothes. Her boots were beside the travelling bag, so she slipped her feet into them and tightened the laces. She was all fingers and thumbs, and groggy from the laudanum. One drop was nothing, really. A mere taste. Still she couldn't help wishing she hadn't taken any at all.

Picking up the bag she looked down at the mound on the mattress that was her pregnant cousin, Cyn, and silently promised to send word to her as soon as she possibly could.

Then she tiptoed round the screen. The edge of a mattress was in her way but she skirted carefully round it. *Bye, Orly*, she whispered in her mind. A stump of candle, set for safety in an empty jar, was guttering close by Orlando's head. His reading light. Its faint glow flickered on his face—on the pale unconscious frown of it as he stirred, but didn't wake. Asleep he looked less like a scholar and more like the eager little boy Ivy remembered from a long time ago.

Goodbye...

Aunt Pamela's chaise longue had been in the same spot for so long that Ivy had no need to feel her way round it. Her aunt was snoring loud enough to bother the dead. She would be upset, Ivy knew, about the loss of her travelling bag and would doubtless suffer the worst headache of her invalid life over the curtailment of her niece's nice little earner. Otherwise, Ivy knew, her disappearance would cause this woman very little concern.

Keeping her eyes on the chaise, just in case her aunt should suddenly shake a leg, Ivy edged closer to the door. Closer and closer she got to it until—

'And where might you be goin', so bright an' early?'

She felt his foot first—the sole of his boot pressed firm against her hip, to stop her moving any further. He hadn't kicked her but it felt worse, somehow, that he had brought her to this sudden, teasing, halt and was leaning back in a chair, against the closed door, his leg braced against her like a cattle prod.

He must have been there for a while, Ivy realized. Waiting for her there in the dark...filing his nails or spit-polishing his buttons...biding his time, anyway, knowing full well that she would try to leave.

'Well, Cousin Ive? Speak up? To the market is it, to be first in the queue for lavender an' late roses? Well, that'll be a first, strike me if it won't.'

He was keeping his voice low, so as not to wake the family.

I could scream, Ivy thought. *I could kick up a right song an' dance. But what good would it do me? Aunt Pamela would only moan about the din. Cousin Cyn would get all agitated again and Orly... Orly would just snuff out 'is blinkin' candle, probably, and pretend to sleep through.*

'Well,' Jared continued, in the same low tone, 'you do 'ave somewhere to go, as it 'appens, but I doubt it's the place you 'ad in mind. I was bein' kind, not wakin' yer too early, but seein' as 'ow you're all set, and the coach is ready and waitin' in the Cut, you might as well get goin'. Come on.'

He picked up her travelling bag and took a firm hold of her arm.

'Be'ave yourself,' he scolded, grinning now as she tried and failed to wrench herself from his grip. 'Be a good girl, Cousin Ive, and I'll come an' wave you off. It ain't too long a journey to Kelmscott, so the boys tell me. And just think 'ow pleased your painter man's gonner be when 'e claps eyes on you again.'

CHAPTER 42

*In which Ivy embarks on a difficult journey and an
unexpected visitor turns up at Cheyne Walk*

Nowhere, in the whole of London, could there possibly have been a more decrepit or ridiculous mode of transport than that which awaited Ivy as she was bundled out of Paradise Row and onto the cobbles of New Cut.

The once handsome hackney coach still bore the arms and crest of some noble family on its peeling sides. But the harness was patched and tied with string, the carriage all out of kilter, like a poorly risen loaf, and the wheels so badly worn they looked set to spin apart at the first bump or hole in the road.

The knots of ribbon and tatty silk flowers decorating this sorry contraption only made it look sorrier, like Miss Havisham in *Great Expectations*. The horses, though, were fit enough, prancing, impatiently, between the shafts.

'Get in,' Jared ordered, tugging open the door and flinging his mother's travelling bag onto one of the seats.

Holding her head high, Ivy did as she was told. *The first crossroads we come to*, she told herself, *the first stop we make I will leap straight out again. I will ... Oh!*

There was someone else in the coach. A crone. A hag. A witch. She was sitting in shadow, her back to the driver, with a big ball of wool and a pair of knitting needles bristling on her lap.

'Watch 'er, Peg,' said Jared, as Ivy took the opposite seat, her spine as stiff as a measuring stick. 'Don't let 'er out of yer sight. And when you get to the manor 'ouse, you and Stan see 'er right up to the door and make sure Frosdick knows she's there. Got that?'

'Goddit,' the crone told him, flashing a grin with more gum than tooth to it. 'She'll be'ave 'erself for old Peg, won't yer, dearie?'

Ivy turned her head away and said not a word.

Jared leered and slapped the coach's blistered frame. 'Right then!' he said. 'Be good, Cousin Ive. Except when it pays to be bad, har-har! Drive on, Stanley.'

High up on the driver's seat, Soup-Eyed Stan—father-to-be and latest recipient of a Jackson family contract—grinned a grin very similar to his mother's and flicked his horses into action. This old coach of his was usually to be seen crisscrossing London, at the dead of night, taking one or two of the other boys to wherever a bit of business needed sorting. A nice trip out to the country, as a favour for his future brother-in-law, was no skin off his nose and would make a pleasant change.

He thought of Cyn, as the horses picked up speed, and his gummy eyes grew sentimental at the thought of the child in her belly. His child. His very own babby. Soup-Eyed Stan didn't need a contract to remind him what this meant. He had every intention of marrying his Cyn and of being a good father.

'Steady there...steady...' he crooned, tightening the reins at a notoriously dodgy crossroads. The horses reared, narrowly avoiding a nasty collision as a hansom cab flew by. Soup-Eyed Stan didn't even flinch, for although he saw the world through a milky fog, and the world he saw was growing more distorted by the day, he had a good feel, still, for animals and roads and considered himself an excellent driver.

By the time the sun was high, the coach was making excellent time and raising enough dust to hide an army. Old Peg had begun to knit, but not before pointing a needle Ivy's way and saying, 'If you don't wanner be civil, dearie, that's fine by me. We can sit in silence, like deaf mutes at a wake, all the way to where we're bound, for all I care. But you try openin' that door, or makin' a bolt for it while we're stopped, and it's a nasty jab you'll be gettin'. All right?'

Ivy had closed her eyes, then. And they were still closed as she considered her options. Right now they seemed pitifully few; for even if she did manage to dodge the point of that knitting needle and get away, she had no money, not so much as a farthing, to get herself back to London.

I should 'ave run from Paradise Row, while I 'ad the chance, she thought, bitterly. *I should 'ave upped and gone while Cousin Jared was out makin' 'is arrangements. I should never 'ave taken that laudanum...stupid, stupid, stupid.*

She thought of Mrs Frosdick and of the awful moment soon to come, when they would meet face to face at Kelmscott Manor. *What will she do when she claps eyes on me? What will she say? And will I be safe in that place while she's around? And if I tell old baldy what 'appened will 'e believe it? Will anyone believe it?*

Sinking deeper and deeper into despair, she pressed her head against the tattered upholstery of her seat and willed her mind to be still. There was no point worrying. It was her own stupid fault that she was stuck here in this bumpy coach, being taken to a place where nothing but harm could befall her.

You don't deserve to get away, said the voice in her head. *From this coach or from Mrs Frosdick. Because you're stupid, you are. Stupid, stupid, stupid . . . and spineless. Don't forget spineless . . .*

So what can I do? What should I do?

Her bottle of laudanum, she knew, was still in Aunt Pamela's travelling bag. And it was almost full.

That's the answer, said the voice in her head. *That's what you'll do. Quickly, the second you get the chance—without getting scared or changin' your mind.*

All right.

Feeling calmer, she opened her eyes. A decision had been made. She wouldn't think about it again, in case she faltered.

'What are you knitting?' she asked the old crone in front of her.

Old Peg looked up, startled. Then she flashed her toothless grin and held up her needles. She was a fast worker, Old Peg, and the thing was taking shape, despite one or two stitches dropped as the coach lurched over bumps.

'That's nice,' Ivy said. 'Cousin Cyn will like that.' And she turned her head away from the sight of the baby's bonnet hanging as soft and white as a torn wing from the points of Old Peg's knitting needles.

Meanwhile, Mrs Frosdick was still nowhere near Kelmscott Manor. She was, however, growing more and more fractious, with every day that passed, over the fact that her dear darling Oscar seemed in no particular hurry to return to Cheyne Walk.

Towards noon a letter arrived that made her so angry she found herself wishing there were servants in the house, so that she might vent her spleen by slapping one.

Dear Mother, the letter said. *Although bitterly disappointed by the non-appearance of Miss Jackson I am having a splendid time. You were right. Fresh air is indeed a tonic and I find myself quite suited to the slow pace of country living. Please send my straw-coloured hat with the wide brim as the weather continues unseasonably warm and my nose is beginning to peel.*

Your loving son, Oscar Aretino Frosdick

With her heart pounding and her blood boiling, Mrs Frosdick went straight into the garden and began cutting things with shears. Roses...the plum tree... Michaelmas daisies just coming into flower...butterflies too slow to get out of her way. *Snick snack*, went the shears, making short work and confetti out of everything they touched. *Bang, bang*, went Mrs Frosdick's furious heart. And when there was nothing left to cut up, she went back into the house and sent her gardening gloves flying, like ailing bats, smack against the parlour wall.

Now what?

She couldn't bear to sit still or be idle. Not yet. So she decided it was high time she went back to number sixteen, to unlock that door.

Yes. Positive action! A gesture of faith in the imminent return of the Italian—and, with him, her own dear boy.

It didn't take long. She had no wish to drag the business out, and no intention of peeping into the room. Nor did she want to linger for longer than necessary on the upstairs landing, like a jittery fool who believed in ghosts—or survival against insurmountable odds.

No. A mighty shove of the swollen front door and into her neighbour's house she went. Down the hall...up the stairs...and along to the locked room.

Had Fing Nolan and the Muck Snipe left that door wide open, the stress caused by Oscar's letter would have paled in comparison to the enormous shock such an unexpected turnabout would have caused our Mrs Frosdick.

It could have gone either way. But the Muck Snipe, without thinking twice, had automatically closed and locked the door behind him.

Turning the key, Mrs Frosdick experienced the smallest of shivers down the bones of her spine. Not of guilt or regret...not even of trepidation...but of simple satisfaction over a job well done.

Back down the stairs, and along the hallway she went, feeling far too pleased with herself to notice that the girl's shabby little travelling bag was not where she had left it and that a rather nice blue and white china bowl had gone missing from the window ledge next to the front door.

Out into the sunshine she went, leaving the front door swinging open. Hah! And why not? Let everyone think the wretched girl had left a clear invitation to robbers on top of everything else.

Halfway down the path she was, and looking forward to tea and cake back in her own parlour, when the garden gate swung open and up from the street stepped... Orlando.

CHAPTER 43

Concerning stewed duck, a lot of laudanum, and acting for the best

S oup-eyed Stan drove like the very Devil. So crazily fast did he go that silk ribbons and flowers flew from the coach's trappings like so many nuts and bolts, and Ivy's first views of the English countryside passed in a jouncing blur of wolf brown, scorcher yellow, and varying shades of green. Not that Ivy cared about the landscape or its colours. Not that she gave a badger's trot.

It was dark when they arrived at the hamlet of Kelmscott and the air smelt of crushed grass and corn. Looking out, as the horses slowed, Ivy saw that the sky here was as black as a swathe of velvet and thickly sprinkled with stars. *Ball gowns*, she thought then, with a small smile. *'Undreds of fancy ball gowns. Or curtains . . . lovely curtains, twinklin' away . . . and enough left over for a velvet bag. A travellin' bag—a special one.*

The air felt velvety too, as she stepped out into it, and although she could barely see her own boots in the dark she could sense this air as a vast expanse, stretching away on all sides—mile after mile of it, with no factories, alleyways, or cobbled streets; no markets, no shops, and no *people* clogging it up.

It made her feel unsteady, this awareness of so much space. Then Old Peg took a firm hold of her arm and began marching her across a courtyard, towards the old stone house that was Kelmscott Manor.

'Now who can that be at this time of night?'

'Papa! It's Papa back from Iceland as a surprise!'

'Papa! Papa!'

'Girls, please . . . Your father would hardly need to knock on his own front door, now, would he?'

The two girls continued to clap their hands and bounce up and down on their chairs. They did not really believe it was their father, out there on the step. But it was so interesting to see the fat painter man's face cloud over at any reminder that their beautiful mother was also a wife.

'Who do you think it might be, Mr Frosdick?'

'Yes, Mr Frosdick, do *you* think it's Papa?'

Oscar wiped a bit of gravy from his mouth with his napkin. He was not good with children and these two, in particular, unnerved him. He rather hoped it *was* old Will Morris, come lumbering home from his travels. For then these precocious little daughters of his might be required to eat their suppers upstairs from now on, leaving the grown-ups in peace.

His hostess and the Italian had excused themselves and left the room, both curious to see precisely who was calling at this out-of-the-way place at such a late hour and without an invitation.

'It is probably gypsies,' he said, intending to frighten the children a little—just enough to pay them back for being seen and heard far too often for his liking. 'A cunning band of gypsies, come looking for chickens to kill, and little girls to sell to a circus.'

The girls regarded him, coolly.

'*Most* unlikely,' said the elder one.

Then Ivy walked in.

'Miss . . . Miss *Jackson*,' spluttered Oscar, his face turning so pink that it looked as if he was choking.

The sisters kicked each other's ankles beneath the tablecloth, their expressions gleeful.

OAF in a tizzy . . .

They didn't dare to look at one another. Hysterical giggles, at this point, would only displease their mother and result in their expulsion from the room. Instead they watched and listened while this unexpected guest was properly introduced and invited to sit down. She was tall and pale, just like their mother, but a lot younger. And her hair was very long, very tangled, and very red. It did not surprise them to learn that she was OAF's model, come tardily from London.

But why had she not come days and days ago, when she was supposed to? And why was she here now? Nobody asked. A plate was brought in for her, along with glasses for wine and water, and a set of cutlery.

'It's duck, stewed with peas,' their mother said, lifting the lid from the china tureen. 'May I serve you?'

OAF's model looked up from her plate. It was the first direct question she had been asked and it seemed she was having trouble answering.

The older girl elbowed her sister and her sister nudged her back.

Their mother was leaning gracefully over the tureen,

the china lid in her left hand and a ladle in her right. She was looking at OAF's model with her eyebrows raised, waiting for an answer or the mere passing of a plate.

OAF's model blinked and cleared her throat. Her face was so white, and she had been so very still and silent up to now, that it seemed to the girls that she might, after all, have come from the place where gypsies dwelled. Or, if not from there, from somewhere equally mysterious— an enchanted forest perhaps, or a palace made of ice.

The men were leaning forward, their faces rapt in the candlelight as they waited for the girl to speak. But their mother, they could tell, was growing impatient, standing there above the tureen, with steam from the duck turning her face as pink as OAF's and the lid in her left hand a little too hot, probably, for comfort.

'I don't eat creatures,' OAF's model said then. And every word was as clear as a bell and far bolder than anyone had expected from such a willow-wand of a girl.

'Oh,' the girls' mother said, snippily. 'I see. Well . . . we'd better see if we can conjure you up something else then. You have no objections, I take it, to food torn forcibly from the ground? A potato, for example? A young lettuce, perhaps?'

Mama in a pucker.

How the girls relished the clanging down of the china lid upon the remains of the duck, and the flouncing of their mother's skirts as she left the room.

'Why don't you eat meat?' the older girl asked.

'Yes,' added the younger. 'Why don't you?'

But OAF's model simply shrugged, and looked down

at her empty plate, unable or unwilling to justify her peculiar stand.

'Jenny and May,' OAF scolded. 'You are quite wanting in manners. It isn't polite to . . .'

'Miss Jackson is a vegetarian.'

It was their mother's fat painter friend speaking.

He was looking at OAF's model in such an absorbed and gentle way that it was just as well, the girls thought, that their mother had gone out for lettuce.

'A whatty what?' the older girl—Jenny—asked.

'A vegetarian,' the painter repeated. 'There was a Society formed—oh, some years ago now—and the movement continues to flourish. Its members claim there are both moral and physical advantages to abstaining from meat and I, for one, although unwilling to embrace a life without bacon, have the utmost respect for those who feel strongly enough to allow no space on their plates for anything that once had a face.'

'Oh my,' breathed Jenny. 'I believe I would like to be a vegetarian. I will begin first thing tomorrow.'

'Me too,' chimed her sister. 'I vow and swear I will never eat creatures again. Ever.'

No one was listening.

OAF's model was looking at the fat painter man as if he had just given her a wonderful and totally unexpected present. OAF, meanwhile, was fiddling with his napkin, casting anxious little glances from his model to his neighbour.

He's jealous! OAF is jealous!

So eager were both the little girls to learn more about this pale, pretty vegetarian that after Ivy had eaten her potato salad and a slice of apple tart they begged to be allowed to show her to her room, and help her unpack.

'Miss Jackson is clearly exhausted after her long journey,' their mother told them, sharply. 'And if she is to begin posing tomorrow for Mr Frosdick she may prefer to go up alone, without any further conversation with anyone.'

'It's . . . it's all right,' Ivy said. 'And anyway, I ain't said good evenin' to Mrs Frosdick yet. Is she . . . is she well?'

'Mother isn't here,' said Oscar, sulkily. 'She chose to remain in London after you failed to keep your arrangement with her to catch the Oxford train.'

'In that case,' the Italian said, smoothly, 'dear Mrs Frosdick will be as relieved as we are to learn that Miss Jackson is safe and well, and here at Kelmscott after all. Ladies, Oscar—excuse me. I have some sketches to put in order before the morning.'

'Then can May and Miss Jackson and I be excused too?' said the child named Jenny. 'You are in the attic rooms, with us, Miss Jackson. It is perfectly civilized up there, so long as you don't mind caddis worms. We collect them, you know, in mugs of water, and if you put apple pips, beads, or anything small in with them they make little coverings for themselves, like coats. Isn't that clever?'

Still chattering away, the two sisters led the way up several flights of steep stairs while Ivy followed on. Aunt Pamela's travelling bag weighed heavy in her hand and her mind was beginning to falter over the decision she had made earlier. About the laudanum.

Mrs Frosdick ain't 'ere, she told herself. *You don't 'ave to do it after all. Not yet you don't. Why not wait awhile an' see what 'appens?*

No, said the voice in her head. *No falterin'. No gettin' scared.*

So when the little girls had shown her the nook in the attic where she was to sleep, and the window out of which she would be able to see the meadows when she woke up in the morning, she fell in straight away with their plan to light a lantern and take the short walk from the house to the privy before they went to bed.

'Are vegetarians scared of the dark?' asked young May, solemnly.

'Some might be,' Ivy told her, reaching into the travelling bag for her bottle of laudanum. 'But I ain't. Are you?'

'A little,' said May. 'But sometimes it's fun to be scared. And outside is exactly the same, isn't it, whether it's day or night? You just see things differently, don't you?'

'Yes,' Ivy agreed with her. 'You do.'

Outside was cooler now, and there seemed to be more stars.

'There is room for three in our earth-closet,' one of the girls whispered. 'But we will stay outside, Miss Jackson, while you go in first.'

The swing of the lantern showed ferns among flagstones and the side of an outbuilding with their three shadows flung crazily against it.

Just inside the earth-closet was a box of matches and a candle in a pretty holder. Ivy lit the candle and closed the door, leaving the little girls outside, scaring themselves silly over a dark shape under the yew hedge that seemed

It had taken all the nerve he possessed to push open the gate and approach the great man's house and only an unshakeable belief in the work he had brought with him had enabled him to proceed—that and the knowledge that neither Ivy nor Oscar Frosdick could spot him on his mission because they were both miles away at Kelmscott.

He had recognized Mrs Frosdick at once, and she him. And while he had been merely startled and embarrassed by their sudden encounter (he hadn't believed, for even half a second, Ivy's tale about being imprisoned by this person) she, poor woman, had been rendered almost apoplectic from shock.

'What are you doing here?' she had shouted, waving her fist right under his nose. 'You're trespassing. Get out!'

Shamefaced and unwilling, at that precise moment, either to retrace his steps or betray his hopes and dreams to a stranger, he had risked the smallest of lies.

'Your son's model—my cousin Ivy—is acquainted with your neighbour,' he had said. 'It is in connection with her that I am here.'

At that she had turned such a peculiar colour that he had felt compelled to grab her arm, for fear she should faint dead away.

'I can tell you nothing, nothing at all,' she had muttered, swaying like bamboo. 'The wretched girl was supposed to travel with me to Kelmscott, only...'

'And that is where she is, I believe,' he had replied, puzzled by her outburst. 'It is on a far more...um ...personal...matter that I have come to consult with your neighbour.'

The news that his idol was also at Kelmscott Manor had hit Orlando like a physical blow—so much so that it had fallen to Mrs Frosdick to take *him* by the arm, and suggest a restorative pot of tea.

That must have been—oh—hours ago, now. There had been a meal since then—something quite delicious—and more brandy than was probably wise. And how Orlando loved the Frosdicks' house! How very much at home he felt among its paintings and books and elegant furnishings.

There were no servants, which was odd, but their absence had made it all the easier for him to relax.

I was born for this kind of life, he told himself, aware of the perfect fit of his body in Oscar's leather chair. *Right now I can only aspire to it, but with luck and the right connections I will soon be on my way.*

At some point in the evening, Mrs Frosdick had apologized for shouting at him in next door's garden. He had readily forgiven her and listened sympathetically while she fretted over her reason for being there—a tunnelling beneath her fence that she feared had been caused by a peculiar armour-plated beast whose name he had already forgotten.

Shortly afterwards—or had it been before?—he had felt compelled to confess his own motives for arriving so unexpectedly at number sixteen. He may even have shed a tear or two but if he did he can't remember, and hopes Mrs Frosdick won't either.

Still, she has been kindness and understanding itself, this woman—and so keen to hear him recite his verses that his confidence and optimism have been completely restored. Concerns about the two artists comparing notes (or rather, letters) at Kelmscott Manor no longer fill him with dread. For even if they *have* become wise to his deception...so what? Mrs Frosdick has not only dined with the Brownings, she is on nodding terms with both Swinburne and Whistler. Mrs Frosdick is a fine woman... a cultured woman...a woman of means and contacts. Mrs Frosdick will open all the right doors for him just as efficiently as her Italian neighbour would have done, of this he is quite certain.

'May I prevail upon you, dear boy, to light a fire in the grate? I find the evenings rather chilly now that autumn is almost upon us.'

Leaping obligingly—if somewhat clumsily—out of Oscar's leather chair, Orlando busied himself with matches, coal, and twists of paper. The chimney had not been swept, so the pull of air was insufficient, but he persevered until a small fire tickled the coals and then returned to his place thinking to recite another of his poems—'The Ballad of the Ghost of One-Eyed Jake', perhaps.

'I must ask you to leave now, dear boy,' Mrs Frosdick said to him. 'It has been such a pleasure, but we are well past the hour, now, at which polite company takes its leave.'

'Of...of course. Forgive me. I...' Jumping straight back onto his feet, Orlando clutched at his poems just in time to prevent them spilling from his knees on to the carpet. The sudden movement made his head spin. That fourth brandy, he realized, had been a drink too far.

Mrs Frosdick was holding out her hands. 'If you will permit me,' she said, 'I will pass your poems on to my neighbour at the earliest opportunity. He will, I am sure, be as thrilled as I was to acquaint himself with such an extraordinary collection.'

Orlando hesitated.

'Or, if you cannot wait for his return,' she added, quickly, 'I will prevail upon dear Robert Browning to proffer an opinion.'

With grateful, trembling fingers Orlando passed his precious verses over.

'Goodbye,' Mrs Frosdick said. 'Do see yourself out.'

Backing unsteadily towards the hall, Orlando paused to give his new friend and benefactor one more appreciative smile. 'Oh, but your fire is dying,' he called over to her. 'It will need more paper, if you wish it to last.'

Mrs Frosdick raised his poems, furled tight in her hand, like a swat, and waved him on his way. 'There is no need to worry about *that*, dear boy,' she told him. 'I will very soon have it blazing away.'

CHAPTER 45

Concerning portraits and worms

In the morning, as soon as she woke up, Ivy put on a clean frock and tiptoed downstairs. The house was quiet, with no one else around apart from a young servant girl sweeping the parlour floor.

Already, in peeps through various windows, Ivy had been intrigued by glimpses of the countryside. It was so *green* out there and so perfectly empty, as if anything that hadn't grown from a seed or been built by a creature had been weeded out by a giant hand, or stomped on by a great big foot.

Letting herself out of the main door, she walked to the earth-closet, marvelling anew at the softness of the air. She could hear birds singing, and see them wheeling overhead in great happy arcs. Otherwise the countryside seemed very quiet. Too quiet.

Back in the house she began climbing the stairs, intending to return to the attic and wait. Doubtless old baldy would be summoning her, before long, so that he could make a start on his wretched 'Oh Feelier' picture. Perhaps it would rain. How she hoped it would rain, for then, surely, she would not have to pose all day in the purple dress in the stupid river with nothing to do except think.

I don't want to think, she thought. *Not about Mrs Frosdick and what she did. Not about Prince and Rosa wonderin' where I am. Not about Jared forcin' me 'ere or that woman sayin' she'd poke me with a knittin' needle. Cos there ain't nothin' I can do about any of it* ...

Miserably, she rounded a bend in the stairs.

She missed the Dogs' Home. She missed London. Most of all she missed her laudanum.

Stop it, she told herself. *Don't go gettin' spineless. It was the right thing to do and you did it. No point frettin' now, particularly as there ain't no shopkeeper 'andy out in them fields to let you 'ave some more.*

Passing an open door she caught a glimpse of a picture up on an easel. It was an unfinished portrait of Mrs Morris and she guessed immediately who was painting it.

'Do come in, Miss Jackson.'

The sound of the Italian's voice made her jump, for she hadn't noticed him sorting through sketches just behind the easel.

Timidly, she entered the room. It was a sitting room, of sorts, hung with vast tapestries showing scenes of banquets and warfare. Morning light streamed in through leaded windows and the easel had been carefully positioned to get the benefit of its rays.

'Would you care to sit?'

Ivy shook her head and stayed close to the door. She felt awkward in the presence of this man. He had been kind, last night, saying all those things about vegetarians. But that only made it harder for her to know what she knew about the theft of his models' clothes, and whatever else Fing Nolan and the Muck Snipe had managed to carry away. And then there was the matter of her looking like his dead wife. Like Lizzie. And all the love nonsense Mrs Frosdick had come out with which she sincerely hoped he had never got to hear about.

'Is ... is Alfred doin' all right?' she asked, for the want of something ordinary to say.

The Italian, still shuffling sketches, smiled.

'Alfred is doing very well indeed,' he said. 'He is here in the village, you know, visiting his family. I can do without his services for a while and he has earned some time off. I understand he has found himself a sweetheart— or re-acquainted himself with one, to be precise. A local girl who hadn't ceased pining since he left to work in London. They are very much in love, by all accounts.'

'That's nice,' said Ivy. She thought of Alfred's freckles, and of his botched attempt to conceal them. She remembered how sweet and protective he had been, on those long walks from Chelsea to Lambeth. And he had been right about the laudanum—she just hadn't wanted to listen.

Could she and Alfred have become sweethearts? Probably, she decided, if she had paid him more attention. But they hadn't really been suited so it was good to hear that he had found happiness, instead, with a girl who loved him enough to pine.

The Italian was saying something else to her:

'Forgive my boldness, Miss Jackson, but I take it you are completely recovered, now, from the grave illness that afflicted you in the spring?'

Ivy frowned.

Wot?

'I ain't 'ad no grave illness,' she informed him.

'Ah,' he said. 'I see. I thought not.'

'Unless,' she added, indignantly, 'you're talkin' about me takin' laudanum in which case...'

'No,' he interrupted, gently. 'I wasn't referring to that.'

He had moved in front of the easel and was considering his portrait of Mrs Morris. Ivy considered it too. Mrs Morris wasn't smiling, but at least she had her eyes open and was looking fit and well. There was a river behind her and long-fingered leaves were dappling her shoulders and being moved aside by her hands. It seemed she had just stepped from the water, even though she wasn't wet.

'It needs a title,' the Italian said. 'I was thinking of *Water Willow*.'

'That's nice,' Ivy agreed. 'That'll do, I reckon.'

The Italian smiled. He had picked up a ruler and was holding it between his eye and the canvas, measuring the distance between one object and another. He didn't look at Ivy as he said, 'If you would consider posing for me, Miss Jackson, instead of for Oscar Frosdick, I would be greatly honoured. Without wishing to sound *too* dismissive of my neighbour's—*ahem*—talents, I can at least guarantee that any study *I* make of you will be saleable, and of exhibition standard.'

Ivy did not know what to say. She looked once again at the painting, *Water Willow*. It was beautiful. She thought of the picture of Lizzie, with her drugged face and closed eyes. She thought of Mrs Morris poised, the previous evening, above the tureen of duck, with a ladle in her hand and a cross look on her face. She thought of all the hours she herself had already spent, standing next to the Frosdicks' roses with a dressing gown cord pinned around her legs.

'Thank you,' she said. 'I'll think about it.'

Meanwhile, back in London, a couple of nasty types woke up from a rum-fuddled sleep and groaned.

'Where are we?' growled one.

'Footpad Alley,' muttered his mate. 'Fing Nolan's place.'

For a moment or two they lay quietly, each one scratching his jail crop and trying to remember how they had got there. The usual, they decided. A bit of business, a drink, and a punch up, followed by a timely rescue from some tavern or other by one of Fing Nolan's lads.

Then: ''Ere,' said one. 'What's wiv the picture? Didn't there used to be a tree up there?'

'Yeah,' the other agreed. 'A big black tree wot the Muck Snipe drew. They must've 'ad a change around.'

'Bit different, ain't it?' said the first. 'That red bird don't look like no feathered critter I've ever seen, and is that doxy dead or what?'

His mate narrowed his eyes, the better to squint up at the sickly-looking woman and the blood-red bird with the flower in its beak.

'I preferred the tree,' he said.

Returning to the attic Ivy found the Morris sisters up and dressed and huddled over their collection of caddis worms.

315

'Look, Miss Jackson,' young Jenny called out. 'This one has a coat like a harlequin's. It's beautiful.'

A mug of water was thrust under Ivy's nose. Inside was a creature—a tiny thing, barely discernable beneath a crust of apple pips, hooks and eyes, and glittery blue beads.

'In the wild they cover themselves all over with teeny-tiny bits of stone and weed,' Jenny explained. 'Papa says they tie things on, *with threads from their own bodies*. They have to do it, you see. It's in their natures. So then, when you catch them, they make do with whatever you choose to put in their water. Isn't this one pretty? I'm going to ask Mama for sequins for my next worm. Gold, if possible. Then May will do one with the pearls from her broken bracelet and we'll see which looks prettiest.'

Ivy stared down at the caddis worm, struggling in the grotesque covering it had created for itself. Then she shuddered and turned away.

The girls came running after her, across the attic floor. 'You haven't unpacked yet, Miss Jackson,' said May. 'Can we help you?'

'If yer want,' Ivy told her.

Sitting on her bed, she watched as the children unbuckled Aunt Pamela's travelling bag, vying to be the first to take something out and hang it up. They were like puppies, she thought, only a lot more exhausting and— she couldn't help but think it—nowhere near as lovable.

'You have a letter here, Miss Jackson,' said Jenny, holding up a badly creased envelope. 'It was sticking out of a pocket and it hasn't been opened yet. Don't you want to know who it's from?'

Ivy considered the crumpled missive. It had been months, now, since she had given it any thought at all and its contents were still neither here nor there, so far as she was concerned.

The two sisters, however, were turning the envelope over and over, their faces bright with curiosity.

'You open it,' Ivy said to them. 'And tell me what it says.'

CHAPTER 46

Concerning the madness of Ophelia

The lavender dress was so baggy and long that Ivy needed help getting into it.

'Is he using real flowers as well?' asked Mrs Morris, tugging and pinning the waist with what seemed to Ivy like unnecessary force.

'I don't know,' Ivy said.

The children, who were lolling nearby on a window seat, sighed.

'You look like a bride, Miss Jackson,' said May.

'OAF, OAF,' whispered her sister, 'plight me your troth ... O darling OAF . . .'

'Girls,' their mother said, crossly. 'Go to your lessons. Immediately.'

With the little girls gone the parlour seemed suddenly cooler.

Mrs Morris tweaked hard at the lavender bodice, making a tiny hole with her fingernail beside a ridge of embroidered forget-me-nots. 'When this gown gets wet,' she said, 'it will probably be transparent. Do you mind?'

Ivy didn't give a monkey's burp.

'I've got me shift on,' she said. 'Underneath.'

'Yes, I can tell.' Mrs Morris's voice was terse as she

318

stepped back and took stock. 'It rather spoils the effect, actually, so don't be offended, will you, my dear, if Mr Frosdick asks you to take it off. As a full-time artist's model, on a generous retainer, you cannot afford to be coy.'

Before Ivy could reply the parlour door flew open and in bounded Oscar, raring to go.

'I say,' he declared, gazing at Ivy in pink-faced rapture. 'I was right about that dress, by Jove I was. You look divine, Miss Jackson. Utterly divine. Now all you need to do is look raving mad as well. For she was quite insane, Ophelia, by the time she drowned. Stark, staring . . .'

'Are those my roses? Please tell me those are not my roses.'

Cut off in mid-speech, Oscar looked down at the wicker basket he had brought in with him—a basket foaming prettily with the sweet-scented heads of four dozen freshly-picked blooms.

'Well . . . yes,' he stammered. 'They are. But I didn't take them all. Not all. It is quite the wrong season, you see, for forget-me-nots, and there are no poppies to be had either, since the harvest.'

Mrs Morris looked at him as if she couldn't, for the life of her, understand what he was doing here—as a species of life on earth, never mind as a guest in her house.

'You are the limit, Mr Frosdick,' she told him, icily. 'The absolute limit . . .'

And the look on her face, as she swept from the room, was quite different from the one in *Water Willow*.

'I say,' huffed Oscar, more offended than contrite. 'Anyone would think I had kicked her precious daughters in the shins or taken an axe to the dovecote. Surely she understands—I cannot paint Ophelia Drowning without flowers and must make do, this late in the season, with whatever I can find.'

He jiggled his basket petulantly.

'They're wilting already,' he moaned. 'We must make haste to the river and get started. If you had only come when you were meant to, Miss Jackson, there might still have been poppies out there. Now—to work!'

Without a word, Ivy followed him out.

'Carry this please,' Oscar said, thrusting his folded easel into her arms. 'I would take it myself, but am already over-burdened with the flowers and my satchel.'

The easel wasn't heavy but it was an awkward shape. And with both hands full it was impossible, Ivy found, to control the sweep of the lavender gown.

Skirting cowpats in the yard, she heard a loud tapping on glass and looked up to see the Morris children waving through a window and laughing like cats at the sight of OAF swinging along like a bridesmaid, with his basket of roses, and poor Miss Jackson bringing up the rear, weighed down by paraphernalia.

I know, I know, thought Ivy, grimly. *This is stupid, this is. Stupid, stupid, stupid . . .*

By the time they had crossed the yard, and begun walking through a meadow, the hand-embroidered thistles Oscar had admired so much on the hem of Ivy's gown were trailing real burrs. And Ivy herself was close to tears.

'Not far,' called Oscar, adjusting his satchel of brushes and paints. 'Nearly there.'

Stumbling on, Ivy spied the river glinting beyond a

line of trees. She could hear rooks cawing and see their nests—great ramshackle piles of sticks which for some reason made her think of the houses at Paradise Row.

The tops of the trees were making a loud shushing sound, even though the sun was shining and the breeze felt light. It seemed to be the only sound for miles around, apart from the rooks, and Ivy didn't like it. It made her think of ghosts. Very lonely ghosts, stuck out in the middle of nowhere and craving a change of company.

They crossed over a little bridge, with brambles either side. Ivy looked at the blackberries growing thick among the thorns. She had only ever seen them at the markets before and had assumed they grew on trees, like the Frosdicks' plums.

A prickly stem snagged at her head. She pulled hard to free herself, leaving a few long, red hairs behind among the berries.

'Careful,' scolded Oscar, who had turned to check on her progress. 'Don't scratch your face whatever you do.'

When they finally reached the river they had to walk a little way, to a bend where a particular willow grew.

'Look, I've tied a rope to its trunk,' Oscar said. 'So that you've got something to hang on to. Otherwise you might easily drift away—the current is quite strong.'

Quickly he set up his easel, fussing over the height and turning the whole thing this way and that until he was quite satisfied.

Ivy had taken off her boots but was loath to approach the bank for there were stinging nettles in the grass, and the water lapping beneath the willow fronds looked equally cruel.

'Come on,' Oscar chivvied. 'In you go. Believe me, you'll be perfectly safe in these shallows, so long as you hang onto the rope. Only, just use your left hand if you will, so the contrivance isn't obvious. I mean it, Miss Jackson— into the river with you, please. For if my elderly mother can oblige me by sitting blindfold up a tree while the grass below her freezes, you can surely pose, quite happily, in a bit of sun-warmed water.'

Shut up, Ivy willed him. *Shut up about your mother*.

Gritting her teeth she picked her way to the bank.

'This ain't warm,' she protested, dipping her toes. 'It's blinkin' freezin'. And I can't see the bottom.'

'You'll soon get used to it,' Oscar told her. 'Now hold onto the rope and *in you go*. That's it. That's the way! Now...lie flat on your back...that's it, don't flail around. Ah...that's not going to work. We can't have Ophelia clinging to a rope like a stranded mountaineer, can we? Not if she's supposed to be drowning. What happens if you let go with the left hand? Ah...no good. You're twizzling. Out you come.'

Having hauled Ivy back onto the bank, Oscar fished up the rope and set about fashioning the end of it into a loosely knotted loop. Drenched and shivering, Ivy watched him. *What?* Had her pose for Oh Feelier Drowning been so terrible that he had decided to try Oh Feelier Hanging instead?

'There,' Oscar said, eventually. 'That's better. If you slip this loop up over your legs and then tighten it around your waist it will leave you with both hands free. I just hope the rope is long enough, so it won't look like you're sitting up...'

The rope *was* long enough, just about. Still, Ivy had to lie at a most awkward angle, her heels and elbows grinding into the silt of the river bed so that the current did not spin her round or tilt her to one side. You could see the rope, too, where it entered the water but Oscar didn't seem to mind about that.

Nor did he seem all that bothered when most of the rose petals he scattered around Ivy's floating figure simply drifted away like fairy boats.

'Lie back a little,' he instructed from the bank. 'So that your hair swirls around your face. That's it! And look up at the sky. That's perfect. Now—you're certainly looking deranged but can you sing?'

'Wot?'

'Ophelia was singing as she drowned. I can't remember what Shakespeare wrote, exactly, but any old nonsense will do.'

'I can't 'ear yer,' Ivy snapped. 'I've got water in me ears. It's 'orrible. I ain't posin' like this—it ain't comfy.'

Reluctantly Oscar fetched a large stone which he lowered into the river, and told her to place under her head.

'It rather spoils the line of your neck, in relation to your shoulders,' he observed sulkily as she adjusted her pose in the freezing water. 'But since your comfort is important I am prepared, just this once, to accede to your wishes. Now—stay exactly as you are. I really *must* make a start.'

CHAPTER 47

In which Ivy, having reached the end of
her tether, must either sink or swim

I t took less than three minutes for Ivy to seriously
regret having raised her ears above water-level. For
Oscar was in the mood to talk. Not to converse, since
that would have required having to listen, but to talk. For
a very long time. About himself.

He was extremely happy, here in the countryside, he
told Ivy. So happy that he found himself disinclined to
leave and return to London. And so, being a man of
action as well as words, by thunder, he had made some
enquiries and found a splendid little house to rent, just a
trot away at Lechlade.

'I'm afraid mother will be a little put out,' he remarked,
dabbing happily away at his canvas. 'For I do not intend
for her to move in with me.'

Put out? She'll be furious! It's the worst thing in the world that
could happen to her. For one gleeful moment Ivy forgot that
her fingers and toes had gone all pulpy and that something
had just nibbled her neck. For she could imagine no form
of retribution more fitting for the ghastly Mrs Frosdick,
than being parted from her beloved son. *She'll be so mad an'*
so heartbroken that she won't be able to stand it!

'However,' Oscar continued, 'I would certainly expect
you to take up residence with me.'

Whaaaat?

The thrill Ivy was enjoying at the thought of Mrs Frosdick's imminent change of fortune turned to a shudder that had nothing to do with the temperature of the river or the attentions of its fish. And she turned her face from the sky so sharply that the boulder supporting her head wobbled and slipped in the mud.

'I . . . I can't,' she said, resuming her pose with great difficulty. 'It ain't . . . it ain't possible.'

Beneath the daisies and forget-me-nots on her water-logged bodice she could feel her heart thumping.

Perhaps he was joking. Perhaps he was pulling her wet and muddy leg.

But Oscar Frosdick, as well she knew, was not a great one for jokes.

'I can quite see that it might look—*ahem*—a little unconventional,' he said. 'And I do understand that you have your reputation to consider.'

He paused and cleared his throat.

'But there is, of course, a very obvious way around such an awkward dilemma.'

Flat on her back though she was, with her arms, spine, and legs held rigid against the tug of the water, Ivy could see that Oscar had turned the brightest shade of pink it was possible to go if you were neither a piglet nor a rose. And that he was keeping his eyes firmly fixed on his canvas as he worked up to the most crucial statement of all concerning this appalling scheme of his.

Only, it wouldn't be a statement, would it? It would be a question. That was the usual way of it, to allow a girl time to think . . . to decide.

And so it was a question Ivy waited to hear, even after she had guessed, with horror, what it was going to be and was already fumbling, with river-numbed fingers, to loosen the knot at her side.

'I intend to marry you,' Oscar said. 'As soon as possible. I am a man of considerable means, Miss Jackson, as you are aware. You will want for nothing, and neither will your family.'

She thought she would never do it. She didn't think she had the strength. But as Oscar babbled on, and whatever was taking shape on his canvas got frantically daubed with Prussian blue, the knot came undone and the rope lassoing her to the willow tree loosened and gave way.

'So, my dear Miss Jackson, I shall of course make a formal approach to your guardian, to ask for your hand. But is there anything you wish to say at this point?'

'Yes. Me 'ands are freezin', thanks to you. And you ain't 'avin' 'em. Nor any other bit of me neither . . . Oops!'

He had been right about the current, old baldy. But Ivy knew no fear as the lavender dress billowed out all around her and she began to float downstream.

Could she swim? Of course not. No more than she could sing.

But she could still touch the muddy old riverbed when she put down both her feet and dry land, with its fringe of trailing willows, seemed reassuringly close as she half scrabbled and half drifted along.

Very soon Oscar Aretino Frosdick was little more than a stick figure, waving his arms and jumping up and down on the bank.

Goodbye! Goodbye!

The current was fiercer now and the river seemed to be widening.

So when she saw the punt wedged in a clump of rushes she waited until she was almost upon it and then struggled and staggered and splashed and fought until her hands touched its wooden sides and the river let her go.

It was hard work, hauling herself up, and as she did it the punt shifted. Just in time she clambered in, before it slid from the rushes completely and began to glide away.

Carefully, so as not to tip out or do anything else wrong, Ivy got herself seated and looked around for the pole. There it was, at her feet, right where it was supposed to be. In a minute she would grab it and take control of this craft. But for now she simply sat, her long hair streaming, the sleeves of the lavender dress trailing, and the September sunshine gilding the water and the willows and the thick clumps of rushes and warming her through and through.

In a minute she would think about heading for the bank, and about returning to Kelmscott Manor to collect her things: her pale dress, her dark dress, her flannel petticoat, slippers, and shawl, her 'I' for 'Ivy' brooch, her handkerchief—and her money. For the letter the Morris girls opened that morning had contained a crisp five pound note; an 'extra little something' sent by Oscar Frosdick to be absolutely certain of retaining her services for *Eve After The Fall*.

It was enough money, Ivy knew, to take her anywhere she chose to go. By train or by carriage. Anywhere at all.

And it had been right there in her pocket all the time . . .

She was coming to a bend in the river, with a couple of small buildings just visible through the trees. And in the distance, above the shushing of willow fronds and the cawing of rooks, she heard a different sound. An urgent, happy sound—the barking of a dog. Rosa Pavitt would have called it a good omen. She would be sure to tell Rosa about the barking of the dog.

There were children, now, racing along the river bank and calling something out. And a fisherman sat with his mouth wide open and a look of total astonishment on his face as the punt went sailing by.

The children had reached the water's edge and were laughing and pointing their fingers. But Ivy didn't care. She didn't give an otter's thrash as she rolled up the sleeves of the lavender dress and reached down for the pole.

For Ivy had a plan.

A mighty grand plan.

Tate Britain, Summer 2004

'Right, Year Ten, gather round. Kayleigh—are you with us? Now—who can tell me something— anything—about this painting here?'

'It's Victorian, miss.'

'Well, yes, Leanne. That rather goes without saying. Anyone else? Come on, Year Ten, what have we learned so far about the Pre-Raphaelites? Robert?'

'Is it to do with death, miss?'

'Thank you, Robert. The *Beata Beatrix* is indeed to do with death. It was painted some time between eighteen sixty-four and eighteen seventy by Dante Gabriel Rossetti— one of the best known of all the Pre-Raphaelite painters— and is one of his most fascinating works.

'Rossetti's inspiration for this painting, Year Ten, was an account written by the thirteenth-century poet, Dante, about his love for a girl called Beatrice and his grief when she died young. But it is also a memorial to Rossetti's own wife, Lizzie Siddal, who took a fatal overdose of laudanum in eighteen sixty-two and whose face he painted from sketches and memory to represent the dying Beatrice.'

'Did she top 'erself, miss? His wife?'

'Yes, Daniel, it seems she did. It was hushed up for a long time to avoid a scandal, but she apparently left a note pinned to her nightie asking Rossetti to look after her younger brother, Henry, who had unspecified learning difficulties.'

'She looks like a druggie, miss, doesn't she? A druggie needing a fix.'

'That is certainly one way of looking at the *Beata Beatrix*, Leanne. In fact Rossetti appears to be inviting precisely that interpretation through his use of symbolism. Which images show... Yes, Hannah?'

'The poppy, miss. It's what you get heroin and stuff out of.'

'Correct, Hannah. Laudanum, which so many Victorian ladies took to steady their nerves, is—like heroin—a derivative of opium. And this white flower here is an opium poppy. And this bird, although it recalls the symbol of the dove which, in Pre-Raphaelite paintings represents...?'

'The Holy Spirit, miss.'

'... Thank you, Kayleigh... This bird is such a screaming shade of red that it is clearly symbolic of danger.'

'Miss—who are those people in the background?'

'Well spotted, Robert. The figure on the right is the poet, Dante, and the one on the left is Love. Just behind them is the bridge over the river Arno in Florence, where Dante and Beatrice lived. But it could just as easily be seen as the old Battersea Bridge that spanned the River Thames near Rossetti's home in Chelsea.

'It has always fascinated me—try listening, Leanne, as it just might interest you as well—it has always fascinated me, Year Ten, that Rossetti is known to have made at least six replicas of this painting and that, in the later ones, the woman looks less like Lizzie Siddal and he substituted the red bird and white poppy for a more conventional-looking white bird and red poppy.

'Now—which group has been looking at representations of women in Victorian art? Hannah? No—you're landscapes, aren't you. Kayleigh—right, then, what did your group think about the Pre-Raphaelite paintings in this room?'

'Well...we thought the women were a bit of a sad lot, miss. There's one dying of consumption, another weeping because her husband's been lost at sea, another looking fed up because she's about to marry some old boy...oh, and there's one over there who's wasting away under a bridge because her husband kicked her out for being unfaithful and now she's destitute.'

'Thank you, Kayleigh. Madonnas and magdalens... beautiful angels and seductive sirens. Oh, those Victorian painter men! And many of the women and girls who posed for these paintings got tarred with the same brush, being variously said to have been sickly, neurotic, promiscuous, or empty-headed. Lizzie Siddal was actually a talented artist in her own right, but it's as Rossetti's red-haired muse that she is best remembered This wasn't Rossetti's fault. He actually encouraged her to paint. It was more to do with the whole culture and ideology of Victorian England which denied women opportunities and then defined them as inferior.'

'What about the other models, miss? Like that one over there—the one with black hair, lying in the snow.'

'Ah yes, Saint Eulalia—slain for refusing to worship Roman gods. I'm not sure who the model for Saint Eulalia was, Hannah; Janey Morris had dark hair but I don't *think* it's her. Janey was married to the Pre-Raphaelite designer and poet, William Morris. She was an embroideress— extremely talented—but, again, it is as the face in Rossetti's paintings *Proserpine, Water Willow,* and *Mrs William Morris in a Blue Dress* that she is best remembered. She was a very good friend of Rossetti's and modelled for him a lot, after Lizzie Siddal died.'

'So that's not her then, miss, lying in the snow?'

'No. A number of Pre-Raphaelite models were ordinary girls picked out in the streets for the way they looked. "Stunners" they were called by Rossetti and his circle. We know the colour of their hair and the shapes of their faces. And we know who some of them got married to, and how many children they had. But as for the rest; well—we can only imagine.'

Julie Hearn was born in Abingdon, near Oxford, and has been writing all her life. After training as a journalist she went to Australia where she worked on a daily tabloid newspaper. She then lived in Spain for a while before returning to England where she worked as a features editor on a chain of weekly newspapers as well as writing freelance for magazines and the national press. After her daughter was born she went back to her studies and obtained a BA in English and an MSt in women's studies. She is now a full time writer. Her first novel, *Follow Me Down*, was published to much critical acclaim in 2003. *Ivy* is her third novel for Oxford University Press.

Also by Julie Hearn, *The Merrybegot*

The Confession of Patience Madden
The Year of Our Lord, 1692

G ood day, brothers. I am ready to talk to you now. Ready
to tell you the truth. Pray forgive the croak in my voice
It has been ... it has been ...
Water? Yes. Thank you ...
Are you listening? I can barely see you. It is so dark in here ...
Are you ready?
Then I will begin.

I never meant it to end the way it did. Grace might have done,
but not me. Grace was fifteen, as artful as a snake, and already
on the slippery slope to Hell. But I, Patience Madden, could have
stopped any time—uncrossed my eyes; made my arms and legs
be still; and called a halt to the filthy words jumping out of my
mouth like toads. I could have spat the pins from under my
tongue and admitted they came not from the Devil but from the
cherrywood box our mother kept tiny things in.

I could have sat up in bed, looked around at the villagers come
to whisper and gawp, and said No. Stop praying for me. Stop
bringing me bay leaves and splashes of holy water. For I don't
deserve your lucky charms, nor any help from the Lord. Neither
does my sister. She deserves them even less. It was her fault. She
started it. And now she's hurting me. Yes, she is. Pinching me black
and blue beneath the coverlet, lest I weaken and tell you the truth.

Grace, I whispered, on the third evening, after our neighbours had drifted away to feed their hogs, their children, or their own nosy faces. Grace, I'm scared. I want to get up. Grace, I'm hungry.

Be silent, she hissed. Or, if you can't be silent, call out some more about imps at the window, and a crow in the corner. That was good. They liked that. We'll do more with the imps and the crow.

She promised me I would not have to behave like this for much longer. In a day or so, she said, we would stage our recovery. Wake up all smiles, ready to put on our itchy bonnets, and do our tiresome chores, like good, obedient girls.

A few days more, she said, and our lives would go back to normal. As dull as scum, but blameless.

It did not happen like that. It went too far.

We went too far.

April 1645

The cunning woman's granddaughter is chasing a pig when she learns there is to be no frolicking in the village on May morning. Minister's orders.

'Bogger ... that,' she pants. 'And bogger ... this ... pig. There's no ... catching ... him ...'

Clutching her sides, she gives up the chase, and collapses, laughing, against the gnarled trunk of a tree. Above her head, pink blossoms shake like fairy fists. Spring has arrived. A beautiful time. A time when it feels absolutely right to think of dancing barefoot in the dew, and absolutely wrong to dwell on the new minister, with his miserable ways and face like a trodden parsnip.

'That's what they be saying,' the blacksmith's son tells her. 'No pole. No goin' off into the woods. No nothing. It ain't godly, Nell, to frolic so. That's what the minister reckons.'

Nell picks a blade of new grass and begins to chew it. Her stomach rumbles beneath her pinafore, but she is used to that. Out of the corner of her eye she can see the pig rooting around. It is a bad pig. A bothersome pig. Her granny will sort it out. This is how:

A Spell to Sooth a Truculent Pig

First, catch your pig. Do it on a Monday, on a waning moon, when the time be right for healing. Point him to the north, and hang on tight. Rap his snout three times with a wand of oak, and call: 'Powers of earth, tame and soothe this creature that he may become docile and no longer a bogging nuisance.'

Wait seven beats of the heart, then let him go.

So mote it be.

A light breeze frisks the orchard. There are things Nell ought to be doing, but she stays where she is, squinting up at the blacksmith's son and thinking about May morning.

'And who be you wishing to frolic with anyway, Sam Towser?' she chuckles. 'As if I couldn't guess ...'

The lad reddens. He is a month short of sixteen and all swept through with the kind of longings that can tie up a boy's tongue and have him tripping over everything, from clods of earth to his own great feet, twenty times a day. He has a mop of corn-coloured hair, and a cleft in his chin so deep it might have been pressed there by his guardian angel. He is too ungainly; too unfledged, as yet, to be truly handsome. But he will be. The promise of it is all about him, like the guarantee of a glorious day once some mist has cleared.

'No one,' he mumbles. 'I got horses to see to. No time for fumblin' around with some daft maid on May mornin', nor any other time.'

'Pah! That's a fib!' Nell flings both arms wide and twists her face to look like a parsnip. 'Beware, sinner! Beware what you say! Repent! Repent! For Satan loves a fibber, and will carry you off to burn in Hell. In Hell, I tell you, where fibbers go. And frolickers. And women who wear scarlet ribbons, or sweep their hearths on Sundays …'

'Hush … Hush up, you daft wench …'

'Repent! Repent! For I am your minister. God's representative in this heathen place … Repent! For though my nose drips and I do not know a hoe from my …'

'NELL, hush!'

'…elbow, I know a sinner when I see one. And a fibber. And a frolicker. All rolled into one vile, wretched …'

'Right!'

'… body … and a … Yieeek! …'

He has pounced and is tickling her—tickling her to what feels like a giggly death, while the sun pours down like honey, and the truculent pig looks on in mild surprise.

'You two! Have a care! Mind that tree, and stop your messing.'

A woman has entered the orchard. She stands some distance away, almost in the nettles. Her face, beneath a bonnet the colour of porridge, is grave.

'What?' Nell scrambles to her feet. 'What is it, Mistress Denby? What's happened?'

The blacksmith's son gets up. There are twigs and fallen

petals in his hair. He looks like Puck. He looks drop-dead frolicsome.

'Gotter go,' he mutters. 'I got horses to see to.'

The woman and the girl pay him no mind. They have already jumped the stile and are hurrying away, along the crooked path leading down to the village. Women's stuff, he supposes. Someone getting born. Or dying. Or doing both in the space of a few breaths.

He doesn't want to be seen trotting at the heels of womenfolk, towards whatever, or whoever, needs their attention in some fusty room. The sun is high, now, and he has his own ritual to perform.

The apple tree he chooses is truly ancient; its timber as knotted as a crone's shins; its blossom strangely pale. No one knows how long it has stood here, or why it was planted alone. Much older than the rest, it continues to bear fruit so sweet that to press cider from it, and drink the stuff, is said to send the mind dribbling out of the nostrils and the legs in several directions at once.

It is to this tree the Apple Howlers come, on Twelfth Night, to scare away evil spirits. It is here that they form their circle—a raggle taggle of villagers, young and old, banging pails and pots and howling, 'Hats full! Caps full! Bushels, bushels, sacks full!' loud enough to wake the dead.

It is on these branches, and around this trunk, that the Howlers hang their amulets and leave cider-soaked toast for the piskies. The orchard swarms with piskies. Everyone knows that. Little folk in rags, their skin as rough as bark, their heads sprouting lichens and moss. A few are downright malicious, the rest merely troublesome and high-spirited. All are uglier than dead hedgehogs as greedy as swine. Over the hills, in a neighbouring county, lies fairy territory—a prettier species, by far, the fairies, but just as pesky, so rumour has it … just as demanding of treats, and remembrance.

Be good to the piskies, the old folk say hereabouts, and they will be good to you. Treat them with respect on Twelfth Night and they will stay by the trees, watching over the fruit until picking time comes.

The cider-soaked toast has been eaten long ago by robins and other things. But the amulets are still here, swaying gently at the end of their strings, like small, hanged felons.

'May I?' says the blacksmith's son, before pressing the point of a horseshoe nail into the old tree's trunk.

Yep, something replies, the sound of it such a faint rasp that the blacksmith's son assumes the pig has farted.

Slowly, carefully, he begins to cut. Not his full name— Samuel—for he isn't sure of all the letters. A single 'S' is the mark he makes, the down stroke wobbly as a cater-pillar against the wood. He can't spell the other name, either. The one that is on his mind day and night. The one he only has to hear, in passing, for a fluttering to start in his belly, as if larks are nesting there.

He knows his alphabet though. Just. And he knows, from the way the girl's name is said, which letter he needs to entwine with his own. It is one of the tricky ones that sounds different, depending on the word. As the metal point of the nail forms the letter's curve he finds himself wishing it made a soft sound like the beginning of 'gentle'. He would have liked that. It would have seemed significant.

The girl's name, though, begins with a hard 'G', like 'gallows' or 'god'.

When he has finished, he steps back to inspect what he has done. And then he sees one. At least, he thinks he does. There and gone it is, between knots of blossom, its face as coarse and grey as the tree, its small, bright eyes fixed intently on the 'S' and the 'G'.

'Oh ...'

He looks quickly, all around, and then back again. Nothing. There is nothing there. A trick of the light, perhaps? But no ... His sight is good, and he isn't given to fancies.

He stays a minute more, half dreading, half hoping to see the thing again. What did it mean? Was it lucky, to see a piskie when you were a month short of sixteen and so desperate to get your hands on a certain someone that you would probably die of frustration if it didn't happen soon?

Did it mean that he would?

Did it?

It takes just seconds for the blacksmith's son to convince himself that he has been sent an auspicious sign. That, come May morning, he will be frolicking away to his heart's content with the girl whose name begins with a hard-sounding 'G'.

She will be all over him like a vine, yes she will, for all she is the minister's daughter and seems as distant and cool as a star. He will have her. No doubt about it. For they are joined, already, in his mind and on the tree. And their union has been blessed. He has the piskie's promise.

The blacksmith's son feels light on his feet as he swings himself over the stile, and he is whistling as he strides away.

'*Silly young bogger* ... ' goes the sighing and the rasping among the topmost branches of the trees. '*Silly ... little ... whelp.*' And the letters 'S' and 'G' begin slowly turning brown, the way a cut apple will do, or naked flesh beneath hot sun.